All You
Need is
Greece

BOOKS BY SUE ROBERTS

My Big Greek Summer
My Very Italian Holiday
You, Me and Italy
A Very French Affair
As Greek as It Gets
Some Like It Greek
Going Greek
Greece Actually
What Happens in Greece
Take a Chance on Greece
There's Something about Greece

Christmas at Red Robin Cottage

SUE ROBERTS

All You Need is Greece

bookouture

Published by Bookouture in 2023

An imprint of Storyfire Ltd.
Carmelite House
50 Victoria Embankment
London EC4Y 0DZ

www.bookouture.com

ISBN: 978-1-83790-542-3
eBook ISBN: 978-1-83790-541-6

For my family. I love you all.

ONE

'Do you even like dogs, Beth?'

My friend Jess pulled a face as she looked over my shoulder as I read an online advertisement looking for volunteers for a dog rescue in Greece.

'Er, hello. Of course I do. I grew up surrounded by dogs,' I tell her, thinking of our own Labrador retriever and my gran's slightly crazy boxer Mitzi that had a habit of leaping onto the chair in her kitchen and eating the food from her plate when her back was turned. 'And I'm addicted to that programme about Battersea Dogs Home. I would have a dog here, if the landlord would allow it.'

'Well, you learn something new about someone every day.' Jess laughed. 'I just never had you down as a dog lover. But then, how would I have known that, with dogs not being allowed in these apartments.'

Jess is my next-door neighbour and friend, who I met when we both moved in here two years ago. We've recently toyed with the idea of sharing an apartment and halving the rent, but ultimately decided that we like our own space, so put in the extra working hours to pay for it.

I smooth my long chestnut hair into a ponytail and pick up my bag to take the short walk to work at the local supermarket, where I am employed as general manger. I have already received two texts this morning from staff calling in sick, so it looks like it is going to be a busy day. I've furiously texted a few other part-time staff who so far have decided to ignore me. In a way, I can't blame them. They have probably made plans for their day off and why not? It's still a bit of a bugger, though; I can only hope the shop isn't too busy later.

Jess and I finish our coffee that she has popped in for. She calls by most mornings, and then walks to the shop with me, before heading to her job in a local solicitor's office. Today she has taken the day off work to visit her gran, so will nip into the bakery next door for some Chelsea buns to take round.

'You don't fancy a shift at the supermarket, do you?' I joke. Although, given the staff situation, maybe I'd take her up on it if she said yes.

'No, thanks! Let's just say I wouldn't have your tact and diplomacy when it came to dealing with tricky customers,' she says, grinning. 'Besides, I wouldn't want to let my gran down.'

'Ha-ha, fair enough. I just thought, you know, with you having a day off work...' I give her exaggerated, pleading eyes.

'During which I have promised to mow my gran's front lawn and paint her kitchen ceiling,' she reminds me.

'Worth a try.' I shrug.

'Are you coming out later?' she asks. We often head to the local pub for drinks and, sometimes, a karaoke song or two on a Friday night. 'I'll be ready for a few drinks by then.'

'I might do. It depends how tired I am after work, especially as we are short-staffed.' I'd planned wine, chocolate and a catch-up of the latest TV drama starring David Tennant.

'Oh, come on, it will do you good,' she says gently. 'You can't mope around on your own in the flat on a Friday evening. I'm sure Marco isn't doing the same,' she says, before quickly apologising, and saying that was a little insensitive of her.

'It's okay, and you're probably right.' I manage a smile.

TWO

As I arrive at the store, there's already a small queue of locals standing outside as I open up and I wish them a cheery good morning. I guess if sales are buoyant, the shop won't close down, like several others have along our high street, and that is something I have to be thankful for.

A text pings through from one of our students as I'm opening up. Thankfully she says she will cover for one of the sick employees and will be here in twenty minutes. It's not as bad as having two staff off, as at least the shelves will be refilled, and I might actually have the chance to nip to the loo.

I rush around all morning, but by lunchtime it is a little quieter and my mind starts to wander. I know Jess didn't really mean anything by bringing Marco up, and she might have a point. He always liked being busy, and I can't imagine that's changed much now.

It was me who ended things with Marco and, although I still miss him terribly, I wasn't prepared to wait forever for a wedding. We'd been engaged for two years after being together for three, and I got the feeling he had gone cold on the idea of marriage. The sparkling engagement ring on my finger might as well have been a piece of costume jewellery. The final straw for me was when I pinned him down over booking wedding venues for next year and his silence said it all. He quietly ignored the bridal magazines I left out on the coffee table, even tidying the room and placing them in a magazine rack. Was it too much to expect my fiancé to be at least a little bit excited about planning our wedding? It was time to face facts. Our nuptials were never going to take place.

I met Marco at a local Italian restaurant on our high street, one of the businesses that still seems to be thriving in our market town. As he tended our table one evening, the tall, dark-haired Marco singled me out for extra attention, and by the end of the evening he had asked for my number. I tried to play it cool but there was no way I could ignore him. Especially with those startling blue eyes that contrasted perfectly against his beautifully styled dark hair and olive skin. Of course, my friends warned me off, saying he was a charmer and he probably chatted up all the diners in his family-run restaurant, but it seems he didn't and we quickly became a couple. After two years, we rented a flat together and began to save for a future. That was until two months ago when we split, and I have had to work many extra hours to keep up with the rent on the flat, but I can't be with someone who doesn't want to commit to marriage. It matters to me, and it doesn't to him. There is no compromise.

When I ended the relationship, Marco seemed genuinely heartbroken, and told me how much he loved me, but that he wasn't sure he believed in the institution of marriage. I couldn't see how we could go on after that, because I do believe in marriage, and longed to celebrate wedding anniversaries every year and have the dream marriage my parents never managed to achieve. Following the split, I had been thinking about getting away somewhere.

So, the ad for the volunteers at the dog rescue in Crete that I saw this morning could be perfect. The only problem was, the volunteers had to pledge six weeks, and there was no way I could be away from the supermarket for that long. Perhaps I could negotiate a shorter stay if I got in touch.

Maybe out there, in the Cretan hills, I might have the chance of shaking all thoughts of Marco from my head. Especially being amongst the animals.

'You're really going then? Who will I walk to work with in the mornings?' asks Jess.

It's Friday evening and we're sitting in a booth at Charlie Parker's Bar and Jazz restaurant, having decided to avoid the karaoke night at the local pub when we saw a hen party heading in there, already the worse for wear.

Judith, the lady who runs the rescue, was lovely when I called and asked if there was any way I could come over for four weeks. It meant I was taking almost all my annual leave at once, but my deputy manager was very keen to put her recent management course training into practice, freeing me up to go.

'I'm sure you'll manage. And it's only for a few weeks. I just need to get away, somewhere completely different and try and fall out of love with Marco.' I sigh.

'You have to come home some time and he will still be here when you do,' Jess reminds me, always one to give me a reality check.

'I know that, but, well, I might feel differently after a break.'

I can only hope.

It was difficult to walk past the Little Italy Trattoria in town without glancing inside and torturing myself with memories of the evening I first laid eyes on Marco, and how he smiled at me every time he set something down on our table, making my heart race.

'Don't hate me, but is marriage really that important to

you?' asks Jess, taking a glug of her wine. 'You and Marco were so good together. Does it really matter?'

'Yes, it does. I mean, if I thought he didn't want to get married right now, but would like to one day, I could maybe live with that. But he is vehemently against the idea of marriage, full stop. He says it's an outdated institution that shouldn't be forced upon people, and who needs a piece of paper etc... I hoped we might have had children one day, and would definitely want to be married then.'

'Is anyone really bothered about that these days?' she reasons.

'Maybe not, but I am. Anyway, I don't want to talk about Marco, talk of him is off the menu this evening. I am more interested in this one,' I say, picking up the food menu and studying it. 'I'm starved.'

We dine on tasty chicken fajitas and finish up with an Eton mess for dessert and a zesty cocktail. It's Friday night after all, and I'm not in work until lunchtime tomorrow. There is a trio of musicians playing an easy going set of jazz music, and, glancing around, I notice lots of couples enjoying the ambience.

'I've had a lovely evening, Jess. It was just what I needed. I'm glad you persuaded me to come out tonight,' I tell her, feeling merry and relaxed, as we step outside onto the pavement into the August evening.

'I'm glad you enjoyed yourself.' She links arms with me as we take the short walk to our block of apartments, less than ten minutes from the high street. As we cross the road, I notice Marco and his father further along, closing the metal shutters of the restaurant. As he glances in my direction, our eyes meet and my heart sinks. He gives a wave and I wave back, before walking on.

The sooner I get away from here for a while, the better.

THREE

'I hope this dog place brings you some comfort.'

Jess wraps me in a hug as she drops me off at the airport in her temperamental old car that thankfully didn't decide to conk out en route.

'And when you come back, maybe we ought to have a cheap girls' weekend somewhere,' she says. 'I bet the others would be up for that. I saw a rental online for a refurbished cottage with a hot tub not far away from here.'

The others are a group of girls we met in the pub one Friday evening and quickly became friends with; a couple of them also attend the yoga class at the community centre. They are not exactly close friends like Jess and I, but a friendly bunch who I have grown closer to, especially these past couple of months.

'Sounds good. And thanks, Jess. You really are a great friend.'

'Even though I won't work in the shop when you're short-staffed?'

'Yes, despite that. Anyway, I would quite like to keep the customers I have, thanks,' I tease, although I think Jess is right when she says she might not possess the correct customer service skills when it comes to dealing with a difficult customer.

'Cheeky.' Jess gives me a final hug. 'So, go on, off you go, you don't want to miss your flight.'

'Oh gosh, I am doing the right thing, aren't I?' I ask Jess, as I am suddenly filled with doubts.

'Of course you are! Besides, my mum was in the shop the other day, and she said your deputy manager was telling everyone that she is in charge next week. I bet she's polishing her badge right now, she'll kill you if you don't go.' She laughs. 'Seriously, though, it will do you good, putting a bit of distance between you and Marco. It might give you some clarity. I'll miss you, though.'

'And I'll miss you too. Oh, of course you are right, I know you are, I'm just having a last-minute wobble, that's all. It's only for a few weeks.'

'That's the spirit. Text me when you get there. Safe journey.'

Standing in the queue for check-in, I can hardly believe I am doing this alone. Not that I have a problem with solo travel, I have done it before visiting friends, but it feels strange not to be texting Marco and telling him I will call him when I land in Greece.

The check-in queue is far longer than I expected, so I plug my headphones into my phone and listen to some music to while away the time. I'm looking forward to getting through to the airport lounge and having a drink.

I collect my suitcase from the baggage carousel, then head to arrivals. Judith has kindly arranged for a guy called Lars to collect me from the airport. Walking through, a young woman suddenly stops dead with her suitcase and I almost trip right over it.

'I'm so sorry.' She looks mortified. 'I bent down to pick this up.' She lifts up a book.

'No harm done,' I say brightly, as she had a genuine reason for stopping. I often wonder why people do that in supermarkets, with no apparent reason. It causes no end of arguments at the store when people stop without warning in the middle of the aisles with their trolleys.

She smiles and we carry on walking in the same direction, before we end up standing close to each other with our suitcases, scanning the people holding up names on cards. I can't help noticing her chewing her nails, and looking a bit anxious.

'Where are you heading?' I ask, a little unsure if I ought to try and engage the young woman, who is maybe in her early twenties, into a conversation.

'Near Hersonissos.' She looks up and I see that she has beautiful green eyes and delicate features behind her glasses. Her dark, wavy hair is threaded into a plait, her figure hidden beneath a baggy blue sweatshirt and jogging pants.

'Oh, me too. Whereabouts?' I ask.

'A village in the hills. I'm going to be staying at a dog rescue for a while.'

'It's not by any chance called Pine Forest, is it?' I ask.

'Yes.' She nods. 'Do you know it?'

'No, not exactly, but I'm heading there too. Are you one of the new volunteers?'

'I am.' She smiles. 'I take it you are too?'

'I am, indeed. Well, I'm pleased you're heading there too, I've made a new friend already.' I smile brightly. 'I'm Beth.'

Her face breaks into a genuine smile then. 'Nice to meet you, Beth. I'm Hannah.'

'And I guess you must be waiting for Lars too, although I think we are a little early.' I glance at my watch.

'I'm glad I've met someone who is heading to the rescue as,

to be honest, I was worried about coming here alone, but, well, you seem nice,' she says honestly.

'Thanks. So do you. What were you worried about?'

'I don't know.' She gives a little shrug. 'I've always been good around animals. People, not so much. Unless I know them well, that is,' she adds.

I'm about to ask her why she has decided to travel all the way to Greece and work with complete strangers, when she speaks again. 'So I decided to do something a bit adventurous. We're always being told to challenge ourselves and get out of our comfort zone, aren't we? I thought it was about time I tried.'

'I suppose we are, although we're also encouraged to take ice-cold swims in lakes. Can you imagine? No, thanks.' I give a little shiver. 'And to have smoothies with kale for breakfast. Ugh! I tried kale once. It tasted like petrol.' She smiles, revealing a row of neat, white teeth. 'Not that I've ever tasted petrol, of course, but you know what I mean,' I say, before diving into a packet of cheese and onion crisps as my stomach gives a little rumble. I offer her some but she politely declines.

'Don't get me wrong, I do eat healthily. Well, mostly,' I admit, glancing at the bag of crisps in my hand. 'It's just that every week, there seems to be a new fad or some expert telling us that various foods are now bad for us. Bacon sandwiches are killers apparently,' I say, thinking of how I would be reluctant to give up my Sunday morning treat. 'Anyway, I think it's really brave of you to travel alone, especially after what you have just told me.'

'Thanks. And as we're heading to the same place, perhaps we were meant to be friends.'

Talk turns to books then, as she is currently clutching one in her hand, and her face visibly lights up. I listen with feigned interest as she talks about the Gothic horror story, then I tell her I don't read books and she looks mildly horrified.

'What. Never?' She frowns.

'Well, hardly ever. In fact, no, never.'

'How come?' She seems genuinely perplexed.

'Reading is a bit too solitary for me. Also, I don't seem to have the concentration to ever get to the end of a book.'

'Maybe you just haven't found one that really grips you,' she says, determined that I should give it another go.

'Maybe. I guess I don't see the point in reading about things when you can be out there actually doing them.' I might not have been doing as much since ending things with Marco, but I'd always preferred being busy with other people to sitting quietly.

Thinking about it, I don't think I have read a whole book in my life. I passed my GCSE English by watching the film version of *Macbeth* rather than studying the text, and I watched *An Inspector Calls* at the theatre. I prefer to learn visually, watching and doing things, rather than reading about them.

'But you can't do all of the things you read about,' she argues. 'Otherwise, I'd be flying around outside right now on a ten-foot-long blue dragon,' she continues, and I burst out laughing.

'Okay, fantasy, sure, I take your point,' I concede. 'But most other things you could aspire to do in real life, surely?'

'If you're lucky enough.' She looks serious for a moment. 'Sure, books can provide inspiration, but some people aren't able to follow their dreams for various reasons. A lot of people live vicariously through books.'

'I must admit I hadn't really thought about that before,' I say, suddenly counting my blessings.

'It's true. Chatting to people in the library, where I have a Saturday job, I've discovered books are a lifeline to some of them.'

'I can imagine. Maybe I have just been put off reading by my English teacher at school, who always picked on me in class to give an answer. Usually when I was staring out of the window and daydreaming about what I would be doing after school with my friends,' I confess, and she laughs.

I smile then when I think of how surprised that teacher would be to learn that I successfully manage a busy supermarket, as she often told me daydreaming would get me nowhere.

'Stories are about the characters for me,' continues Hannah. 'It's good to see how other people live their lives and get inside their head.'

'I'm not sure I want to get inside the head of a ten-foot blue dragon.'

'You know what I mean.' She rolls her eyes, but there is a smile on her face.

'I do, I'm just teasing. Anyway, each to their own. And I do read magazines sometimes. Did you know that a male seahorse carries the babies? And that they have to eat non-stop, as their stomachs work differently and never really fill up. Imagine that, being able to eat constantly and never put on an ounce of weight.' I finish my bag of crisps, before scrunching up the packet, and placing it into a nearby bin.

'I knew they carried their young, but I didn't know they eat non-stop. I guess you learn something new every day.'

'And from one who doesn't even read books.' I wink, and she laughs.

We find somewhere to sit while we wait, chatting easily to each other. I can't wait to arrive at the dog sanctuary and meet the animals, and have cuddles with the dogs, maybe even the donkeys. I'm looking forward to making friends with the other volunteers too, especially if they are as nice as Hannah. I really admire her for doing something totally out of her comfort zone, despite my joking with her about the pressure in life to do just that. I hope this experience in Crete lives up to her expectations. And mine.

I realise I haven't given Marco a thought for the last few hours, which is a record for me. Maybe getting away and meeting new people really is exactly what I needed.

FOUR

It's not too long before a tanned guy with a grey trimmed beard comes racing into the arrivals hall, holding up a board with our names on. He spots us quickly, apologising profusely as he approaches.

'I am so sorry, I got caught in traffic. I hope you haven't been waiting too long.'

'Don't worry about it, hardly any time at all. And it has given Hannah and me a chance to make friends already,' I tell him.

'That's nice.' He smiles. 'And I'm glad you haven't been waiting long. My name is Lars. Welcome to Crete.'

We head outside towards the car, where I feel the warm sun on my face as Lars kindly loads our suitcases into the boot.

As we leave the airport I am overwhelmed by the beautiful scenery as we climb higher along the mountain roads, taking in the verdant forest, a glimpse of the gorgeous sea in the distance. It feels so refreshingly different to be here, away from the busy town back home and the constant stopping and starting at traffic lights. There is such a sense of tranquillity here, I can already feel my shoulders relaxing as I take in my surroundings.

Lars is welcoming and friendly and patiently answers my seemingly never-ending questions about the dog rescue.

'The number of dogs had dwindled down, and Judith was thinking of a quiet life. For about two weeks.' He laughs. 'When more dogs needed rescuing, Judith didn't hesitate. I cannot imagine her doing anything else,' he tells us.

Hannah is sitting beside me with her nose in a book, only lifting her head occasionally to peer out at the breathtaking scenery.

'This is some place,' I say as we drive along. 'It must be a dream living here.'

'It is indeed,' Lars replies with a smile. 'Although I have only lived here for a few short months.'

He tells us his story as we drive, revealing that he came out as a volunteer, before falling for Judith, the owner of the rescue. When he speaks, it's clear he thinks the world of her.

'It seems you are never too old to fall in love,' he says. 'In fact, I have asked Judith to marry me.'

'That is such a wonderful story, congratulations,' I tell him, thinking not everyone is against the idea of marriage. Being around a loved-up couple is probably the last thing I need right now, but I'm happy they have found each other.

Hannah lifts her head from her book and congratulates him too.

I think of my own engagement ring then, tucked in a drawer back home, and feel a little pang to the heart. Marco insisted I keep the ring when I broke things off, telling me he hoped that one day I would change my mind about us parting. We'd rowed and I'd asked him why he had bought me a ring in the first place, if he was so set against marriage. He admitted then that he wasn't sure why he had bought a ring, but he just knew it was something I wanted, which annoyed me even more. It felt like I was just being placated. For a minute, I think about our apartment, the time we spent making it a cosy home, scouring furniture shops and local websites where we sourced a fabulous second-hand dining set. We had even decked out the small balcony with fake turf and a tiny black-metal table and two chairs set. In the evening, a string of bulbs threaded through the balcony fence gave it a romantic touch when, during the summer months, we would sit outside and share a bottle of wine, enjoying the view of the town and the viaduct in the distance.

Driving on, we pass several pastel-painted houses dotted about, and high on a hill I glimpse a white church with the blue and white Greek flag outside, billowing gently in the breeze. A few seconds later, we pull up inside the wrought-iron gates of a large farmhouse-looking building, and are greeted by the sound of barking dogs.

'We're here. Welcome to Pine Forest Rescue,' says Lars as he opens the door for me and Hannah to climb out. At once I inhale the scent of the surrounding pine trees as Lars unloads our suitcases.

A pretty woman wearing a blue dress with a white cardigan over the top, with swept-up grey hair that is the same colour as her eyes, comes to meet us and introduces herself as Judith. She welcomes us warmly before offering us a cold drink.

'You are the first ones to arrive,' she explains as she takes some fresh lemonade from a fridge. 'Or maybe you would prefer a hot drink, as the weather is a little cool,' she continues, but we stick with the offer of lemonade, as it feels warm to us.

In fact, the weather is just perfect, hot, but not stifling as Lars had told us it had been during the summer months.

'I'm not sure I could have coped with your summer heat-wave,' I tell Judith.

'Maybe I have acclimatised to the weather,' Judith tells us. 'Although the summer was exceptionally hot, even for the locals.'

'Well, it's good to be here. It's such a beautiful area and certainly warmer than back home.'

'I burn easily, which is why I didn't come earlier in the summer. I thought this time of year would suit me perfectly,' says Hannah.

'Well, you are both very welcome,' says Judith as she pours us a drink and places some delicious-looking scones onto a plate, with some butter and strawberry jam.

'Home-made,' she says about the jam. 'Although I can't take the credit for the scones, my niece, Tania, made them. Hers are so much nicer than mine,' she admits.

Judith asks us about our work back home and Hannah tells us that she is studying English literature, and that the late summer months work for her other plans too.

'I'm not back at uni until mid-October, so I thought it would be nice to enjoy some time in a completely different place.'

Hannah hopes to become a librarian one day, which explains why she works weekends at her local library. I already can't imagine her doing anything else.

'You must be good with people if you manage a shop,' says Judith, when I tell her about the supermarket.

'I like to think so. Although it isn't all plain sailing.' I tell her about a bloke who recently tried to return a pizza and get a refund after he'd eaten three quarters of it. 'I do love it, though. You never know what you are going to come across in any one day.'

'Sounds a bit like here,' she says, chuckling.

After our cold drinks, Judith takes us on a tour, first showing us to the room that Hannah and I are sharing. We then head off to meet the animals, who are all completely adorable. A gorgeous white terrier melts my heart with his large brown eyes and tiny little bark that is so endearing.

'Hey there, fella.' I pet the friendly dog and he wags his tail excitedly. Most of the dogs are delighted to meet us, one or two older dogs pottering slowly over, and giving us a sniff before wandering off again and curling up in their dog beds.

I dread to think what would happen to these animals if places such as this didn't exist. Especially for the older ones, who at least have the chance to live out their last days in relative comfort here at the rescue, as older dogs are so much harder to rehome.

'It's about time for the second feed, so your arrival time has worked out perfectly,' says Judith, who we follow to the food preparation area.

After the dogs have been fed and watered, Hannah and I walk the dogs that haven't been out with volunteers today. We take a circular walk of the area, getting our bearings, and when we arrive back at the rescue, a blue car has just pulled up and a middle-aged couple climb out. The blonde woman is tall and willowy, the gentleman dark haired and deeply tanned. The colour is so intense, I can't help wondering if it is a spray tan.

'Hi!' The woman raises her hand and waves as we approach. 'Oh my goodness, are these some of the pooches?' She bends down and pets the dogs, making kissing sounds and calling them little beauties, and the air is filled with a cloud of her floral fragrance. Her face is remarkably unlined, yet I would maybe place the couple in their late forties. There is definitely an air of elegance about them, as even dressed casually in jeans and cotton shirts, they display a definite sense of style.

'I'm Doll and this is my husband, Michael,' says the attractive blonde. 'Well, it's Dorothy really, but my dad always called me Doll when I was a little girl, and the name just kind of stuck.' She smiles a perfect smile, and the husband grips my hand so firmly with his handshake I almost visibly wince. I can see Hannah have the same reaction, and try to hide a smile.

'Great to meet you, ladies.' He smiles an equally sparkling white-toothed grin as his wife.

Once we are all inside, Judith shows Doll and Michael to

their room, and soon the pale-yellow sun is disappearing behind the hills as evening falls, and an indigo sky slowly begins to take its place.

'Well, isn't this just wonderful,' says Doll, tucking into a simple supper of chicken souvlaki, pitta breads and salad. 'Just what we both needed: simplicity and mountain views. I can't wait to get out there walking with the dogs in the morning.'

'Me, too,' agrees Michael. 'We've always loved dogs, haven't we, Doll?' He turns to his wife. 'But being away so much, we have never really kept them as it wouldn't be fair.'

'What do you do for a living?' I ask, intrigued by the fact that they are away from home a lot.

'We are professional dancers,' says Doll. 'We've just finished a tour of Europe, actually.'

'She's being modest,' says Michael, taking a sip of bottled beer. 'When she says professional dancers, we are triple world champions in Latin American dance.'

'Wow, that's amazing,' says Judith. 'We're honoured to be in the presence of world champions.'

'Thanks.' Doll shrugs. 'It sounds a bit like bragging to me, introducing yourself as a triple world champion, so I tell people I'm a dancer to begin with. Michael, on the other hand, likes to let everyone know from the get-go!' She laughs.

'Too right.' He grins. 'All that blood, sweat and tears to get where we are, I want everyone to know what we have achieved.' He laughs. 'Although I wouldn't have it any other way, or I wouldn't have met you, my love.' He gives her a kiss on the cheek and she smiles.

'Anyway,' continues Doll. 'It can get a bit exhausting now that we are getting a little older, although obviously we keep ourselves fit. Being here in the forest is the perfect place to recharge and relax, away from the glitz and sparkle of the dance world. I mean, I know it will be hard work looking after the animals, but it's a different type of exertion.' She smiles at

Judith, letting her know she doesn't underestimate the hard work in looking after the animals.

Doll and Michael tell us some funny stories from their early competition days, including a malfunction with an outfit, involving a see-through dress that Doll was unaware of when she went braless during a competition dance.

'No wonder we won that one,' jokes Michael. 'Most of those judges were blokes. You probably made their night.'

'Oh, behave.' Doll rolls her eyes. 'We were by far the best that evening.'

'Just teasing, my love. Of course we were the best, no contest.' He takes a sip of beer.

Hannah says little throughout the evening, preferring to just listen, joining in the conversation every now and then and smiling in all the right places. Just after ten o'clock, she stands and wishes everyone a goodnight.

'Oh, I was about to bring out some melon,' offers Judith, but Hannah politely refuses.

'I always read before bed, so I thought I might get a couple of chapters of my book in now.' She smiles. 'I imagine it's an early start in the morning.'

'Well, you are right about that,' agrees Judith. 'The animals aren't ones for having a lie-in.' She smiles. 'Goodnight then, see you in the morning.'

'Probably sensible,' I say, although, in truth I could sit here all night, chatting to the interesting people sitting around the table. It's a world away from my life back home, and already I am savouring the change, absorbing every minute of this new environment.

'I won't be far behind you, and don't worry, I won't chat.' I wink at Hannah, suddenly wondering if us sharing a room is going to be a good match. I needn't have worried, though, as half an hour later, when I retire, I smile to myself at the sight of Hannah snoozing gently, her book open on the top of the covers.

I quietly place it on her bedside table before sliding into the bed on the other side of the room myself.

It doesn't take long for me to start drifting off, but before sleep comes, I can't help but smile at my time in Greece so far. Something tells me I am going to like it here.

FIVE

Four volunteers arrive the following morning to walk the dogs as the sun makes an appearance once more in a clear blue sky. A handsome couple from over the road also appear to take some of the dogs out and Judith introduces the woman as her niece, Tania, and her boyfriend, Nicos.

'So pleased to meet you all.' Tania beams a welcoming smile. 'Things have suddenly gotten a little busy again here at the rescue, but my aunt lives and breathes the dogs,' she tells me as we walk and fall into step together.

Hannah is walking a little behind, with two small dogs on each lead, chatting away to them as she walks, which makes me smile.

'Judith's wonderful, isn't she?' I say to Tania. 'And Lars was telling me all about how they found romance and recently got engaged. It's such a lovely story.'

'It really is. I'm thrilled for her, she never thought she would meet someone else over here. Her whole life has been the animals since my uncle passed away.'

'I imagine they were a lot of comfort to her. It's obvious how much she cares for them.'

'They were. The dogs were like family to her and to my uncle Ray, as they never had any children,' she reveals.

We stroll along, watching the sun filtering through the leaves of the trees, casting moving patterns on the road below. One or two of the trees have leaves that are slowly turning a pale yellow, others in various shades of green like jewels decorating the branches. I take lungfuls of the invigorating mountain air as we walk.

'I was engaged recently,' I find myself telling Tania as we chat about Judith's upcoming wedding.

'You were?' She turns to face me and suddenly the whole marriage thing comes tumbling out and, to my surprise, I can feel tears building in my eyes. Although we have only just met, Tania is so easy to talk to. Too easy. If only I didn't miss Marco so damn much.

'That's a tricky one.' We've arrived at a field, which Tania tells me is an unofficial dog park, adopted from some unclaimed land. She lets the dogs she is walking off lead and throws a ball. They all race off after it at top speed.

'Tell me about it.' I sigh. 'If either one of us had compromised, then we would be sacrificing our beliefs. I miss him, though I kind of wish I didn't. It's part of the reason I came here, to put a little distance between us.'

'You're bound to miss him. You can't just switch off your feelings for someone,' she says kindly, touching my arm. 'But then it's hard not to stick by your beliefs too, I guess.'

Nicos is walking up ahead chatting to another bloke of a similar age. Tania tells me all about how she met him when he inherited the pink house across the road from the rescue.

'Oh, that's a beautiful-looking house. And gosh, it sounds like this is quite the place for romance, given it is such a small village.'

'I know! Sometimes, I can hardly believe I actually live here. Romance was the last thing on my mind when I came to visit my aunt,' she tells me. 'But I thought Nicos was lovely as soon as I saw him, despite him being very quiet. It turned out he just had things on his mind at the time. There was a lot going on with his ex,' she reveals.

'If only relationships weren't so complicated.' I sigh.

'That's life, though, hey. And Panos is single if you're interested, although maybe he's a bit too young for you.' She giggles as she points out a young man who is walking behind Hannah. They look around the same age.

'By at least ten years, I'd say. And I'm definitely not looking for romance,' I insist, looking at the young man. 'Anyway, the only reason I came here was for the love of dogs,' I say, thinking of my favourite show back home. 'Loving animals is far less complicated than humans.'

'I take your point,' Tania concedes, before telling me all about the local family bar that Panos runs with his sister, which is owned by their mother, their father having passed away last year. I might not be interested in Panos, but the bar sounds like a perfect place to visit.

'You should come for dinner one evening,' says Tania, as we talk about the tasty delights to be found around here. I already feel she could become a good friend whilst I'm here, and I thank her. 'In fact, I'll invite a few people over for a BBQ next week,' she suggests. 'I have to warn you, though, if you think this lot are lively, I have a rather crazy Hungarian Vizsla. We may have to cage him until dinner is over.'

'Ah, he sounds like fun.'

'You might not say that when he sits eyeing your food, or even worse steals it, given half a chance,' she says and I think of my gran's boxer dog who was the same.

'He does sound adorable, though. Is he a red Vizsla?'

'He is. Smudge lives with us, along with his little friend Annie. They were at the rescue for over a year.'

She takes her phone from her pocket and shows me a photo of the pair.

'Oh, I love them already. Smudge's fur is the same colour as my hair, I just know we are going to be friends,' I say and she smiles.

When we arrive at a small stream, the dogs take a dip and Tania's handsome partner, Nicos, comes over to her. Hannah stands looking around, then Panos gestures to a seat beside him on a large flat rock. She smiles politely before joining him, then she reaches into her rucksack for a book.

'Do you enjoy book?' Panos gestures to the novel. His English is not as fluent as Nicos's, although maybe he has never really left the village, spending his days working at the family bar.

'Yes.' Hannah smiles. 'It's a bit heavy at times. But I like it.'

'Shall I carry it for you?' He grins.

'No, I mean heavy going. I...'

'I joke.' He smiles, a wide smile that lights up his handsome face, framed by dark curly hair.

'Oh, I see.' She smiles and I'm charmed by the scene unfolding in front of me, pleased that there is someone here around Hannah's own age for her to chat to.

'I also love to read. Sometimes I try and read English novel, to help with the language, but it is almost impossible.' He shakes his head.

'That's a good idea, though, to read books, and pick out some words. I don't know enough Greek words to even attempt reading something as short as a pamphlet in Greek.'

'What is pamphlet?'

'Pamphlet is a brochure. Or leaflet?' She reaches into her bag and pulls out a leaflet about a museum.

'Ah, *prospektous*,' he says.

'That actually makes sense,' says Hannah. 'I have learned a new word.'

'Maybe I could help you. Then also, you could help me with English words,' he offers.

'Sure.' She shrugs, her cheeks colouring a little.

'Shall we make a move back?' Tania stands and leads us in a circular walk back towards the rescue.

The sun is beautifully warm, caressing my arms and legs, and by the time we have returned I feel incredibly relaxed. When Tania and Nicos leave, I notice them holding hands as they head back across the road, clearly besotted with each other, and I swallow down a feeling of personal regret.

Doll and Michael have stayed at the rescue today, feeding the donkeys and replenishing the food as well as cleaning the kennels. We have a rota, so tomorrow they will walk the dogs and we will do the cleaning, although we all muck in as and when required. Doll is working with Lars, and he is laughing at something she has said.

Hannah and I are contemplating a swim, which horrifies Judith, who doesn't think it's warm enough, but it definitely is, at twenty-one degrees. After swimming side by side, we are sitting on the sunloungers, sipping a drink.

'You're a really good swimmer,' I comment. Hannah looks as cool as a cucumber, whereas my cheeks are burning and I feel like I've had a real workout just trying to keep up with her.

'I enjoy it. I used to swim for the county,' she tells me as she sips her drink.

'You did? Wow, that's amazing. No wonder I couldn't keep up with you.'

'My swimming teacher actually told me I might make the Olympics one day,' she says casually. 'But I'm not sure I really had the fire or the discipline, and that's what you need, isn't it?'

'I suppose it is. Plus, I imagine it's a gruelling schedule. I don't suppose you could get up at the crack of dawn and all that stuff unless you were really passionate about it. Especially in the winter.' I give a little shiver at the thought.

'Exactly. Besides, I think my dad wanted it more than I did, fulfilling his own dreams through me. He was a good swimmer, but he never quite made it. I'm not sure he's quite forgiven me for giving up,' she says, and I think of all of those parents who try and live their own unfulfilled ambitions through their children.

'Well, we have to do what makes us happy. And books obviously do it for you.'

Her eyes light up at the mention of books.

'Oh, definitely. I do still enjoy swimming, but books are definitely my passion. I just love being surrounded by them in the library. I get super excited when new ones arrive.'

I'm not sure I've found my passion in life. It definitely wasn't my lifetime ambition to work in a supermarket, but as I'm the manager it pays quite well. And I do love meeting the customers. It was my first job after leaving an ill-fated college course in hairdressing, which I was completely unsuited to. I soon settled into the high street store in my local town, the only problem initially being that my mum thought I could give her freebies, notably alcohol. She would often appear inside, intoxicated, and would start shouting at me when I asked her to leave empty-handed. Thankfully, the manager at the time was super understanding. They dealt with everything tactfully, even sending me on a short break when I was upset, burning with shame and embarrassment. Eventually she stopped coming into the shop and moved out of the area. I'm not exactly sure where to – I only hear from her when she wants some money. Even that is less frequently these days, which probably means she has hooked up with yet another bloke.

'Maybe I ought to persevere one day, and actually read a

whole book.' I smile. 'Although I do learn rather a lot from reading magazines. For example, did you know that cows kill more people than sharks,' I tell her.

'Are you sure you haven't made that one up?' Hannah looks at me doubtfully.

'It's hard to believe, but it's actually true. Sharks kill around five humans a year, whereas cows kill around twenty-two people per year. Another little fact I gleaned from reading *National Geographic* magazine on my lunch break in the shop. It's where I learned about the male seahorses carrying the babies.'

'How fascinating. I've always been a bit wary of cows when out walking in the countryside. It's the way they stare at you,' she says. 'And maybe you just need the right book. Schoolbooks can put people off for life when you have to study them. It's different and nice to just read for pleasure.'

'If you say so,' I reply. We chat for a little longer, but I can see Hannah itching to dive back into her book, so I plug my headphones into my phone and listen to some of my favourite music. As I settle into the sunlounger, I reflect on how nice it is to get to know someone so different.

SIX

'Have you seen Lars?'

It's the following morning, and Judith is looking for her fiancé, who seems to have disappeared without a word.

'Last time I saw him, he was cleaning out the donkey stalls with Doll,' says Michael as he winds a green hose up and hangs it near the outdoor tap. 'Come to think of it, Doll has disappeared too,' he says, glancing around.

'She's in the kitchen,' I tell Michael. 'Or at least she was a few minutes ago.'

Judith looks a little bemused, saying that it's unlike Lars to go off without telling anyone, but at that moment he appears behind her.

'Oh, there you are.' Judith's face breaks into a smile as she turns to see him emerge from the donkey area. 'I was looking for you! Can you help me with something on the computer?'

'Coming.' He smiles. Once he's followed Judith inside, Doll also appears from the donkey stalls.

'I think those animals are my favourites. Especially that poor old Freddie with the damaged leg. I've taken to giving him a bit of fruit from the breakfast table.' She smiles. 'They love pears, don't they?' She winks. 'As well as carrots. It must get really boring eating straw all day.'

'Maybe to us, but don't forget it's their staple diet,' Hannah reminds her.

'I know, but a little bit of crunch must be nice for them. Every now and then.'

With the morning's work done, Judith gathers us together and tells us it's coming time to do some fundraising down at the harbour.

'It is something we do once a month and is vital to keep some money in the coffers to keep the rescue going,' she explains.

'Have you ever done a crowdfunding page?' asks Hannah, removing her glasses and giving them a wipe with the edge of her T-shirt. Her eyes really are a striking shade of green.

'We did think about it,' says Judith. 'But there are quite a few dog rescues in Crete, so I can't imagine the response would be that great.'

'Might be worth a try even so. And maybe you should try Star Beach as well as the harbour for the fundraising. A lot of British people use that beach and they are mad about dogs, aren't they? Just look at us coming all this way to volunteer.'

'You know, that might not be a bad idea. Good thinking, Hannah,' says Judith and Hannah looks pleased with herself. 'On Friday, we will do exactly that.' Judith gives a wry smile. 'Well, when I say we, I mean you guys. Lars and I will stay here and look after things. I can't stand for as long as I used to.'

'Great,' I say, thinking a day at the beach might be a nice place to get a bit of a tan if I wear shorts and a sleeveless top. Even if it is a fundraising exercise, I am already looking forward to it.

.   .   .   .

'Does anyone fancy the bar later?' I ask when all the chores are done. I have a couple of pretty dresses in my suitcase and it might be nice to put on a little make-up, especially after mucking out the animals. Plus, a nice glass of wine might help me sleep, as despite being tired yesterday, I tossed and turned last night, thoughts of Marco annoyingly popping into my head. So much for coming here to forget about him.

I wish I could drop the idea of getting married, as Jess had suggested. Goodness knows why I'm so set on it. I wasn't exactly shown the best example of marriage, what with Dad's anger issues that led to Mum's drinking and eventually their messy divorce. Maybe I aspire to have everything that they didn't, welcoming children into a secure, loving marriage.

'I will,' says Hannah at once, surprising me with her keen-ness, whilst Doll and Michael decline, saying they will stay here with Judith and Lars.

'It does close around nine, although sometimes it stays open a little later, if business is good,' warns Judith. 'It's more of a daytime bar, serving customers with drinks after they have climbed the dozens of steps up to the church.'

As we get ready, I ask Hannah if she ever wears make-up, as I apply my own in front of the small dressing-table mirror. I never feel properly dressed without it, especially for an evening out.

I pull my long hair up into a bun and pull a few strands around my face, before changing into cropped white trousers and a tight-fitting green top and I am ready to go.

'No. I wouldn't have a clue where to start when it comes to make-up,' she admits.

'Well, you certainly don't need it. You're very pretty and you have lovely eyes,' I tell her. 'I bet they would stand out even more with a touch of mascara.'

I offer her my mascara wand and a pot of clear lip gloss.

'Thanks, but I'm not sure,' she says politely.

'No worries.' I smile. 'But help yourself anytime, you don't need to ask me.'

'Thank you, Beth.'

I leave the make-up on the dressing table and go off to tidy away the things I have left in the bathroom. When I return, Hannah is dressed in light blue jeans and a floral blouse. Her long dark hair is let loose; the make-up on the dressing table remains untouched.

'You look lovely,' I tell her and she smiles, a little self-consciously. 'Thanks. I wasn't sure if the blouse was a bit loud, but I guess it does still feel like summer here.'

'I'd say colourful, rather than loud, and it suits you perfectly. And goes well with those jeans.'

'Thanks. Maybe it does look good.' She looks at herself in the mirror, turning this way and that to double-check.

'You are most welcome. And there is no maybe about it, you look great.'

Before we leave, Hannah grabs a canvas tote bag and pops a couple of books into it. I was amazed to discover that she had packed six books into her suitcase to bring here.

'Don't say you're going to read in the bar?' I tease her, laughing.

'No,' she says, looking sheepish. 'I was going to give one of my books to Panos.'

'That's alright then. We don't want to dent the bar's profits by sitting reading instead of drinking,' I say and she looks a little embarrassed.

'Gosh, sorry, I'm just joking,' I say quickly. 'I'm just thinking of these people who read in cafés for hours, only buying one coffee.'

'I do that. Although I do generally buy a cake or something else too.' She laughs, but I wish I could stop putting my big foot in my mouth. 'I also noticed a bookcase downstairs in the kitchen. I'll pop a book or two there, once I've finished, for some of the other volunteers,' she says thoughtfully.

Walking along to the bar, the heady scent of flowers, pine and wild rosemary fills the air. A bird flies overhead and settles on a tree branch high up, chirping in the early evening. It's so peaceful and pretty, and the sky is gently changing colour from a light blue to a a soft shade of pink, signalling another fine day tomorrow. We are just turning a corner, about to make the ascent up the hill to the bar, when a car passes so quickly that we are practically flattened against the bushes at the side of the road. I wave my fist at the inconsiderate driver, who comes to an abrupt halt in the middle of the road.

'Uh, oh,' says Hannah a little nervously. 'Do you think he saw you make that gesture? I hope this isn't a case of road rage.'

'I'll give him road rage. He nearly bloody killed us! Fancy driving like that, on these roads,' I rant. 'Anyway, I only raised my fist. I could have been far more impolite.'

I'm marching towards the car, Hannah flapping her hands and telling me we might get murdered, which, although dramatic, makes me back off a little. As I slow, my anger starts to dissipate and I stop, about to turn around, when the door of the car opens and out steps the most drop-dead gorgeous man I think I have ever seen.

'I'm so sorry,' says the man, dressed in a light-blue suit and white shirt, holding his hands up. He has large brown eyes and a chiselled jaw, and looks as though he has just stepped off a catwalk.

'You ought to be more careful,' I say; my rage has completely subsided and Hannah gives me a knowing look and raises an eyebrow.

'Of course, apologies once more,' he says earnestly. 'I guess I am so used to these roads being quiet. It is nice to be away from the city and be able to really drive this car.' He gestures to his sleek, silver BMW. 'Please, let me buy you both a drink to say sorry.'

'Hmm. Well, we were just heading to the bar actually,' I say nonchalantly. This guy is seriously hot.

'And where are my manners.' He shakes hands with us both. 'My name is Artemis.'

SEVEN

Panos isn't at the bar when we arrive, but a young woman is serving the few customers up here. She must be his sister, though, as she looks exactly like him. After Artemis orders our drinks – a beer for Hannah, wine for me and Artemis – the young woman brings the drinks over and introduces herself as Helena.

'You look so much like your brother,' I can't help commenting. 'We met him the other day walking the dogs.'

'Yes. We are twins.' She smiles.

Hannah glances around the bar, and I wonder if she is disappointed that Panos is not here this evening.

'Where is your brother now?' I ask, as I feel on Hannah's behalf.

'Just taking something to my grandmother's house. He will be here shortly,' she says, before disappearing back to the bar.

'So, do you live here?' I turn my attention to Artemis.

'No, but my mother does and I grew up here. I came to visit her today, to bring her something.' He takes a drink.

'That's very kind of you.' Such a handsome man has such a big heart.

'I've been visiting my mother more often recently, as she had a fall earlier in the year. She has been out and about a lot with her new friend, determined to live life to the fullest. Last month they went into Heraklion to watch an expensive show at a theatre.'

He looks slightly uncomfortable before continuing, 'But I do worry that she is doing too much. And being out here... It's nice, but she is so far from anything. I live on the other side of Hersonissos, close to the main harbour.'

'It is a gorgeous place. I'm not sure I could live here either, though. It's a bit too quiet for me, except for the barking!' I say. 'Although the rescue is the perfect place to spend a few weeks, away from everything.'

'You are trying to get away from everything?' He takes a sip of wine.

'Not exactly. But they do say a change is as good as a rest.' I'm not about to spill my guts to this guy.

'It is quiet up here,' says Artemis. 'But there is plenty of action down in Hersonissos.' He holds my gaze for a moment. 'If you like, I could show you around sometime.'

'Sounds good. Will your wife be joining us?' I gesture to his wedding ring, and he lets out a deep sigh.

'We are separated.' He slides the gold band up and down his finger. 'Yes, I wear the ring because I thought we might make up. But I do not think she is coming back.' He drains the last of his drink and orders another one.

'But you hope she will?' Hannah asks, averting her gaze from the bar area, where she has no doubt been keeping an eye out for Panos.

'No. Well, to be truthful I'm not sure,' he says. 'There have been lots of weekends away with her girlfriends lately and it seems she wants to be single again.' He shrugs as Helena brings over his fresh glass of wine.

'I'm sorry to hear that.' I can't help feeling a bit sorry for

Artemis, and my mind drifts to marriages and Marco before I can stop myself.

'Maybe it is good for me. Now I am free to talk to beautiful women whenever I please.' He leans in closer and I can smell his expensive aftershave. 'You have something in your hair,' he says. Then, 'May I?'

He extracts a leaf from my hair that had floated down from a nearby tree, and smiles. I can see how easy it would be for any woman to fall under this guy's spell. He has such a confident way about him and there is no denying his good looks.

We chat for a bit longer, before Artemis pushes his untouched glass of wine towards me.

'Please. I should not really have ordered another drink as I am driving. But maybe I will see you tomorrow. If you are free?'

'I'm working at the rescue,' I remind him.

'But surely you have free time?' He looks at me, seeming certain I will take him up on his offer.

'I do in the early evening. But I'm not sure what my plans are tomorrow.' I glance at Hannah, but she has taken one of the books from her bag, and is engrossed in reading. I hope she doesn't feel excluded. 'Anyway, it was nice to meet you, Artemis, but this is kind of a girls' night out.'

'Of course.' Artemis glances at his watch. 'I must be off anyway. Shall I pick you up tomorrow? At say, seven, at the animal rescue. I can show you somewhere a little livelier.'

'I never agreed to that.'

'I know you didn't. But I am hoping that you will.' He smiles as he grabs his keys from the table and stands to leave.

Maybe I ought to go out with him. I am here to try and get over Marco after all. What better way than a little holiday flirtation with a very handsome guy? Having a little fun surely can't hurt, can it?

'I'm not making any promises. It depends how busy we are

tomorrow, and if I can be bothered doing anything in the evening,' I say casually.

'Okay. Well, at least you will think about it. Goodnight, ladies.'

'Sorry about that.' I turn to Hannah. 'I hope you didn't feel left out. I expected him to buy us a drink, then be on his way.'

'Oh, it's fine, it wasn't for long. He's a bit full of himself, isn't he? But wow, he's so good-looking.'

'He is, isn't he?' I say as the roar of his car can be heard, followed by the sound of the horn beeping as he drives out of sight.

'"Flashy" is the word my mum would use,' says Hannah.

'And I think she would be right.' I giggle. 'The complete opposite to Panos, I'd say.' I nod to the figure who has just arrived at the bar, wearing blue jeans, Converse sneakers, and a black T-shirt.

'*Kalispera.*' Panos strides towards us and Hannah visibly brightens. 'How are you?' he asks.

'I'm good thanks. And you?' She tucks a strand of hair shyly behind her ear.

'Very well. I am pleased you are here, actually. I hope maybe you help me?' asks Panos, turning to Hannah.

'Help you? In what way.'

'Remember we talk of books. I need to improve my English. Could I maybe send you emails?'

Panos goes on to explain that a friend of his improved his English by sending emails to an English friend, and in turn they would pick up some Greek.

'Kind of like a pen pal?' says Hannah.

'Pen pal?' Panos looks puzzled.

'Yes. Someone you write letters to, although in this case emails.'

'I see. Yes, like that.' He smiles.

'Oh, and I brought you this. There are not many English

books for sale around here, I noticed. Maybe you could read this.'

'Thank you.' He turns the book over and slowly reads the blurb.

'No offence, but it is quite an easy read,' says Hannah. 'No super long words.'

'Perfect. Lovely jubbly,' he says and we both burst out laughing.

'That isn't something a lot of English people say, apart from Del Boy,' I say.

'Yes! *Only Fools and the Horses*! My grandmother watches it. I learn a lot of English from TV programmes.' He smiles proudly.

'Oh dear,' says Hannah. 'Let's hope he doesn't make any politically incorrect remarks if he watches those old shows.' She giggles, when Panos heads to the bar.

He returns with some olives and crisps in bowls and places them on the table.

'*Efcharisto*,' says Hannah and he replies with '*Parakalo*', which means 'welcome'.

'Is the word "olive" the same in Greek?' asks Hannah.

'It is "*elia*". You say "el e ya".'

'And "crisps"?'

'"*Tsips*". You say "teeps".'

'Thanks, I think I will remember that. "*Tsips*" sounds a bit like "crisps".'

'My pleasure,' Panos says, smiling, before going off to serve a couple of people who have just arrived at the bar.

Sitting beneath a tall olive tree, we watch a few other people come and go. Soon enough, there is only Hannah and me left in the bar, just after nine fifteen. Helena begins to wipe nearby tables and glances at her watch.

'I think it's time for us to call it a night,' I say, finishing the glass of wine that Artemis left. 'Helena and Panos seem far too polite to tell us to leave, but Judith did mention that the bar closes early. Don't forget to give Panos your email address,' I remind Hannah.

'Oh, I'm not sure,' she says, but Panos is already striding towards us.

They exchange contact details, and Hannah is smiling shyly as they do.

'Goodnight then,' we say to Panos as we gather our things.

'*Kalinychta*,' says Panos.

'*Kalinychta*,' repeats Hannah, picking up her bag with a smile.

'That was nice,' I say to Hannah as we walk home, feeling mellow. It's a little cooler now, so I pull on my denim jacket.

'It was,' says Hannah.

As we walk, passing through the trees, we listen to the sound of chirruping crickets that sound every evening here. The path towards the rescue is quite dark, so I find the torch on my phone to guide us home, and Hannah does the same. In the distance across the valley, lights are glowing in the houses like flickering candles.

'Maybe lacking a cocktail menu, but the wine was decent enough.' I smile.

'Don't worry, I'm sure you will find a cocktail bar tomorrow evening when Artemis takes you out,' says Hannah.

'That's if I decide to go with him. I haven't actually made my mind up yet.'

'Yeah, right,' she says, smiling at me.

Just then, a rabbit darts out across the road and we both scream, before bursting out laughing.

'It seems it isn't just drivers who like to speed along these roads,' I say, linking arms with Hannah as we stroll downhill with our flashlights.

EIGHT

The sun burns brightly in a clear blue sky once again the following day. Just seeing it instantly lifts my mood. I'm happy to soak up the hot weather at the moment, and like the thought of going home with a nice tan. The forest will be bathed in a soft amber glow in a month or two, as some of the leaves change colour, creating a tapestry of autumnal shades alongside the evergreen pines.

I'm enjoying the warmth while stroking Freddie, the poor donkey with the bent leg, who, despite this, is cheerful and loving. There are several other donkeys at the rescue, including Willow, an elderly female who has recently retired after a life of transporting goods and people throughout a village. She was found cast aside wandering, as some are once they are of no use to their owners. But today, she is enjoying the sunshine, only recently having ventured from her stall.

'Living your best life now, aren't you, boy?' I stroke Freddie's nose and he brays contentedly. Judith had told me all about another old donkey called Eric, and how he blows hot and cold, which has proved to be true. Today he's in his stall ignoring everyone. But tomorrow, who knows?

'Right, that's the donkeys sorted,' I say, joining the others, having mucked out, filled the feeders with fresh hay, and made sure there is plenty of water. Doll and Michael have fed the dogs and are hosing down the paths outside the cages.

'Gorgeous day, isn't it?' Doll is wearing shorts and a T-shirt, her long, toned legs testament to her years as a dancer.

'Fantastic,' says Michael, turning his face to the sun. 'I might actually get a real tan out here. This spray tan will wear off soon enough,' he tells us, confirming my suspicions. 'We get them done when we have a dance tour,' he explains.

'Will you ever retire?' I ask as we head towards the kitchen for a drink.

'I don't like to think about it,' says Doll. 'Dancing is all I've ever known.'

'Much as I love the dancing too, I can't wait,' says Michael. 'It's getting harder to drag myself out of bed in the winter. I wouldn't mind retiring to the sun. I could sit in it all day.'

'As if. You would be bored stiff after a week.' She rolls her eyes at her husband and laughs.

'I'm not sure I would, my love. Imagine basking in the sunshine, reading and drinking wine, or taking long beach walks. And if we did get bored, we could teach dance classes somewhere.'

'We?' She laughs.

'I couldn't do it without you, you know that. We're like Fred Astaire and Ginger Rogers.'

Hannah asks who they are and Doll says she feels ancient, so I don't like to say that I don't know who they are either. I think I may have vaguely heard about them starring in some old movies.

'Well, I like the sound of the sunshine and wine bit,' says Doll, carrying two empty food sacks to a large bin. 'I quite fancy Spain, I've always been partial to some tapas. Maybe some-where along the Alicante coast. I'm not so sure about the dance school bit, though. When I retire, I want to do just that,' she says firmly.

'Of course. But surely Portugal, my love?' says Michael. 'We already have friends there, remember.'

'Whatever. Anyway, we're not ready for the knacker's yard just yet, are we?' She smiles. 'So let's not have this conversation right now.'

Lars appears just then, and tells us he is off to a large supermarket several miles away. 'Would anyone like anything bringing back?'

'I wouldn't mind going,' Hannah whispers in my ear. 'I need a couple of pens and a notebook. Will you come too?'

'I thought you were being brave and getting out of that comfort zone?' I say, but then feel a bit mean when she goes a little quiet.

'Of course I will come. I could probably do with a new mascara,' I tell her and turn to ask Lars if we can join him. He says he will wait outside in the car, whilst we nip inside for our bags.

We drive down the windy mountain road, enjoying the scenery, and I smile at the mountain goats, some standing high on craggy rocks, one or two meandering down the roads. Turning left, we drive along a road lined with olive trees, and dotted with buildings that include rustic farmhouses, and a white building with a green roof that Lars informs us is an olive oil factory. There isn't a cloud in the sky and it's a world away from everything back home.

'I see you like your books.' Lars turns to Hannah in the back seat, who is staring out of the window, an open book on her lap.

'Yes, I do. I was hoping there might be one or two books in the supermarket actually,' she tells him. 'Although they will probably all be in Greek.'

'You do see the occasional English book, although it's mainly in the larger, touristy towns. I think Judith has some books, but perhaps they are not the kind someone of your age might be interested in,' Lars tells her.

'Thanks. I pretty much read anything so I'm sure I can find something.'

As we approach the coast road, I eye the sparkling water that looks so inviting on a day like this.

'Hey, Hannah, look at that sea. I could dive right in, especially in this nice weather. I wish I'd brought my swimming costume now. My new mascara can wait,' I say, staring out of the window at a speedboat in the distance skimming across the water.

'It does look like a nice quiet beach. Perhaps we could come here one day?' suggests Hannah.

'Sure, why not?' I say, thinking it might be nice for a walk one evening, especially if the current warm weather continues.

We pull up outside a large supermarket that is bright and airy inside and sells just about anything you could possibly need, alongside the usual Greek souvenirs. I buy a bottle of ouzo and some plastic shot glasses, just in case anyone fancies staying up and chatting one evening. I also buy a pink sarong, as I'd forgotten to bring one, and some giant bags of crisps. Judith feeds us well, but I'm a bit of a night-time muncher, a habit I'm trying hard to break.

Hannah has bought a notebook, pen and a Greek novel that, judging by its cover, is a romance. Armed with our goodies, we make our way back to the rescue. Hannah has also bought a huge bag of assorted toffees that she passes around as we drive.

Lars gives us a driving tour on a different route on the way back, passing tiny churches, and a small maritime museum, as well as several shops, bars and restaurants. There's a sign for Malia as we approach the highway, and I wonder whether I might actually get the chance to visit whilst I'm here. I'm not sure if it's Hannah's thing, though, as she seems keener on her suggestion to visit the quiet beach we passed earlier. As we drive, she buries her nose in her new book, saying some of the Greek words out loud.

'I'm sure I'm not pronouncing these words properly. It's pretty difficult,' she says, closing her book with a sigh.

'I'm sure Panos will help you,' I remind her.

'I'm sure he will.' She smiles at the mention of his name. 'And I will help him with his English. We can't have him saying "lovely jubbly" all the time, can we?' She laughs.

'Oh, I know. If he keeps watching those old TV programmes, I dread to think what he might come out with. I worry he might say something to upset someone, especially nowadays.'

We go quiet as we admire the views again, before Hannah surprises me and starts chatting to Lars instead of reading.

'So, when are you getting married then?' Hannah asks him as we start driving up into the hills again.

'It was supposed to be next summer. But recently we decided, why wait? Especially at our age.' He grins. 'So the wedding is going to take place in a few weeks, before the weather becomes a little unpredictable. Tania and Nicos have offered to have the wedding at their place, as they have a large garden. Everyone in the village is invited.'

I juggle the dates to figure out whether I will be gone before the wedding but it seems it will take place two days before I am due to leave. Despite my mixed feelings over weddings at the moment, already I can't think of a nicer couple to celebrate a wedding with. Maybe if I can't face it, I will offer to stay with the animals. That is, if Judith wouldn't consider it rude of me.

'I'm so happy for you and Judith. And what a beautiful place. I can't imagine a better venue to hold a wedding reception than at her niece's house, especially with the beautiful forest backdrop. I imagine the photographs will look incredible.'

'I'm sure you are right. And I feel very lucky to have found Judith. I never thought love would happen for me again,' he tells us honestly. 'But it seems it can creep up on you when you least expect it. Even for an old guy like me.'

'I think love can happen at any age, if you are open to it. Although I don't think of you as an old man,' I tell him truthfully, as his penchant for early morning hikes and long swims would give a man half his age a run for their money.

I think of my mum then, and how she is always in love and rarely without a man. Then again, some of her relationships could not exactly be described as loving; she just hates being alone. I'm not sure she has ever been really happy in a relationship, and despite everything, I really hope there will come a time when she is. Perhaps she cannot be truly happy until she learns to love herself.

As we continue travelling back, with the car windows open and the sun beaming down from the sky, I'm so thankful to be here. And I realise I haven't thought about Marco today. Not until talk of weddings came up, at least. It seems I can't help thinking of what might have been.

NINE

As we pull in back at the farmhouse, Judith is in one of the garden areas talking to an older lady, with black hair piled up on her head, and wearing a blue patterned top and a pair of white trousers. They were laughing at something when we arrived, but as we join them Judith quickly introduces us to her friend Yolanda. She is a striking-looking woman with a familiar look about her that I can't quite place.

'*Kalispera*, it is nice to meet you, but now I go.' She speaks quickly in a strong Greek accent. She finishes her drink and picks up a bike helmet. 'I need some honey, so I am driving to the honey farm. I need to get back out on my bike again.'

'Well, it isn't far, I suppose, but do be careful,' says Judith.

'*Nai, nai.*' She waves her hand.

Judith walks her to the gate and Yolanda loops her straw basket over her moped and climbs on and a few minutes later, the sound of a moped can be heard driving off.

'Gosh, will she be alright on that?' I ask Judith as we head inside with the shopping. 'Those hills are pretty steep.'

'I'm sure she will be fine,' she assures me. 'Her house is the green one at the top of the hill, and it's a bit much walking up and down, especially following her fall. Lars offers to drive her around, but she is fiercely independent. I did worry when she first started driving her moped, but try telling her that,' she says, raising an eyebrow. 'Thankfully she didn't break any bones when she fell, and she is determined to grab life with both hands. She often says to me, "The day I stop going out and about is the day I lie down in my grave."'

'She sounds a bit like my gran,' I tell Judith. 'She still walks around the less salubrious parts of town with her walking stick, which she doesn't actually need, but says it's for protection.' I can't help smiling.

Judith laughs, then tells us all about the accident her friend had a few months ago and how she bounced back so quickly. 'That's when she decided to get the moped, so she could get about, including coming here to visit. Really, she is as fit as a fiddle. I draw the line at riding pillion, though. Usually she just heads down here, and Lars take us out in the car. We enjoy a little clothes shopping and lunch now and then.'

'That sounds nice,' I say, thinking of how I enjoy doing that back home with friends.

After the second animal feed of the day and a chat with Eric the donkey, who is happy to hang out with us for a bit today, we do some general cleaning. Once I've finished up, I head inside to take a shower and change into a flowery dress. I tie my long hair back and offer my help in the kitchen, but it seems Lars has everything under control this evening, with the tantalising smell of a casserole on the go. Just then, Hannah, who has been outside sitting beneath a tree with her laptop exchanging an email with Panos, walks into the kitchen.

'Beth, there is someone here to see you,' she says, gesturing towards the gate. As I walk closer, I spot the sleek outline of Artemis's silver BMW. He is leaning on the roof so confidently.

'So, have you made your mind up then? Would you like to go out with me?' He smiles that million-dollar smile that surely any girl would find hard to resist.

'You don't give up easily, do you?' I casually reply, although I think my mind is already made up.

'Did anyone ever achieve anything by giving up easily?'

He walks towards me, looking smart and sexy, dressed in dark jeans and a patterned, fitted shirt that shows off his toned physique.

'Where did you have in mind?' I'm trying to play it cool, but there is no doubt that Artemis looks seriously hot this evening.

'A little restaurant I know, on a beach.' As he walks closer, I notice that he smells wonderful too. 'That is, if you haven't already eaten? If so, maybe a drink?'

'Actually, no I haven't eaten.'

I must admit, I decided not to eat, in case Artemis had a restaurant in mind.

'So would you like to join me? The food is very good.'

He holds my gaze with his large, dark-brown eyes.

'Okay sure, why not,' I find myself saying, before stopping myself from adding, 'How could I resist?'

I nip inside and tell Judith I will be dining out with a friend I met at the bar. She tells me to be careful and asks if I am sure I know what I am doing, going off with someone I barely know.

Maybe she has a point. I don't really know this guy, but I figure as his mother lives around here he isn't likely to try anything untoward.

'Oh, don't worry. I'm sure he can be trusted,' I tell her as I grab my bag. 'He said his mother lives in the village.'

'Oh, right.' Judith looks a little puzzled, but tells me to have a nice evening all the same.

· · ·

'You look good,' Artemis comments on my cotton dress, as I climb into the passenger seat. 'Black looks great against your wonderful hair colour.'

'Thank you. And you look good too, I like your shirt,' I say, feeling flattered by his remark.

I wonder whether his wife chose it for him, but decide not to ask.

We drive for around fifteen minutes, before pulling into a quiet beach as the light is beginning to fade. Stepping out of the car, I notice a string of bulb lights stretched across the entrance to a beach bar gives it a romantic feel. Several tables sit outside on a wooden decking area, overlooking the sea and the gently rolling waves.

'This is nice,' I say when we arrive at the restaurant and are quickly shown to a table by a young waitress. Looking around, I spot a couple walking hand in hand further along the beach.

'I like it here,' he says, ordering some drinks from the waitress, who hands us a menu. I wonder whether this is where he brings all of his dates and half imagine the staff in the kitchen gossiping about his latest squeeze.

'Do you come here often?' I ask, and he smiles. Gosh, that's a damn perfect smile.

'Not at all,' he says, just as the waitress arrives with our drinks. 'I have been here with my wife, but not for a long time. Even then it was only occasionally.'

'How long have you been on your own?' I ask, and he takes a few seconds to answer.

'I will be honest with you, not long.' He takes a sip of his beer. 'But things haven't been right for a while. As I said, she prefers the company of her friends these days. Things can change between people over time.'

He manages a bright smile. 'How about you? I take it you are single too?'

I've just quizzed him about his personal life, yet I don't feel like discussing my own situation right now. Maybe it's best to stay away from the subject of relationships and just enjoy the evening.

'Single, yes,' I say, perusing the menu. 'Shall we order?'

Maybe this evening should be all about relaxing and having a pleasant evening, not discussing our love lives. I came here to get away from thinking about that, after all. Marco and I are over and I don't see how we can ever reach a compromise.

'Of course,' he says, snapping the menu shut and not asking me any more questions, probably feeling relieved that I am not doing the same.

When the waitress returns, he orders our food in Greek. Then I watch his gaze follow the pretty young waitress as she returns to the kitchen with the order.

'You really do have beautiful hair,' he says, lifting a strand and letting it run through his fingers, and I wonder how many women have fallen under his spell. He does seem rather taken with my hair, but maybe he doesn't come across too many redheads in Greece.

'Thanks. I have my mother to thank for it,' I tell him.

At least there is something I can thank her for. And my long legs.

We eat our delicious food; I opted for the fish of the day, a tasty red mullet, with fluffy rice and roasted, herby potatoes, whilst Artemis chooses a tasty-looking moussaka. When we finish, he orders a Greek coffee and I enjoy a cappuccino. As he sips his drink, he studies me closely.

'What?' I feel like I am about to blush under his gaze.

'Nothing. I am just looking at you. I bet you never thought you would go on a date with a man who almost ran you over. I'm surprised you are here.'

'I'm a little surprised by that myself,' I tell him honestly.

'What made you accept?' He swirls his drink around his glass, his eyes never leaving mine.

The large glass of wine I have downed has completely relaxed me, but I'm hardly about to tell him it is because he is extremely attractive and a perfect distraction for my broken heart.

'Why not? You told me your mother lived locally, so I figured you weren't an axe murderer. I'm not sure Hannah is completely convinced, though.'

I tell him about her panic when I raced towards the car, after he almost mowed us down and he laughs.

'I told you, I expected the road to be empty. I have learned my lesson, I promise.' He holds his hands up.

Talk turns to work and he tells me he works for a large bank just outside Heraklion in sales, and I talk about the supermarket back home.

'Do you enjoy your work?' he asks.

'I do, actually. I love meeting people. The staff can be a bit unreliable at times, but thankfully there is usually someone to cover. How about you? Do you enjoy working in a bank?'

'I do. Part of my work involves organising mortgages for people, among other things. It's a good feeling telling someone they have been accepted for a mortgage, making the dream of their first home a reality.'

'Yes, I can imagine that feeling good. I don't quite get the same satisfaction pointing someone to the coffee aisle, but I do enjoy chatting to the customers, especially the older ones who can be a little lonely.'

As we chat, I am relieved that my suspicion that Artemis is actually a nice guy seems to have been confirmed. After we drain our coffee and he settles the bill, we head to his car. My heart flutters as he opens the door for me to climb inside. Yes, he might be a little showy, his aftershave a little bit overpowering and his watch expensive-looking, but he is also a gentleman.

'Thank you,' I say, climbing inside, after a perfectly lovely evening.

I sink back into the leather passenger seat and enjoy the drive, feeling relaxed and mellow.

When he drops me back at the rescue, he gives me a gentle kiss on the cheek and says goodnight.

'Thank you for this evening, Artemis. I had a good time,' I tell him.

'The pleasure was all mine.'

As he drives off down the hill, I surprise myself by wondering if he will ask me out again.

TEN

'Gosh this is just so difficult.'

The next day, the morning feeds done, Hannah is in the kitchen, grabbing a moment to send an email to Panos.

'I have to keep checking Google Translate to reply.' She sighs. 'It's taking far longer than I expected.'

'Maybe keep the messages a little shorter?' I suggest, as glancing at her laptop there appears to be rather a long email to be deciphered. 'It might be a bit less daunting.'

'You're probably right.' She smiles, before finishing up and closing her laptop.

'So how did your date go last night?' she asks, waving a cafetière and offering me a coffee and I nod.

'Absolutely great, as it happens. Artemis took me to a lovely restaurant on a quiet beach, although I wouldn't exactly call it a date.'

'But it sounds romantic.' She looks at me from under her glasses and smiles.

'It was a romantic setting, I guess, if romance is what you are after, which I'm not.' I keep telling myself this, but last night

I'll admit I did have a good time. But it's just nice to have a little attention from an attractive man, isn't it?

'I believe you.' She grins.

She fills two mugs with coffee and places one down in front of me, as Judith appears from the donkey area, enquiring if we have seen Lars.

'Does he have a habit of disappearing?' I say, thinking of yesterday when she could not find him then either.

'Not usually, no.' She frowns. 'Oh, never mind, I'm sure he's around somewhere. Anyway, while you're here, I thought about what you said.' She turns to Hannah, who offers her coffee, but she declines. 'I only have one in the morning, love, or I'm running to the loo all day,' she confides.

'Maybe it's the caffeine? You should try decaffeinated,' I suggest.

'I did once, it made no difference. I think it's just my age.' She laughs.

'Sorry, you said you have thought about something I said?' Hannah looks a little puzzled.

'Yes, about doing some fundraising at Star Beach. I know people often book September breaks before the weather changes, especially the English as it's cheaper to travel here after the main school holidays. So I thought more about the fundraising tomorrow, and I definitely think you should head there instead of to the harbour.'

'Great, yes, I can't think of a better place to raise funds than at a beach,' I tell her. 'Let's hope it's still busy.'

'With any luck,' says Judith. 'Especially as the weather is set to be fine again tomorrow.'

'Great. I'm sure Doll and Michael will be thrilled too.'

It's Friday tomorrow, and I remember that Tania has invited everyone for a BBQ at their place on Monday evening, which I am really looking forward to. The week has flown by and I realise Marco has been in my thoughts less and less over the week. Keeping busy must be the key to not dwelling on things too much, or maybe it's mixing with different people and seeing new things that is distracting me from my life back home.

'Good. That's settled then.' She smiles.

Just then, Michael appears with a new bale of straw to take to the donkeys. Judith fills him in on the plans for tomorrow, but Doll is nowhere to be seen.

We tackle the jobs around the rescue, and an hour later, I'm returning some cleaning liquid to the utility area, when I spot a car pull up outside the gates. Out step Lars and Doll, then to my surprise, Lars heads through the front gate, but Doll disappears out of sight, heading towards a rear entrance near the pool. A few minutes later she appears from the bushes by the path between the house and the pool. What on earth is going on?

'That was a long shower,' Michael comments as Doll strolls over to join him and Judith and she tells him she was sorting out some laundry, before taking a shower.

'Keeping tabs on me?' She giggles.

'I don't think I've ever been able to do that, Doll.' He laughs. 'Just don't go off walking alone, that's all. There are some steep drops out there in the forest. Not to mention snakes.'

'Now you're just trying to frighten me, you know I hate snakes,' she says and Michael laughs.

'I can't say I've ever come across any snakes. Thank goodness,' says Judith, before she heads off to the office.

Why on earth would Doll tell her husband that she was in the shower, when she had gone out with Lars? And why did Lars not tell Judith where he was going?

I don't have time to dwell on it too much, though, as it's a busy day at the shelter and by late afternoon, we are having a break and enjoying a cool drink. The weather, although not as hot as yesterday, is still pleasantly warm, the bright blue sky dotted with just a few wispy white clouds.

'Not long until the wedding, hey, Judith, I bet you feel excited,' I say, sipping a glass of Judith's delicious home-made lemonade.

'Oh yes. I'm really looking forward to it, especially knowing that Tania is here too. And it's so good of her and Nicos to offer to host it at their place, the garden is perfect.'

'It really is a lovely-looking place; I'm sure the wedding will be wonderful.'

'My friend Yolanda says she will decorate the front of the house with balloons and ribbons. She is very creative and makes the most beautiful cushions for her home,' Judith tells us.

'Have you been friends for long?'

'Over ten years, since we first moved here to Crete. We lost touch a bit after my husband died and I got so busy with the animals, but when she had her fall and I had my knee operation, we reconnected and have been inseparable since!' She chuckles. 'She has been really helpful, especially persuading the local priest to conduct the wedding outside of a church, which is not something he is usually keen on, apparently.'

'What a lovely thing to do. And if there is anything I can do to help, I would be happy to,' I offer, before wondering what I can do. I'm not particularly creative, but I guess I could do something. The more I get to know Judith and Lars, the more I feel I want to help towards their big day.

'Me too,' adds Hannah.

'Well, that's very kind of you both, but hopefully we will have everything sorted. The people in the village are all going to bring some food and Tania is baking the wedding cake – she is a wonderful baker. It won't be a fancy affair, but everyone is most welcome, of course.'

'I think it sounds just perfect,' I tell her. I imagine the garden overflowing with people, music mingling with the sound of their laughter, and a beautiful wedding cake taking centre stage on a table in the garden. I can picture the pretty pink house covered in balloons and banners.

'I hope it will be. We don't want anything too flashy at our time of life.' She smiles.

The word 'flashy' makes me think of Artemis and how my very first impression of him may not have been entirely fair. He was courteous and polite last night, listening and asking questions about me, hardly talking about himself at all.

'And it's a shame the animals can't join us, but can you imagine?' says Judith. 'We won't be able to leave them alone all day, but a few hours celebrating will be just wonderful. But I can't leave them alone for too long.'

'I'm sure people will pop over and check up on them,' I reassure her. 'It's your big day! In fact, I don't mind doing just that, and I'm sure the other volunteers will help too. You don't need to worry, the animals will be in good hands. That's definitely something I can help with.'

I don't expect to be fully involved in the wedding celebrations, and even though Judith has kindly invited the volunteers, she barely knows us. Although maybe there is still a part of me that is trying to avoid a wedding ceremony by offering to look after the animals.

It's just after six, when I receive a text from Artemis telling me has a day off work tomorrow, and do I have any free time at all. I tap out a reply saying we will be at Star Beach fundraising for most of the day for the rescue.

Great, I have always liked Star Beach. I might see you there x, he replies.

I'm surprised that the thought of seeing him again seems quite appealing. Suddenly I'm really looking forward to tomorrow.

ELEVEN

Star Beach is busy this morning, as people enjoy the last weeks of the summer sun, and we set up our stand beneath a tree on the wooden boardwalk approaching the beach. The footfall is constant, especially as we are quite close to the beach bar. Strategic positioning, as suggested by Michael, seems to pay off as after an hour we collect quite a few donations, wearing our bright yellow T-shirts emblazoned with the Pine Forest Rescue logo, with a silhouette of a dog in the corner. Judith has even provided us with a little card reader for people to ping a donation across, aware that people are carrying less and less cash.

'This seems to be going well,' I say, as a coach load of tourists pull up, some of them stopping to chat and donating a little something, others heading straight for the sand, beach bags slung over their shoulder.

'Ah, it's gorgeous here,' says Hannah, eyeing the pine forests rising beyond the sea in the background. The busy beach bar is gently pumping out music, making the most of the last of the warm weather, and a couple of guys are chatting to a group of young people at a stand hiring out speedboats and pedalos. I'm told the weather can be a little unpredictable here at this time of year, although it is warmer in Crete than other Greek islands as it is the most southerly. Judith told me that she had a walk with the volunteers after Christmas lunch last year, as the weather was so mild.

'Lovely day, isn't it? I've always loved this beach, we used to bring the children here when they were younger,' says an Englishwoman wearing a pink T-shirt with the slogan 'I Love Strictly', chatting to Doll. She cleverly moves the conversation to the dance show, and the woman's mouth falls open when Michael joins them and tells her the pair are world champions in Latin American dance.

'Never! That's wonderful. I'd love to see a live show. Do you tour?' asks the woman excitedly.

'We do. We have actually just finished a dance tour around some European cities,' Michael tells her. 'We will be touring in the UK again next year, all being well.'

'How exciting! I would love to see you both dance, and Latin American just happens to be my favourite,' says the woman, clearly overjoyed to be in the presence of triple world champions.

He glances at Doll.

'Although we're not actually dressed for it, we can show you a bit of a dance if you like?' he offers and the woman is speechless.

Doll asks Hannah if she has Spotify on her phone, and a few seconds later, a tune, perfect for a salsa dance, starts playing. Michael takes Doll by the hand and pulls her to him, moving to the rhythm of the music as easy as breathing. Soon, a small crowd has gathered, mesmerised by the couple's dancing. They aren't the only ones, as it's like nothing I have ever seen before. Even dressed in casual clothing, Doll and Michael are pure magic.

When the dance comes to an end, a thunderous applause follows and even the bar staff have walked around to the other side of the bar to get a better look. Coins and notes appear from the crowd and are pushed into the collecting tin.

'That was amazing!' I tell Michael and Doll. 'You've made a huge difference to the collecting with that impromptu show. Judith will be absolutely thrilled.'

'It was nice to dance. And I really enjoyed the audience's reaction,' says Michael, lapping up the attention, particularly from the woman in the *Strictly* T-shirt. She looks as though she might just pass out with excitement.

'Of course you did,' Doll says with a laugh. 'Any chance to show off. Although, I must admit, that did feel good. It's lovely to get such a great response, it shows we still have it, I suppose.'

'Use it or lose it, my love.' He kisses her and I think of how in love they must be, to have an enduring marriage, living and working together for so many years.

A couple of hours later, we are about to break for lunch when a handsome man strides towards us, attracting admiring glances from a group of women dining at a table nearby. I notice at once that it is Artemis.

'*Kalispera,*' he says, removing his glasses and kissing me on both cheeks. Out of the corner of my eye, I see Doll give Hannah a nudge and Hannah smiles. He is dressed casually, in beige shorts and a tight navy T-shirt that hugs his body in all the right places.

'Artemis, hi, you made it.' I smile, feeling happy to see him.

I introduce him to the others, and he shakes their hands warmly.

'How is the fundraising going?' he asks, before peeling a fifty euro note from his wallet and handing it over.

'Very well, actually. Gosh, thanks, that's very generous of you,' I say, placing it into a petty cash tin and locking it, as the collecting tin is now full.

'All for a good cause.' He smiles. 'Now, can I steal you away for a drink?'

'Sure. It's good timing actually as we are about to break for lunch. Please join us,' I offer.

'I'm okay for a bit, but I might just grab an ice cream,' says Hannah. 'You guys eat first; I'll look after the stall.'

'I'll grab the ice creams and stay here with you, love,' says Doll, whilst Michael says he will go for a bit of a walk along the beach to stretch his legs after the dance.

'It looks like it is just you and me then,' says Artemis, heading to an empty table at the beach bar and picking up a menu. We are soon dining on Greek salads, with fabulous local olives and delicious cocktails in the busy bar overlooking the sea. Loved-up couples are holding hands across tables, sipping drinks and stealing kisses, alongside families with children tucking into burgers and chips or cooling ice creams. The soft, white sand leads to the blue sea, where people are riding speed-boats or swimming, enjoying the pleasant weather. A lady offering Thai massages threads in and out of the dining tables and a bloke sitting on his own drains his beer and heads towards a sunbed with her.

'Have you ever had one of those?' I ask Artemis, nodding towards the masseur, who is setting her green mat down onto the bloke's sunbed.

'No. Have you?'

'Actually, yes. A couple of years ago on holiday, when I was feeling a bit stressed. I fell asleep for an hour afterwards, it was amazing.'

'I can think of another activity that would give you a nice, relaxed sleep,' he says cheekily.

'I bet you could.' I laugh it off, but it's hard not to feel a twinge of something. He is so damn attractive.

'It really is so good to see you again.' Artemis slides his hand across the table and gently takes hold of mine.

'Good to see you again too,' I say, trying to keep my tone light. I am not here for romance, so despite the undeniably pleasant feeling, I slowly release my hand from his. I watch the masseuse apply long, slow strokes of her hands, before kneading the shoulders of her male customer. I'm lost in a daydream for a moment, imagining Artemis rubbing sun lotion into my back, massaging it in with his strong-looking hands, easing any tension and lulling me into a relaxed state, despite telling myself I do not want a holiday fling. Not after Marco.

'That does look amazing, actually,' he says, following my gaze.

'Hmm? What?'

'That massage. Maybe we should go to a spa and have one, side by side,' he suggests.

'I'm not sure I have time for such things,' I say, bringing myself back to reality. What on earth am I thinking? 'And, if I'm honest, I prefer to be outdoors than getting hot and steamy indoors.'

'That's a shame.' He grins and I roll my eyes, but smile.

We finish up and head back to the stand and the others find a seat for lunch at the beach restaurant. A trio of women chat to Artemis about the rescue, and he charms them easily, even though he doesn't actually work there. Before they leave, they reach into their pockets and drop some coins into a tin, a blonde in a blue kaftan giving him backward glances, which he is very aware of, as she walks towards the sand with her friend.

'What time are you leaving here?' he asks as the others return to the stand after their meal, and the afternoon draws to a close.

'In around an hour, I imagine. We're getting a bit low on soft toys for the children.'

Judith told me that she purchases boxes of second-hand soft toys and washes them to give out as little gifts for the children, along with a little sticker or a pencil when their parents make a donation.

It's almost four o'clock now and many of the day trippers have drifted off, whilst some families are just arriving with young children for a swim after school, as the sun begins its descent a little earlier at this time of year.

'I thought we might go for a swim, now that the fundraising has finished,' suggests Artemis, who has hung around with us until the end of the day. 'I could drive you back later to the rescue.'

'How do you know I have packed a swimsuit?'

'Have you?'

'As a matter of fact, yes, I have.'

I had thought about having a swim but wasn't sure if I would have the time, being here to fundraise. As things have quietened down now, though, I would like nothing more than a refreshing swim in the inviting blue sea.

'Sure, why not? That sounds good.'

We pack everything away into the truck and I tell Hannah that Artemis will drop me back at the rescue later.

'Have fun,' says Doll with a wink and Hannah whispers in my ear, 'I thought you weren't looking for romance.'

'I assure you I'm not. I just fancy a swim in the sea, that's all.'

'If you say so,' she teases.

'I do. And we will literally be half an hour behind you. You don't think Judith will mind me getting back a bit later, do you?' I ask, suddenly wondering if it's okay to be out a little longer.

'After raising all this money? I doubt it.' She smiles.

'Okay, see you in a bit then.'

I head to the ladies and get changed into my swimsuit, wrapping my new sarong around me as I approach the water. Artemis is at the water's edge dressed in swimming shorts and revealing an impressive body. For a second, I feel a little self-conscious removing my sarong and placing it on the sand. As I quickly run towards the water, I can feel his eyes following me.

We swim beneath the balmy sun, the water pleasant, but not as warm as I imagined it to be. For a second, I lose my footing on some stones below the water. Artemis steadies me in his arms and the touch of his skin against mine feels so good. I hadn't realised how much I have missed being held like this and for a moment I stay in his embrace, savouring the feeling of being wrapped in a man's arms.

'Are you okay?' His face is inches away from mine, and I'm shocked by my own thoughts as I wonder whether he might move closer and kiss me with those very attractive lips. But he doesn't, and I'm even more surprised by my disappointment.

'Come on, I will race you to that boat.' He smiles, pointing to a small speedboat moored up further into the water, not far away.

Swimming side by side, it feels so good to be here in the open, blue-green water, laughing and just being in the moment, for a short time at least. If there is any way I can forget about my situation back at home, this is surely it. The boat is actually a little further away than it looks, and by the time we swim back I can feel the muscles in my thighs protesting a little. I really ought to get out there and do more walking, like I once did. Despite the aches, I really enjoyed it.

'That was wonderful,' I tell Artemis, as I sit on a rock towelling myself down, before wrapping my sarong around my waist.

'I enjoyed it too,' says Artemis. 'I can't remember the last time I spent an afternoon at the beach, which sounds strange, given that it is on the doorstep. But maybe I have always preferred the city,' he admits. 'I like the buzz.'

'Even though you were raised in the village?'

'Yes. Maybe it is because of that,' he admits. 'I was keen to leave as a teenager as there wasn't much going on. And, honestly, I have no desire to ever live there again. Not now,' he says, not elaborating, even though there's a slight tension in his jaw as he finishes.

'I guess we have to figure out what we prefer when we get older. As children we have no choice in where we live, I suppose.'

I recall the place me and Mum lived in after she separated from my dad. It was a run-down house on the wrong side of town. I wouldn't want to return to anything like that, now I can choose.

'Exactly. Now, would you like a drink before we set off?' He gestures towards the bar.

'Thanks, but I'd better not. I said I wouldn't be far behind the others. And there is still work to do back at the rescue.'

'Sure.'

We grab our things and stroll towards his car, along with throngs of people who have spent the day here and are heading back to their hotels or homes for the evening.

On the way back, I look forward to having dinner with everyone, and seeing the animals. The fundraising day has been wonderful, and I think Hannah was so right to suggest having it at the beach. Even though the harbour must be busy, it has been far nicer fundraising here, with so much to distract your attention, than I imagine it would be over there. I am thrilled that the money raised will help the shelter a little longer, as I have completely fallen in love with the dogs, the donkeys, and the beauty of the forest setting. I can't wait to meet the Vizsla and cockapoo at Tania's place on Monday evening. But, I have to admit, I have really enjoyed the opportunity to take a dip in the sea, and to hang out with Artemis at the beach too.

In the car, I place a bottle of water into a drink holder and our hands brush for a second as Artemis changes gear. He turns to me and smiles and I get that warm feeling once more, the one that I am doing my very best to ignore. Although I am slowly beginning to wonder why I am ignoring it. Maybe I should just relax and see what happens, reminding myself that I am not with Marco anymore.

'Thank you for the lunch today, Artemis, and for driving me home. It really was lovely to see you again,' I tell him when he drops me outside the rescue.

'My pleasure,' he says, kissing me lightly on the cheek before he departs. 'I will call you.'

Heading inside, I think that maybe I would like Artemis to contact me again. Today has been a lot of fun and I feel good. I can hardly wait to see what tomorrow brings.

TWELVE

Judith is more than thrilled with the collection today, and delighted by the story of Michael and Doll giving an impromptu dance to the people at the beach.

'Isn't that wonderful! That's it then. I'll be sending you out to dance to a crowd more often now, in exchange for a donation or two. I'm sorry I missed it.'

'That's actually not a bad idea,' says Michael. 'We could set up a place for a show. Isn't there an old amphitheatre not far from here?' He rubs his chin in thought.

'We are supposed to be here recharging our batteries, not putting on shows,' Doll reminds him, although she doesn't seem to be protesting too much.

'But think about it. We could put the word about, and maybe ask for donations rather than selling tickets. We could sort the music out.' Michael is on a roll now.

'The old amphitheatre isn't far from a busy village, actually,' Judith tells him. 'Come to think of it, the village square is surrounded by restaurants. Maybe you could do a bit of a show there instead. If you really want to, that is.'

'Even better!' Michael beams. 'Captive audience there with the diners in the restaurants.'

'We could pass around a hat for donations,' says Doll, clearly warming to the idea.

'That's sorted then. Maybe next week, we could speak to the restauranteurs and ask them to advertise a dance evening in the square. I'm sure they would be up for that as it would be good for business after all. They could advertise it on a chalk-board, along with the menu outside their restaurant. World champions here, for one night only.' Michael seems to be getting carried away with himself now, and Doll tells him to calm down.

'But I couldn't ask you to do that,' protests Judith, surprised but clearly excited by their generous offer.

'You didn't ask, we offered,' says Michael.

'Well, you did,' Doll whispers to me, but she is smiling.

'I haven't packed any of my dance dresses, though,' says Doll. 'Although there is probably a place in Heraklion where I could buy something? I wouldn't mind a trip there anyway.'

'Any excuse for a shopping spree,' says Michael, with a smile. 'But, of course, I'm sure we could manage that, my love.' He kisses her on the cheek and she smiles. 'Me, on the other hand, I have a suit packed for such an occasion, as you never know when an opportunity might present itself.'

'Why does that not surprise me?'

Lars has made the most wonderful moussaka this evening, served with a crunchy Greek salad, and we dine outside beneath the ancient olive tree that is threaded with lights. Just after eight, Judith and Lars nip inside for some blankets that they offer around, before lighting a fire pit. It's warm and cosy, and after toasting some marshmallows, talk turns to beaches in the surrounding areas.

'I would definitely like to go back to Star Beach,' says Hannah. 'That water looked very inviting,' she continues, finishing her drink. 'I do enjoy sea swimming but the beaches back home are a bit of a drive away. And very cold.'

'Of course! Hannah is a bit of a champion swimmer.' I tell the others how she used to swim for her county.

'That's wonderful,' says Judith, asking Hannah all about her swimming and she modestly tells them her story.

'Anyway, that water wasn't as warm as it looked, let me tell you,' I say to Hannah. 'Which was surprising, given the hot sun.'

'You went swimming?'

'Yes, with my new friend.' I dive into a slice of juicy melon, wondering if I ought to fetch the ouzo and the shot glasses, as the conversation is flowing and the evening is turning out to be very relaxed and enjoyable. Then again, maybe not. We have work to do tomorrow and I'm pretty sure I would only regret it in the morning.

'Oh, was that the guy you went out with the other evening?' asks Judith.

'Yes, it was.'

'I meant to ask you, what's his name? There aren't that many houses here in the village, so I probably know him, or his mother at least,' she says.

'Oh, it's Artemis,' I tell her and she draws back, visibly surprised.

'Do you know him?' I ask and she quickly recovers her smile.

'As a matter of fact, I do, yes. He is the son of my friend Yolanda.'

'He did say he grew up here, but I didn't realise you would be so close with his mother! He seems like a nice guy and it's good to make some new friends, but I'm certainly not looking for romance,' I tell her, and she smiles but says nothing.

'Right, that's me. I think it's time I got to bed,' says Hannah.

'I have one more chapter of my book left and I'm dying to find out what happens.'

'I'll join you. And I don't mind if you leave your lamp on,' I tell her, thinking I might send a few texts to my friend Jess, as it's still early in the UK.

'I think that's our cue to wrap up the evening,' says Lars, and the others follow suit.

'Goodnight,' says Judith, looking a little perplexed. Maybe her friend hasn't told her about Artemis's separation from his wife. Or maybe he hasn't told his mother everything yet. That would explain her concern. But he has been nothing but honest with me, so I have no reason to doubt him. Do I?

The rescue is its usual hive of activity on Saturday. It's warm but with more clouds than yesterday, and many volunteers arrive to take the dogs out for long walks, enjoying the beauty of the forest.

Hannah and I set off with Lars for the dogs' afternoon exercise. It's a very pleasant walk, as we take a slightly different route and stumble across a dilapidated farmhouse, almost obscured by overgrown grasses and weeds. As we pass through, Lars points to a pit he filled in after Annie the cockapoo slipped down into the bottom of it.

'Thankfully it wasn't very deep. But the building needs knocking down altogether,' says Lars. 'It has gone past the refurbishment stage but it's difficult in Greece. Finding out who the owner is, or was, is so tricky. Buildings are often just left to rot.'

'That's such a shame. I bet it had so much potential, if someone had taken it on and refurbished it a little sooner.'

'I imagine so.'

'Saying that, it's a little remote, though. Do many people pass through here?' I ask Lars, as we make our way through a patch of long grass.

'Dog walkers mainly. The occasional hiker too, but only if they get a bit lost, as it's not on a footpath. We first discovered this route chasing after Annie.'

A little further down, I get a glimpse of the sea in the distance, the foamy waves crashing against the shore. The temperature is starting to cool a little, and here in the forest, the pine trees stand tall, their evergreen colour in contrast to the local forest maples and oaks, their leaves softly changing to a palette of earthy shades.

I'm looking forward to the BBQ on Monday evening, and to chatting with Tania and Nicos, who seem like a gorgeous couple, and clearly madly in love. I know that they aren't married, but maybe it isn't something they have thought about? Tania did tell me they have only been together for a few months. I can't help wondering if I ought to relax a bit, if that's my first thought about the happy couple, and not consider marriage as the be all and end all of a relationship. But, despite spending time in the company of the glorious Artemis, my heart still feels heavy when I think of Marco.

We head on, taking a detour past the village bar where Panos and Helena are cooking something on the charcoal, smoke spiralling in the air. The dogs raise their noses and bark at the scent as we pass them. The bar is quite busy this after-noon, with tourists who have probably been to visit the church before the light fades. A few locals are enjoying a drink and a game of dominoes at a table beneath an oak tree and nod as we walk past.

'Maybe one day I will take a walk up there, without the dogs, though. I imagine the view from the top is amazing,' I say, staring at the white church standing proudly amidst the rocks high up.

'I bet it is. I could come too and take some photos. I used to be quite into photography,' Hannah tells us.

'Used to?'

'I did consider taking a course at uni, before I signed up for English.'

'It seems you are a girl of many talents,' says Lars, saying exactly what I was just thinking.

'Not really.' She smiles. 'It's just a little hobby I enjoy. I don't have any fancy camera equipment; I mainly just use my phone camera.'

It makes me think that perhaps I ought to get myself a hobby, as my interests consist mainly of going to the pub and taking a yoga class. I do enjoy being outdoors, though, and being here has made me realise I ought to get out walking a little more, perhaps even join a local walking group.

I have a memory of taking the bus to a nearby country park with my mum, when I was younger, and walking across fields skirting a golf course. One time, we walked along a country road passing an ancient church and stumbled upon a huge blackberry bush, bursting with fat juicy blackberries. Mum pulled a carrier bag from her handbag, and we picked a load, filling the bag, and laughing at our purple-stained fingers. Back home, we called into the shop for a ready-made crumble mix – Mum wasn't much of a baker – and enjoyed blackberry crumble and custard after tea. I hope she looks back on those days from time to time with fondness, as I do. She was happy then.

Panos calls Hannah's name and waves as we pass the bar and she waves back with a broad smile on her face.

'You like him, don't you?' I say, as we take a left turn and walk downhill back towards the rescue.

'Yes,' Hannah admits with a shy smile. 'He's nice. And I'm actually learning a little more about the Greek language, as he is such a good teacher.'

'I'm sure he's grateful for the chance to improve his English too.'

'I think so, yes. He's a quick learner. I think he could have gone far, had he had more of an education,' she reveals. 'He told me his father died two years ago, and his mother has been in poor health ever since. He and Helena have had to keep the bar running, as there is no one else, only their elderly grandmother.'

It makes me wonder how many young people sacrifice their own desires to continue working in the family business. I guess we take for granted the opportunities that present themselves in life, if we are fortunate enough to have them.

'What does his mother do with her days? I don't recall ever seeing her at the bar.'

'Not much apparently. Their gran lives with them, and Panos says she has tried to persuade his mother to come to the bar occasionally and at least get some fresh air, but she doesn't leave the house much, apart from tending to the garden.'

'I think I have seen his gran at the bar. Is she the elderly lady dressed in black?'

'It is. Panos says she is quite the character, apparently.'

As we approach the rescue, we pass the pink house belonging to Tania and Nicos, and the dogs with us go crazy, barking and straining at their leads. As we draw closer, I can see why. A handsome red Vizsla and an adorable black cockapoo are running the length of the fence in the rear garden, barking and going crazy too. The Vizsla, who must be the infamous Smudge, leaps so high I'm convinced he might just leap over the chicken-wire fence.

There is a chorus of barks back and forth between the two groups of dogs, before we move on and leave the two dogs to continue racing around the garden in excitement.

'How sweet that they are all saying hello to their friends,' says Lars as we walk on, explaining that Tania often brings the dogs out on walks with the rescue dogs, even though they have a large garden to play in.

Back at the rescue, Judith has filled a table with home-made breads, cooked meats, and cheeses along with a quiche and jugs of water and orange juice. She asks if we would like to take lunch in the kitchen, but we are all warm from the long walk, so after settling the dogs in their cages, we opt to dine outside.

It's so beautiful I could happily sit here all day, watching the sunlight filter through the branches of the trees, warming my legs and relaxing. Even after a few days, I can feel myself settling in and thinking even less about Marco, but maybe that's because I don't have to walk past the restaurant every day. Living so close to each other, there is always something there to remind me of him. I'm not sure if I can fall out of love with him in a few short weeks, but maybe trying to put some distance between us is working. Especially as I find myself spending more time in the unexpected company of a certain handsome Greek.

We're clearing away the plates when I feel my phone vibrate in the pocket of my shorts. As if reading my thoughts, it's a text from Artemis asking if I would like to go for a drive with him tomorrow, to a restaurant high in the hills close to a monastery. I smile, tapping out a reply to tell him that would be very nice, and I will contact him later.

Out of the corner of my eye, I see Judith watching me and wonder why she has a look of quiet concern on her face.

THIRTEEN

'*Kalispera*, how are you today?'

Hannah is saying the words over and over to one of the dogs.

'Careful, people might start getting concerned if you keep talking to yourself like that,' I joke, as the little terrier cocks its head from side to side as if it really does understand what she is saying.

'Oh, Beth, hi. Panos tells me I am getting the pronunciation right with some new phrases, but that I should practise a lot, otherwise I will forget them.'

'Oh, I completely get that. I did one of those online Spanish courses once, and learned a ton of words and phrases. As soon as I stopped practising, I forget every single one.' I laugh. 'Although I did remember *"Tengo el pasaporte en la maleta"*, which means "My passport is in the suitcase". Really useful when you are trying to order food in a restaurant,' I say, and she laughs.

'That's exactly it. If you don't put it into practice daily, you do forget. Which is why it's so great to talk with Panos online each day. Already his English is improving. My Greek not so much.'

'Give it time. Plus Panos already had a good grasp of English,' I remind her. 'You never had any knowledge of the Greek language, did you?'

'No, of course you are right.'

Finishing the afternoon chores, I'm heading inside to the bathroom, when I bump into Judith coming out of her office.

'Beth, do you mind if I have a quick word with you?' she says, steering me towards the kitchen.

'Of course. What's on your mind?' I ask cheerfully.

'Well, I hope you don't mind me saying, but I spoke to my friend Yolanda this morning. Artemis is her son.'

'Oh yes, you mentioned that. She's the lady who was here when we first arrived, I remember her,' I say, recalling why she looked familiar, as she has a strong look of her son.

'Yes, that's right.' She smiles. 'Anyway, the thing is, during our chat she told me that Artemis has only been separated from his wife for a few weeks. I hope you don't think I am prying, I was just wondering whether you were aware of that?'

'He told me he was separated, if that's what you mean,' I tell her, although I am surprised by the news that it is so recently.

'I'm glad he told you.' She nods. 'But the thing is, it's not the first time he and his wife have broken up. They have what you might call a volatile relationship.'

'Oh, right. Thanks for the heads-up but the truth is I am not long out of a relationship myself. The last thing I am looking for is romance. It's just nice getting to know new people, and being shown the area a little bit by someone local.'

All the same, hearing about the history of their marriage does make me feel a little unsure of whether I ought to see him again. I certainly don't want to be implicated in any divorce proceedings further down the line.

'As long as you are aware.' She smiles.

'Sure, he did tell me he was recently separated, but I admit I didn't realise that it was quite that recently. Thanks, Judith.'

'No problem. And I hope you don't think I'm gossiping, but my friend also tells me that he is a bit careless with money. He often borrows from her. I feel it's only fair for you to be armed with the facts, but of course it is entirely your business what you do.' She touches me gently on the arm.

'And I appreciate you looking out for me, I really do. But I'm not planning on falling for him. As I say, I'm recently single myself. It just feels nice to dress up and be taken out.'

'Of course. I understand that. I'm glad we had this little chat.'

Judith is so lovely. Already I can tell she is the type of person you could confide in and tell just about anything, and it would go no further. Tania is so lucky to have her as an aunt. I would have loved an aunt like her to talk to when I was growing up, especially as Mum had her own problems and wasn't always present.

My thoughts turn to the drive to the restaurant in the hills that Artemis suggested, up near the monastery. Would it be wise to carry on seeing him? I wonder. I think about it, but ultimately decide that a friendship between us can't do any harm. And the more time I spend with other people, the less my head is filled with thoughts of Marco. And that can only be a good thing.

The next day, the sun is shining once more and Artemis calls me to confirm if I would like to take a drive to the restaurant near the monastery this evening.

'Do you think we should?' I ask him, getting straight to the point about his very recent split. 'As you are so recently separated. I don't want to be implicated as the other woman in a divorce case.'

He's quiet for a minute before he speaks. 'Maybe it will not come to that. Things are complicated between me and my wife.'

'So you complicate things even more, by taking me out?'

He lets out a deep sigh. 'I can understand your concern but I really think, this time, my wife and I will stay apart. We are not good for each other.'

'Then you must understand, I'm not looking for romance. It's only fair I get that out in the open right now.'

'Me neither. And maybe I would be a fool to jump into a new relationship too. But I do enjoy your company,' he tells me honestly. 'Is there anything wrong with that, if we are both free? Besides, I really want to try the restaurant. I have heard many good things about it.'

I stop myself from asking whether he can afford it, given what Judith told me about his financial situation. I will make sure we split the bill.

'Well, alright. Maybe you could do with a female friend, maybe even a little advice. Not that I'm really qualified for that.'

'Any ladies in my life tend not to be friends,' he says, and I can imagine him grinning at the other end of the phone.

'Well, maybe it's time to change that.'

'I will collect you at seven thirty.'

'Okay, see you later.'

The day passes with its usual routines; the sun shines in the sky, beaming down on us as we work hard and walk the dogs. I'm told the winters here can be quite cool in the hills, but it can get extremely hot in the summer months. Judith told me the temperature in early August this year was stifling. Apparently, there had even been a fire at the rescue due to the heat started by a campfire that was abandoned. Some of the volunteers helped to get things in order, rebuilding the donkey shelter, and Lars it seems paid for the wood, which Judith was truly grateful for.

Artemis arrives at seven thirty to collect me as arranged, and exchanges pleasantries with Judith outside, as she is just returning from Tania's house.

'I am not sure Judith thinks much of me,' says Artemis as we sit in the car about to leave.

'I can't imagine Judith thinking badly of anyone,' I say in her defence, as she is such a wonderful person, and has been so kind to me already. 'Maybe she is just looking out for me, she probably knows about your on-off relationship with your wife. She is your mother's friend after all,' I remind him.

'That could be true,' he muses. 'Although I am sure my marriage is definitely over this time. The longer we are apart, I have no desire to be with her again.'

As we drive, I glance up at the vast granite monastery that is bathed in soft, golden sunlight and watching over the valley like a beacon in the sky. Olive trees stand in straight rows sloping down the hills, with nothing else in sight, apart from the odd farmhouse dotted about.

After a while, the landscape changes to smoother roads and taller, softer trees and village houses appear, some with goats or chickens in the garden. As we climb even higher into the hills, with a landscape of nothing but olive trees once more, we approach a white building with a sign outside that tells us we have arrived at the Olive Garden restaurant, beneath the monastery. We approach the tall, black-metal gates, and announce our arrival at an intercom and the gates are opened, allowing us into the gravelled car park. The entrance to the building is strung with fairy lights, and even from outside it looks expensive.

'Wow, this place looks amazing,' I say as we park up, and I take everything in.

'So do you,' he says, his eyes flicking over my short floral dress, my long chestnut hair let loose this evening.

The courtyard is dotted with pots of colourful flowers and tall grasses in terracotta pots.

Inside, the restaurant is plainly furnished yet stylish, with lit candles in black sconces displayed on white rough stone walls. Colourful artwork adorns some of the walls, adding a touch of modern to the traditional décor, dark beams across the ceiling. A friendly waiter shows us to a table near a window that gives a beautiful view across the valley below. I spot the church in the distance and can make out the tiny squares of pastel houses clinging to the hillside in the village.

'It's really lovely here. I hope the food is just as good,' I say, feeling suddenly famished. It has been such a busy day I barely stopped for lunch, just grabbing some fruit with a little yoghurt.

Artemis orders some bottled water and a glass each of a nice Merlot.

'You never really told me much about yourself, as I recall.' Artemis fixes me with his deep brown eyes. 'Only that you were single.'

'What would you like to know?' I ask.

'I'm not sure. What interests you?'

A waiter arrives then with our drinks and some bread in a basket.

'I'm not sure I have a lot of interests. I've been thinking about that recently, actually, especially as I seem to be surrounded by talented people at the rescue.' I take a sip of the delicious red wine, before diving into the topic I've held off on a little with him. 'I was engaged, up until recently. I was content enough with my job, my home and being with my fiancé. Gosh, that makes me sound really dull.' I laugh.

'Not at all. So you were engaged? What happened?' He takes a piece of bread and butters it.

'I'm not sure. I thought being engaged would lead to settling down and getting married, but it appears my fiancé had other ideas.'

Suddenly I'm telling him how much I wanted marriage, and how Marco is so firmly against it.

'Yet he bought you a ring?' He frowns slightly.

'I know. Figure that one out. Although maybe he did mean it at the time, and just went cold on the idea after a while. I suppose that can happen.'

'And there was definitely no one else involved?'

'No. At least I don't think so.' I frown.

That thought had never really occurred to me, yet he does meet lots of women at the restaurant. But no, surely not. It was me who broke things off, and Marco seemed heartbroken when I did. It was always a mystery to me why Marco was so set against marriage, given that his own parents had been happily married for thirty-five years.

'Well, I am a great believer in things working out just the way they should if they are meant to be.' He raises his glass and I do the same.

'Cheers to that. And to happy ever afters.'

We dine on the most delicious casserole, rich with red wine and herbs and crunchy oregano roasted potatoes. We finish with coffee and a delicious custard pie, called a *galaktoboureko*, drizzled with syrup.

At the end of the meal, I offer to split the bill but Artemis won't hear of it.

'But it's pretty expensive,' I protest, but he urges me to put my money away.

'Really, I insist. Maybe I have a little more money now that I am no longer married. My wife liked to spend a lot,' he says, as he settles the bill and we head out of the restaurant.

It's just after ten thirty when we drive home, the full moon casting a gentle glow over olive groves and a feeling of peace and serenity. Under any other circumstances, I would be thrilled to have enjoyed such a lovely evening, anticipating how the night might end. I'm not sure why I feel that can't happen. I'm single after all but Judith's comments have given me doubts. And I feel a strange loyalty towards Marco, especially since I opened up about things to Artemis, which is ridiculous, I know.

'You are quiet. Are you okay?' asks Artemis, piercing my thoughts.

'Yes, I'm fine, really. I'm just thinking of how different it is here. It's so peaceful,' I say, not wanting to ruin the evening talking about my ex.

The road home after an evening out back home has the sound of noisy traffic and party revellers, the smell of fast-food restaurants drifting onto the pavements. Here, there is barely a sound.

Outside the rescue, Artemis opens the car door for me, and we stand outside beneath the stars.

'I had a lovely evening, thank you. That restaurant really was wonderful,' I tell him.

'So did I. *Kalinychta*, Beth. I hope to see you again.' He kisses me lightly on the cheek.

'I hope so too. And next time, no arguments, I'm paying,' I tell him firmly.

'So there will be a next time?'

'If you like.'

'I like. See you soon.' He smiles, and then he's gone.

As I walk inside, I place my hand on my cheek, where he has just kissed me. A friendly kiss. That's what we are, isn't it? Friends. Just as we agreed. So why do I wonder what it might have felt like if his lips had landed on mine? And why do I feel so ridiculously torn, disloyal even, as my hands instinctively touches the third finger of my left hand, where I once wore my engagement ring?

FOURTEEN

'Oh no!' Hannah is staring at her computer screen.

'What's the matter?'

'I think I have just told Panos he is fat, when I meant kind,' she says, mildly panicked.

'Bit of a difference.' I can't help laughing.

'I know, oh my goodness, "fat" is "*lipos*" and "kind" is "*eidos*". I've been trying to recall words without looking to check. It's the last time I will do that, they don't even sound similar.'

'"*Lipos*" as in "liposuction". That is how I would remember that word. So, what exactly did you say?' I'm biting my lip and trying not to laugh.

'Thank you for helping me. You are very fat.'

I bust out laughing, and thankfully so does Hannah, as she speedily types out another message, explaining her mistake.

'Maybe I should walk to the bar later, and explain in person,' she says. 'I hope he sees the funny side.'

'I'm sure he will.' I'm still smiling.

'Anyway, how did your date with Artemis go?' asks Hannah, closing her laptop.

'Really lovely, actually. The restaurant was beautiful and the food, oh it was fabulous. It was expensive, though, and Artemis wouldn't let me pay for a thing.'

'Talking of food, are you going to the BBQ later at Judith's niece's house? Tania, isn't it?'

'Yes, I'm looking forward to it.'

'Me too. She called over earlier to ask if we were all going. I said I was pretty sure that you were. It was really kind of her to invite us, wasn't it?'

'It was. Her and Nicos seem like such a gorgeous couple.'

'Will Artemis be coming with you? He must know Nicos, if he grew up here in the village.'

'I think he has other plans this evening,' I tell her. 'He said something about meeting some blokes from work in a bar, and watching a football match.'

We stroll over to the donkey area then, where Doll is furtively feeding the animals some fruit.

'Don't be giving them too much of that, they are not used to it, remember,' says Michael, catching his wife with some apples. 'A donkey's diet is almost completely hay. Remember, Judith told us that already.'

'But they like fruit too. It can't do any harm, can it?' asks Doll.

'Just not too much, is all I'm saying. You're cleaning it all up if they get ill from being over-fed fruit,' he says and she pokes her tongue out at him like a child, although she refrains from feeding them any more apples, slipping them back into a hessian bag.

Doll and Michael have been married for twenty-five years, having met and married young on the dance circuit when they were teenagers. Even after all that time, it's obvious they are still mad about each other. I can't help thinking how wonderful it must be to have an enduring love like that.

The day passes quickly, and just after six, I head upstairs to shower. I glance at my phone, which is charging on the bedside table, and notice a message notification.

To my complete shock, it's from Marco.

FIFTEEN

I read the message that simply says *I miss you x* over and over, before stirring myself enough to dry my hair in the bedroom.

The message has taken me completely by surprise. I wonder how I ought to reply to it. Do I tell him I miss him too? But surely, we would just go around in circles if we still want different things going forward?

I think about Jess telling me that I couldn't be expected to switch my feelings off for Marco, we had almost three years together after all, yet isn't that exactly what I have been trying to do, in coming here? Trying to forget about him. And maybe it was beginning to work a little, especially getting to know Artemis. Until I received the message, that is. Now I feel more confused than ever.

I finish getting ready as Hannah walks into the bedroom.

'Are you okay?' she asks. I'm sitting on my bed, phone in hand, just staring at it and wondering how to respond.

'What? Oh yes. I have a message from Marco.'

I pass my phone to Hannah, thrown into confusion and wondering what I ought to do.

'Are you going to reply?' she asks uncertainly.

'Well, that's the thing. I don't know. What would I say?'

'Thanks? I miss you too? Do you miss him?' Hannah comes and sits beside me on the bed.

'I do. I loved him. Maybe I still do. Oh, I don't know.' I sigh. 'Maybe I ought to just forget about the whole marriage idea. We were perfectly happy as we were, until I went and ruined everything.'

'You say you were perfectly happy as you were, but if you were, you would never have broken up, would you? Obviously, the marriage thing was a sticking point between you both. What makes you think things would be any different?' she asks gently.

'You're right, of course you are. You're very wise, for one so young.' I smile at Hannah, who is wearing denim dungarees with a white T-shirt beneath, her hair swept up into a messy bun.

'Sensible, that's me.' She laughs. 'At least that's what my mother always says. My sister was a bit of a wild one, so I think she drilled it into me from an early age that I was the sensible one, in the hope that I would be.'

'I didn't realise you had a sister. Is she older or younger?'

'A year older. She's settled down a bit now, and has had a steady boyfriend for a couple of years, although she still drifts in and out of jobs.'

'It takes some people a lot longer to figure out what they want from life, I guess.'

'That's very true but I'm not sure my sister will ever fully grow up. Anyway, back to Marco. What's he like?' she asks.

'He's a good man. Wonderful, in fact,' I tell her, recalling how romantic he could be, buying me flowers for no reason, or cooking delicious meals, sometimes bringing lovely food home from the restaurant and setting the table like one at the restaurant, with a candle at the centre. 'And he's funny too. We always laughed together.'

Listening to myself listing off all the good things, an outsider might wonder why on earth things didn't work out between us. But marriage was always the sticking point.

'Wow. He sounds like a dream. Don't tell me he is good-looking too?'

'Oh yes, he's very handsome. He has dark hair, and sparkling blue eyes and—'

'And it's obvious you are still in love with him,' she interjects.

'Maybe it's true.' I sigh. 'I don't know why I thought getting away would help me fall out of love with him, although to be fair I've been busy enough for him not to have occupied my thoughts too much.'

'Busy going out with Artemis?' She raises an eyebrow.

'He's just a pleasant distraction. And we really are just friends, as he is recently separated too. I'm certain neither of us want anything more. I can't deny I like him, though. And he is seriously attractive.'

'Maybe you don't want anything serious, but I've seen the way he looks at you.'

'I think there is definitely a mutual physical attraction. Maybe I foolishly thought a bit of fun might be the answer. A holiday fling, as I am single.'

'Exactly. You are single, so you should take advantage of being on a break. If you think there is a chance you might get back with Marco, you won't be able to sleep with anyone else for the rest of your life.'

'Hannah! I'm shocked.'

'Are you? Well, you ought to think about it. You can legitimately have some fun with someone else for a short while, even if it is only physical. How were you to know Marco would get in touch?'

I shake my head and laugh. Even though she has a point and I have imagined numerous encounters with Artemis and his strong body, including when I daydreamed about him applying sun cream across my back with those strong hands.

'So are you going to reply to the text?' asks Hannah.

'Not just yet. I need to figure out what to say. You have reminded me of our different views on marriage. If I say I miss him too, where do we go from there?'

I pop my phone on to charge as I finish getting ready. I can think about that later.

'Right, what's next on the list,' I say, heading outside to do a final check on the donkeys as we will all be out for a while this evening. Eric has spent a lot of time in his shelter today and Freddie, with the damaged leg, has been walking a lot, but both seem content enough.

I finish my look-in, but before going over to Tania's, I head upstairs and pull my phone from the charger and decide to send a reply to Marco. I'm not sure I can find the right words. First, I simply select a thumbs up emoji, before deleting it, as it seems entirely inappropriate. Unsure again, I pop my phone into my small clutch bag, deciding I will deal with it later. Tonight, I am looking forward to mingling with some new friends. Maybe, as Artemis once said, I need to have faith that things will work out just the way they are meant to.

SIXTEEN

'How are you enjoying being here in Crete?'

Tania passes me a glass of white wine, the smell of lamb steaks filling the air as they sizzle on the BBQ that Nicos is over-seeing. I glance around the garden, the terracotta pots filled with pretty flowers, and the grapes above my head growing down through the pergola. Across the sloping valley, the tall trees rise into the distance, giving just the slightest slice of sea in the background.

'I love being here, who wouldn't? And I knew the dogs would help me feel a bit better about things. I just adore them.'

That is, until Marco has just popped right back into my head, I think to myself.

'I'll introduce you to Annie and Smudge properly later, I know you have only seen them over the fence.'

'Where are they now?'

'They are currently crunching on a bone in the stables to stop them howling. Well, Smudge mainly.' She laughs.

'I can't wait.' I smile. 'Lars told me that you take them out walking with the other dogs'.

'Sometimes we do, yes, but honestly? It's easier if we take

them alone, or things can get a little crazy. They do join up with the dogs at the dog park, though, and have a run around with them. They do love their canine buddies.'

Judith and Lars are chatting to Helena and Panos, who we were surprised to see but learnt that their bar shuts early on a Monday. I stroll over with Hannah to join them when Tania goes to assist Nicos. As she approaches, Nicos snakes his arm around her waist with one hand and kisses her on the top of the head, before she goes off to refresh people's drinks.

'Judith, I wonder next week would you like some girls' drinks at the bar?' Helena asks. 'You know, before the wedding?'

'Oh, you mean like a hen party?' Judith looks completely surprised.

'Yes, yes, a hen's party. I could decorate the bar, have a little music,' she offers earnestly.

'That is really thoughtful of you, Helena. I will think about that.' She nods. 'In fact, no, I won't think about it, I will say yes and thank you.' She claps her hands together, looking delighted. 'A hen party, how wonderful. It's not something I would have even considered.'

'Perfect. Next Friday, then? Six o'clock. I think maybe my grandmother will be thrilled. She was only just saying that no one has parties anymore.' Helena grins.

'Gosh that's a great idea, Yolanda will be thrilled too,' says Tania, when Judith tells her what Helena has just offered. 'She also said she missed parties, and has been so looking forward to this evening's BBQ.'

'I'm sure she will be thrilled,' says Judith. 'She has been complaining that she still hasn't had a chance to wear the new dancing shoes she bought in Heraklion after our last shopping trip.'

Doll and Michael have just arrived, looking glamorous, Doll in an eye-catching black and white dress and Michael in a cream-coloured linen suit. Doll is carrying a huge cheesecake that she had been busy preparing this afternoon.

'Wow, that looks amazing, thank you,' says Tania, taking the cheesecake, which is topped with juicy strawberries and raspberries, and swirls of cream.

'Thanks, I probably won't eat any of it, though. I always eat too much sweet stuff when our dance tours have finished.' She grins.

'Well, it's good to treat yourself, my love,' says Michael. 'Just not too much, hey,' he adds, and I can't help thinking of those donkeys she was secretly passing all those treats to.

Just then, another guest arrives, and Tania passes the cheesecake to Nicos and asks him to pop it in the kitchen.

'I am sure I will enjoy some of that later,' I hear Panos say to Hannah. 'But maybe it will make me fat.' He smiles and Hannah almost spits her drink out.

'Will you ever let me forget that?' she says, and he gives her a cheeky grin.

'I have already forgiven you. I realise, it could not possibly be true.' He strokes his flat stomach and Hannah bursts out laughing.

They look so adorable together, yet their lives are a world apart. Hannah will be returning to university in a few weeks and Panos has his life here, running the family bar. I wonder if he is happy doing it. Does he feel a sense of duty and obligation after his father died? It's strange to think that there are so many people out there in the world who could actually be perfect for us, yet we are destined never to meet them.

The BBQ is a wonderful affair; the solar lights in the garden have slowly come to life, illuminating the lawn and the white lights threaded across the porch look magical beneath the darkening sky. I am introduced to a charming couple, Monica and Joe, who own a holiday home and they tell us all about Tania's talent for upcycling, and how she has transformed some of their furniture.

'That's a great skill,' I say to Tania. 'I remember having a go at revamping a wardrobe once, which was a complete disaster. I basically just painted it pink and the paint peeled off after two days.' I laugh at the memory.

'You need primer or at least a special type of paint. It takes a little practice, although anyone can do it,' she says modestly. 'I have watched a lot of videos on YouTube.'

Yolanda and her neighbours, an older couple who speak little English, sit with Lars and Judith, enjoying the food and conversation. Judith and Yolanda laugh a lot together, I can't help noticing.

Chatting away, eating and drinking, I realise Artemis is not here and wonder whether he had even been invited, even though his mother is here.

'Mm, this is just delicious. Who knew halloumi could taste so good on a BBQ?' I savour the salty cheese, griddled to perfection. It perfectly complements the rich lamb, which has been marinated in garlic, rosemary and red wine. The tables set along the front porch are also groaning with Greek salads, chicken skewers, olives and breads. Music is gently playing, and Yolanda is tapping her feet along to the music. I think of the small communal garden at the flats back home and imagine trying to host a party like this. Maybe it's something I could think about when I get home, getting to know the neighbours a little more.

When most of the food has been eaten, Tania asks if I would still like to meet Smudge and Annie.

'I think maybe I will let them have a run around the rear garden. Some of the guests are elderly, I don't want them startled. Or knocked over,' she explains. I notice her glance at her aunt and Yolanda. It's hard to remember that both of them have recently recovered from injuries. They are both just so full of life. I hope I'm doing half as well when I'm their age.

'I would love to meet them too,' says Hannah, who has joined us, whilst Panos heads over to offer his assistance to Nicos, who is cooking some sausages.

At the stables, which now act as huge kennels as well as a furniture workshop, Tania attaches a leash to the dogs and we walk with them to the rear garden. The dogs are so beautiful, their red and black coats contrasting perfectly alongside each other as they walk.

Off the lead, in the rear garden, Smudge can contain his excitement no longer and jumps up, giving us one of his infamous hugs and has me laughing loudly. Annie says hello, with licks on our hands, before racing around the garden, quickly followed by Smudge.

'Oh my gosh, they are just adorable. I have heard so much about them, it's been a joy meeting them. I'll stay here with them for a while if you like, go and mingle with your guests,' I offer and Hannah says she will stay too.

'You don't have to.' Tania throws a ball and the dogs race after it.

'I know, but I want to.' I smile.

'Me too,' adds Hannah.

'Okay, thanks. I will go and check the guests have everything they need. Do you mind shutting them back in the stables when you are ready?'

'No problem,' I tell her.

'I thought about becoming a vet,' says Hannah as she throws the ball once more.

'And you changed your mind?'

'Hmm, I did at the time, yes. The thought of people bringing their pets in terrified me. It felt like too much of a responsibility if something went wrong, or worse still, if I couldn't make them better. A job in books is less risky.' She laughs. 'And I do absolutely love the thought of working in a library. Being surrounded by books wouldn't feel like being in a place of work to me, it's my idea of heaven.'

Just then, an elderly lady appears with a woman in her forties. As Nicos welcomes them warmly, Panos's mouth visibly drops open. Hannah leaves me to shut the dogs in the stables and goes back to the gathering.

I recognise the older woman at once as Panos's grandmother from the bar. I wonder if the woman who looks maybe in her late forties is her daughter?

'Are you okay?' I hear Hannah ask Panos as I join them.

'Yes, Fine. It is my mother,' he says, visibly shocked, almost rooted to the spot.

Before Panos has a chance to go and greet her, Yolanda is standing and crushing the younger woman in an embrace, raising her arms and saying something in Greek to the elderly grandmother, who is nodding and smiling.

Panos and Helena take their mother by the hand, and she sits with Yolanda, Judith and the group of friends. After a few minutes, Panos introduces us to his mother, who tucks her long dark hair behind her ears and nods politely, although says nothing. We leave them alone again, though, but watching the scene unfold with Panos and Helena with their mother is lovely. As they chat, she begins to smile as she sips some ouzo.

'Maybe it is time for a little more music,' says Nicos, playing some upbeat songs, and the guests begin to clap their hands.

'Perhaps you could show us some traditional Greek dancing,' suggests Michael, puffing on a cigar, Doll wafting away the smoke as it spirals towards her.

'I have not had enough ouzo for that,' says Nicos and everyone laughs.

Later in the evening Tania allows the dogs to come and join us after their good behaviour in the rear garden, and as the food has mostly been cleared away. We stand chatting, as the dogs are sniffing around the hedges. The mountain backdrop is so pretty, an orange sun descending lower behind the mountains.

'You're so lucky to live here,' says Hannah dreamily, glancing across the valley.

'I know. There are times when I can hardly believe it myself. Life really can surprise you sometimes.'

'It can. I would never have imagined myself coming here alone,' confides Hannah. 'I'm glad I did, though. I have met so many lovely people.'

'Sometimes it's good to take a chance in life,' agrees Tania. 'My life might have turned out quite differently had I not done exactly that. Right then, I think it's time to get the dogs back in the stables.' She glances around; Annie is running around with a ball in her mouth, but Smudge is nowhere to be seen.

'Smudge!' Tania calls his name, but he seems to have disappeared. 'Smudge, where are you?'

Just then, Smudge comes galloping into the garden, his face covered in what looks like blood, with Nicos in hot pursuit.

'Oh my goodness!' Tania's hand flies to her mouth. 'What's happened?'

'Don't worry.' Nicos doesn't appear to look too concerned. 'I'm sorry, but I left the kitchen door open. I hope you never had any ideas about having any of that cheesecake.'

'No! Oh my goodness, Smudge, you naughty boy. I hope Doll doesn't see it.'

'Maybe I will keep her wine glass topped up so she forgets all about it,' says Nicos, who is trying hard not to laugh.

Tania grabs Smudge by the collar, and leads him to an outdoor tap to wash him before returning the dogs to the stables for the rest of the evening.

'I hope Panos isn't too disappointed,' I say to Hannah as we stroll over to join the others. 'He was really looking forward to some of that cheesecake.' We both burst out laughing.

Everyone is relaxed and happy and as a lively tune is played, Yolanda stands and waves her hands in the air. Soon, she is joined by some of the other guests and they dance and laugh in the middle of the lawn, shoes off, twirling around and loving life. Helena and Panos's mother sit watching the scene, smiling but not yet ready to dance. Nicos is standing with his arms wrapped around Tania, taking in the scene, and when he turns and drops a gentle kiss on her lips, I feel a pang of regret for Marco and me.

'Come and have a dance,' says Monica, the English owner of the holiday home, who's been entertaining me with stories of her younger days.

I wipe my hands on some kitchen towel and join her on the lawn. I give myself up to the music, and soon enjoy the feeling of wild abandon, barefoot on the lawn, dancing with my new friends. Helena comes and joins us, as Panos and Hannah watch from the terrace, the twinkling lights above them. I notice Panos gesture to the outdoor dance floor, but Hannah shakes her head and he seems happy to stay with her, seemingly happy to be a spectator, taking in the other guests dancing the night away.

When a song with a Cuban beat plays, Michael takes Doll by the hand and leads her onto the lawn. They dance energetically, once more holding those watching in the palm of their hand. There is thunderous applause and whoops of delight when they finish the dance.

'No more ballroom dancing, we aren't on tour,' says Doll at the end of it. 'You are such a show-off.' She takes a long sip of her wine, which Nicos keeps topping up, I notice.

'But people love it,' he protests, clearly revelling in the attention.

'I know that, but we are meant to be resting the muscles after the tour,' she reminds him. 'I don't mind doing the charity dance, it's for the rescue after all, but we are not performing seals,' she says, and Michael gives an awkward smile and shrugs.

'What a wonderful evening,' says Yolanda. 'Now you know I have a sweet tooth. Maybe I will try some of that cheesecake before I leave,' she says, and Tania quickly pulls her to one side and whispers in her ear. Everyone else seems to be getting ready to head home too.

After kissing Nicos and Tania on the cheek and thanking them for a wonderful night, Doll shrugs on her wrap for the short walk back to the rescue. Michael shakes Nicos by the hand, and lightly kisses Tania, then they say goodnight to us all and leave, Doll swaying slightly as she walks.

'Phew. Thank goodness Doll never mentioned the cheesecake,' says Tania as we help her clear up in the kitchen, the sorry mess that was once a lovingly made dessert consigned to the bin.

When the other guests have said their goodnights and filtered off to their homes, Tania thanks us for helping in the kitchen. Panos was most disappointed by the lack of cheesecake and Tania promises to make something sweet to pop into the bar in a day or two, which seems to please him. When we come out of the kitchen, Panos is waiting for us and offers to walk us home.

'Tomorrow morning. Maybe we go for a walk and have a pancake at a place I know. They have the best. The bar only opens at twelve. And, of course, you too, Beth.' He turns to me.

'The morning is a busy time, I'm afraid,' says Hannah.

'Of course. Well, maybe later in the day, if you have a break, we could take a stroll together. That is, if you would like to?'

'Will Helena not mind if you leave the bar?' asks Hannah.

'It is a little quiet now that the summer is coming to an end,' he reassures her. 'She will be okay for around one hour. My mother can come and be with her. I think maybe tonight is a breakout.'

'Breakout?' Hannah looks puzzled.

'Do you mean breakthrough?' I suggest.

'Yes, yes, breakthrough. It is the first time she has been out in a long time.'

'Well, that's just wonderful. Let's hope it is the start of her recovery, getting out and about again,' I say.

'I hope so.'

'We usually have a break for lunch around one,' says Hannah, getting back to the subject of going for a walk tomorrow with Panos.

'About twenty minutes away, on a road to Koutouloufari, there is a kiosk that makes the best pancakes. With fruit and cream. Maybe it will make up for the cheesecake.'

'Even though Tania has offered to make you one?' Hannah reminds him.

'Maybe I just like desserts.' He smiles.

'Okay, thanks. I look forward to it.'

I say goodnight to Panos, and head inside, leaving him and Hannah alone for a moment. A short while later, I'm in the kitchen getting some water, when she enters, grinning from ear to ear.

In bed that evening, I glance out of my window and stare at the stars in the navy night sky. I tell myself I'm happy enough on my own, and of course I am, I don't need a man to make me happy. Seeing all the couples here, though, I realise how much Marco and I worked together. We laughed, we loved, and on this beautiful evening under the bright moon, I miss him. I find myself reaching for my phone and tapping out a reply to his message.

I miss you too. Xx

SEVENTEEN

I've been at the rescue for just over a week and the days have fallen into an easy routine. I love being here with the animals and just wish I could take the little white terrier home with me, but I couldn't afford all the legalities and transport costs and remind myself I am not allowed a dog in the apartment anyway.

It's just after eight next morning and Judith is carrying a bale of straw towards the donkey shelter. The smell of disinfectant lingers in the air, as we have not long sluiced down the whole of the concrete areas around the rescue.

'Where on earth has that man disappeared to now?' says Judith, glancing around looking for Lars, who it seems has gone missing once again without telling Judith where he was going. Recalling the day that I saw him and Doll climbing out of the car, and entering the rescue using different routes, I glance around for Doll, but she is nowhere to be seen either. I stop myself from saying anything, as there is probably a very simple explanation.

'Maybe Doll went with him to the shop at the bottom of the hill,' suggests Michael.

'Oh,' says Judith, looking unsurprisingly a little puzzled.

'He usually asks if we need anything when he pops to the shops.'

'I'm not sure either of them have, I'm just assuming.' Michael shrugs. 'She does this at home sometimes, just vanishes. I'm sure they will rock up soon.' He smiles, unconcerned, even though it seems a little strange just to go off unannounced.

Michael doesn't seem to be the slightest bit perturbed that Doll might have gone off to the shops with Lars, or indeed somewhere else, so perhaps I had better rein in my inner Miss Marple.

I don't have time to dwell on that, though, as there is lots of work to be done.

Half an hour later, a car pulls up and out step Lars and Doll, carrying two bags of shopping.

'There you are.' Judith gives a smile that I perceive to be a little strained. 'I wondered where you had got to.'

'I am sorry, my love.' Lars kisses Judith on the cheek. 'You were on the phone when I left, but I did ask Hannah to tell you I had gone to the village for some feta and olives. I also got some more fruit, I noticed the fruit bowl was looking a little empty.'

'And I went to get some of these.' Doll pulls out some bags of sweets. 'I've been craving them, as I've been off the sugar for a while and I never even got to eat any of that cheesecake.'

I exchange a glance with Hannah, who has just joined us. Luckily Doll hasn't discovered what became of her cheesecake.

'I got extra for us all to share.' Doll smiles, holding up two large bags of mixed jellies.

'Ooh, Jelly Babies,' says Hannah. 'Gosh, Judith, I'm so sorry. I was meant to tell you Lars had gone out shopping,' she continues, suddenly remembering she was supposed to pass on a message.

'No harm done,' says Judith, with a broad smile. 'Especially now that we have stocked up on tomatoes, feta and salad. Thank you, Lars.'

As he walks inside, I see him exchange a glance with Doll and she winks.

Around one o'clock, we break for lunch and Hannah tells Judith she is going for a walk with Panos and will be back later.

'Enjoy yourself,' says Judith, setting the outside table with cold meats and cheeses. It is slightly cooler now it's nearing the middle of September, but we are determined to eat outside beneath the blue sky and forest setting for as long as possible.

'It's the perfect weather for a walk. See you later,' I tell Hannah as she grabs her bag and heads off.

'How are the wedding plans coming long?' I ask Judith as I scoop up some creamy hummus and spread it on a cracker. There are also bowls of white beans in a tomato sauce.

'All sorted I think.' She turns to Lars and he takes her hand in his, clearly in love, despite his furtive behaviour with Doll.

'I thought you might have got married at the chapel,' I say, before piling some Greek salad onto my plate.

'Ah well, I would have liked to. But there are just so many steps. Somehow, I don't think I would arrive like Meryl Streep in *Mamma Mia!*, skipping up those steps. I would arrive as the blushing bride for all the wrong reasons.' She laughs loudly. 'Although, actually, I do have my new knee. Maybe I could have taken things slowly. There is a huge terrace outside the chapel, I suppose the wedding could have been done there.' She reflects. 'But never mind, it's far too close to the date to do anything about that now.' Judith brushes away the idea. 'And my niece's garden is a perfectly lovely place to conduct a wedding.'

'Well, I can't argue with that,' I reply. 'It's a pity there isn't a slope up to the church. Eric the donkey could have carried you up there.'

'Now there is someone I would not rely on on my wedding day.' Judith giggles.

Judith and Lars look so happy together, I'm not sure why I felt something secretive was occurring between him and Doll, but the day they entered the rescue separately was just so strange. I did wonder whether I ought to have mentioned something to Lars, but decided against it as there is probably a perfectly simple explanation for it all.

Lunch over, we take the dogs for a walk, joined by some volunteers who have just arrived. A couple from a nearby village are also here to rehome the small terrier who I have already grown very fond of. Judith is always thrilled when a dog finds its forever home, but she says it saddens her a little too.

'Bittersweet, I suppose is the phrase,' she tells me, as they head off, the white terrier glancing back at us from the rear window of the car.

When Hannah returns from her walk with Panos, she looks happy and relaxed. She tells me they cut through the forest and walked part of the road down into Koutouloufari.

'There is a little kiosk with a few chairs and tables outside, along the path. I had pancakes with fruit and honey. Panos was right about them being delicious. We sat eating them, glancing right across the valley, watching cars in the distance climb the mountain roads. It felt like a little oasis in the middle of nowhere.' She sighs.

'Sounds wonderful. I might head over there myself one day.'

'I'll join you if you like,' she offers. 'I could show you the path through the forest. It isn't too far. Maybe we could even walk further on to the honey farm I spotted in the distance.'

'Great. I love honey.'

We carry on with our chores then, Hannah singing as she does some sorting out of supplies in the utility room, and it feels so good to see someone so happy. There is a slight pang, but she deserves this blossoming friendship or romance.

I had another message from Marco today that was simply a heart emoji. I didn't know how on earth to respond to that and he hasn't messaged me since. Perhaps he is waiting for me to get back home, or maybe he has drawn a line under our separation. If so, was there any point in us both acknowledging the fact that we miss each other? Maybe when I head home I can talk to him face to face, as despite working hard and having the distraction of the surroundings – not to mention the charming Artemis – it seems shaking someone from your thoughts is not as simple as upping sticks and going somewhere. Our feelings travel with us.

In the late afternoon I'm finishing up my chores, reaching up to the top of the wall to hang up a hose, when I lose my footing and fall in a heap onto the dusty path.

'Shit. Bugger.' My hand goes to my knee, and I see that it is slightly grazed.

'Do you need a hand?'

I glance up to see Artemis standing over me, trying hard not to smile.

'Artemis, hi.' I accept his hand and he pulls me to my feet. Today, he's wearing a white shirt, sleeves rolled up, and tan chinos, smelling, as always, quite divine.

'Are you alright?'

'Yes, I'm fine.' I smile brightly, retrieving a tissue from the pocket of my shorts and wiping my knee.

'Are you going somewhere?' he asks.

'Yes, actually. Downhill to the village shop. I figure it won't take me too long. And the walk back uphill should give me a good workout,' I tell him. 'Where are you going?'

'I have just left my mother. I was about to drive to the shops for her, as she needs one or two things. She is feeling, maybe, a little delicate today,' he reveals.

'Well, it was nice to see her enjoying herself. She danced the night away.'

'And obviously enjoyed the ouzo too.' He can't help smiling.

I think of Yolanda throwing her arms in the air and dancing with Panos's grandmother.

'Maybe we could walk to the shop together?'

'Sure,' I reply. 'So how was your evening?' I ask him.

'Good. And the team I support actually won, which makes a nice change.'

'Actually, I wondered whether I might have seen you at the BBQ last night.'

'Were you hoping I would be there?' He turns and gives me that dazzling, self-assured smile.

'I never said that. I just thought you might have been there, as surely you know Nicos, having both grown up around here together.'

'We were never really close friends, and people move on.' He shrugs.

I nip inside for a plaster – which I place over my grazed knee, which is now bleeding slightly – before we set off and fall into step with each other.

Walking downhill around each bend in the road reminds me that it might be a bit of a long walk back and more strenuous than I anticipated. I'm not sure my yoga classes back home have prepared me for all this hill walking and my knee is already beginning to throb a bit.

As we make our way, I glance at Artemis and his handsome profile and wonder how differently I might be feeling towards him if Marco didn't still occupy a part of my heart. Despite his charm, he managed to remain married for twelve years, although I know nothing about his life, whether he was faithful, or anything like that. I've already seen how women openly admire his looks, which must be difficult for any partner of his.

As we pass hedgerows, I hear the distant sound of a tractor in a farmhouse field somewhere, and spot a flock of birds swooping down onto something on the ground below. A car slows down and asks if we would like a lift to the bottom of the hill, and I politely decline.

'Are you sure?' asks Artemis.

'Of course I'm sure. This is the easy part,' I remind him. Heading lower down, the glimmer of the gorgeous sea soon comes into view, a red and white ferry in the distance sailing to an island somewhere. 'I might have accepted the lift if it was on the way back up,' I confess.

'I could always go and get the car for the journey back?' Artemis offers.

'Not at all. I only need one or two things,' I tell him brightly, already looking forward to a bottle of iced cool water from the fridge outside the tiny village shop. Besides, I am enjoying walking with him, chatting and admiring the gorgeous scenery. In the car, we would be up and down in no time at all.

Presently, the narrow road widens, and a handful of houses with blue front doors and climbing plants trailing over their walls appear; a moped here and there leans lazily against white walls in the warm, end of summer sunshine. A black and white cat raises its back and stands, crossing our path and meowing. Then the red Coke fridge appears outside the small village shop.

Inside, Artemis begins a conversation with the shopkeeper and I wish him a *kalispera*, before heading along the narrow aisles in search of some crisps, milk and a tub of hot chocolate that I have been craving before bed. I also pick up a packet of hair bands, as I'd forgotten to pack some and had to borrow one from Hannah. I grab some water from the fridge as Artemis is reaching into the nearby freezer for two Magnum ice creams.

'Thanks,' I say, as he hands one to me after I have paid for my things.

'Shall we eat these over there?' Artemis gestures to a bench on a small hill that overlooks the sea and clusters of village houses clinging to the hillside.

'Sure.' I follow him and we sit side by side, taking in the view.

'How are things in your on-off relationship, if you don't mind me asking, that is,' I ask him.

'Not at all. And they are definitely off,' he says firmly. 'We are not good for each other in so many ways.'

'Not something you could work on together, then? You were married for a long time.'

'People change, I guess. Besides, she is not good for my bank balance.'

'So she likes to spend?'

'Far too much.' He sighs. 'My ex is never happy. She always wants more clothes, perfumes, a weekend away with her friends. Does a woman really need to change her hair colour so often at the hairdresser's?' He shakes his head.

'So she is what you might call high-maintenance?'

'Hmm? Yes, that is exactly right. High-maintenance. Which is fine if she earns enough money to pay for all the things she wants, but she doesn't. She seems to think I earn a lot more than I do. But maybe it is my own fault.'

'How do you mean?' I ask, a little puzzled.

'I mean, maybe I indulged her at first, giving her whatever she wanted, trying to impress her. But that was when I earned bonuses. Nowadays? Not so much. People are much more careful with their finances, not taking out loans and so on.' He reflects. 'Which means less bonuses for us.'

'Surely she understood that?'

'No, because I never told her. I was foolish. I borrowed money from my mother to keep her in the lifestyle she became used to.' He sighs. 'Now my mother, rightly, has put a stop to it. Even asking me to pay the money back. Once she found out it was going on my wife, that is,' He reveals. 'Before that she gifted it to me, telling me I am her only son and why not enjoy some of my inheritance now? She says she will not throw the money at my wife anymore, so I am to pay it back, and have it for my own future.'

'The things we do for love, hey? But, honestly, Artemis, if she has lost interest in you because the funds are running low, then maybe she isn't the woman you think she is.'

'It's true. And maybe it is some sort of payback. I believe many people call it karma.' He gazes off towards the sea, lost in his thoughts for a minute.

'Karma? For what?'

'It's a long story. Maybe I will tell you sometime.'

'They do say there is no time like the present,' I suggest.

'If you insist. For stealing another man's fiancée.' He turns to look at me, his eyes full of something I can't make out. Regret? Sorrow?

I'm shocked when Artemis tells me that he and Nicos were once best friends, growing up in the village together, having adventures, especially when they were younger. I listen as he tells me tales of camping beneath the stars with the boys in the village and building tyre swings on the tall trees, as well as making dens and racing through the forest on their bikes.

'It sounds idyllic.'

'It was. And then I ruined things,' he confides. 'Maybe I always admired Nicos, envied him even. I was attracted to his fiancée, as she was so beautiful,' he tells me, clearly feeling the need to unburden himself. 'So I pursued her. I selfishly thought only of myself. I was maybe not such a nice person back then.'

'We all do things we aren't proud of,' I say gently. 'And I'd say a lot of people become better people as they age, learning from their past mistakes. Don't be too hard on yourself. Your marriage lasted a long time, so it clearly was love.'

'I guess so.' He turns to me and smiles. 'Although maybe I could have been happy with another woman, it did not have to be the fiancée of my friend. Back then, I just thought I could have whatever I wanted.'

'And now?'

'Now? I have to face the fact we have grown apart. She wants time with her friends once more. Maybe having married so young, I can understand that.'

'It happens,' I say, thinking of the number of people in my hometown who married young, and never lasted for the duration.

'And I am taking time to sort my finances out. Pay my mother back,' Artemis continues. 'There is no going back now, my ex has moved in with her mother. I think maybe you are right, the well has run dry, so she will probably find someone richer,' he muses.

I slide my hand across to his and give it a little squeeze. We sit quietly for a few minutes, just staring across the green valley towards the sea, and I think of how similar our situations are. Both recently heartbroken, both unsure of what the future holds, and both maybe regretting choices we have made in our lives. After five minutes, I am the first to stand.

'Are you ready for that walk uphill?' I brandish my bottle of water.

'Ready. Are you sure you don't want me to go up and get my car?' he asks, one last time.

'Positive.' I smile. 'Let's do this.'

EIGHTEEN

We chat as we walk uphill, although conversation is limited when we reach a particularly steep curve and I place my hands on my knees and catch my breath for a minute, taking the opportunity to admire the view all around.

When we finally arrive back at the rescue, Artemis crushes me in an embrace at the top of the hill, watched by Nicos and Tania, who are just leaving.

'Thanks for the talk, Beth. You are a good friend.'

'I must be, if you don't mind hugging a sweaty mess,' I joke. The walk uphill was far more challenging than I dared to admit, and my grazed knee is throbbing a bit.

'And I'm glad you see me in the same way,' I say, thinking that maybe Artemis could just maybe be a good friend too.

'So, at the weekend I was thinking, maybe I could show you a good time in Malia.'

'Malia?'

'Yes, strictly as friends,' he quickly adds. 'Perhaps it would do us both good, two people seeking a little fun after heartbreak.' He places his hand on his heart and I can't help smiling. A Saturday in Malia sounds really good.

After the morning feeds, and clean ups, Judith allows us the rest of Saturday to do as we please and she and Lars stay around the rescue, catching up on any admin work. There are usually quite a few volunteers around who like to walk the dogs at the weekend too.

'Do you know, I like the sound of that. I've been wanting to go into Malia. As long as we are not too old for the nightlife.'

'Old?' Artemis looks indignant, before admitting that he prefers quieter places these days, but thinks a night in Malia might just be a lot of fun.

'That's settled then. I'll dig out my best dress for Saturday,' I tell him.

'And your swimming costume, we could go to the beach first. I liked that black one you wore at Star Beach,' he says cheekily.

'Just friends, remember,' I remind him.

Artemis nods in the direction of Nicos and Tania, and I lift my hand and wave. He doesn't stay to chat to his old friend, and now I know the reason why.

'Did you know Artemis had gone off with Nicos's fiancée?'

I'm chatting to Judith in the kitchen, helping her to clear up after the evening dinner.

'I did.' She folds a tea towel and places it on the table. 'Why do you ask?'

'I'm just curious, that's all. Do you think he is a womaniser?' I ask as I place some cutlery into a drawer.

'I never said that exactly, I know he was married for a long time,' she tells me. 'But obviously, as he is very recently separated, I just thought that you should know. His distant past has absolutely nothing to do with me. I can see how devilishly handsome he is.'

'He told me he and Nicos were once friends,' I reveal. 'I

kind of get the impression he has regrets about what has gone on in the past between them.'

She places some glasses into a solid wooden kitchen cupboard.

'He actually told you that?' She turns to face me.

'He did. Well, not in so many words, but he tells me he thinks he is a nicer person these days,' I say, but Judith doesn't seem so sure.

'You might be right,' she says eventually. 'And truthfully? I don't actually know Artemis too well, only from what Yolanda has told me about him. I do know she loves him dearly, despite once saying that she thought his good looks were a curse. And she has made no secret of the fact that she thinks his ex was a gold-digger.'

'She said that?'

'Yes. Oh, they got along perfectly well at first, for years apparently. His wife was a busy beauty therapist and earning good money. Over the years, though, it seems she would work less and less, only doing a couple of facials a week or a set of nails, before swanning off to the beach with her friends, preferring to spend Artemis's money. This is, according to Yolanda,' she adds.

'Well, I don't suppose I know Artemis very well either, but I just kind of get the feeling he's a good guy deep down, despite being cursed with those good looks. I'm going out with him on Saturday actually, once the chores are done.'

'And why not?' She smiles. 'You are only young once, just be careful, that's all I'm saying. Especially as you told me you are only recently single yourself. It would be foolish to rush into anything else. Sorry, you can tell me to mind my own business if you like, I won't be offended.' She smiles once more.

'I would never do that. And I know that the situation is beyond complicated.' I sigh. 'Artemis is fast becoming a good friend, and that's all. It's nice to have a local show me around.'

For some reason, I don't tell Judith that Artemis is going to take me to some busy bars and show me the nightlife of Malia.

Just then Hannah arrives home after being at the bar chatting to Panos, who has walked her home.

'Hi, how was your evening?' I ask.

'Lovely.' She sits on a chair and draws her knees up to her chest, before wrapping her arms around them, and smiles. 'We have so much in common. We both love books, nature and, as it turns out, chess. We played a game this evening that lasted for over two hours. It's nice to have something that doesn't present a language barrier too.'

'That's lovely. Do you fancy a frappé?' I gesture to the coffee machine that has a cold coffee setting.

'Ooh, go on then, I'd love one. Maybe a decaf one, though. Then it's bed for me. I can't wait to see what happens next in my book.'

'Sounds good. I've read all of the magazines I bought at the airport now, and a lot of Judith's books are period dramas or crime thrillers, which are not really my thing. Maybe now is the time to try and take up reading again.'

'You can borrow mine when I've finished, if you like. It isn't fantasy. It's a story about a woman who sets up a centre for lonely people.'

'Sounds a bit depressing.' I pour some milk and ice into the blender on the coffee machine.

'Helping people sounds depressing?' She frowns.

'Of course not. I mean the thought of people being lonely.'

'Oh, it is. We have to open our eyes sometimes and see what's going on around us. The woman in the story sets up the centre after she realised how lonely her own grandmother was. Anyway, I won't spoil it in case you do decide to give it a go.'

'Okay. Maybe I will, thanks. And I think you're right. Especially regarding old people.'

It makes me think of my friend Jess back home, who has

mentioned how her gran really looks forward to her visits and of the old people in the shop who call in for a chat, some saying that we might be the only people they speak to all day. It would explain why they shop daily for their things, rather than filling their trolley for the week. And, of course, getting out for a little exercise.

I place a frappé down in front of Hannah, and once we've finished our drinks, we head upstairs, where Hannah immerses herself in her book and I listen to a podcast where a well-known couple chat about relationships.

The bloke is talking about how women sometimes find guys off-putting who are 'too nice', opting for the blokes who have a bit of an edge about them, which is crazy when you think about it. Surely we all want a secure, solid type of love, with mutual trust and not a sniff of uncertainty. I recall an old school friend once saying that she would never date a boy her parents approved of, as they would be too dull, favouring the bad guys on the motorbikes who were much more fun. Daft when you think about it. Surely the world needs more nice people in it?

I then find myself thinking about Hannah and her empathy for others. And sure, I contribute to the food bank, and we have a trolley at the supermarket for shoppers to drop something into, but maybe I could do a little more. I know, for example, one old woman in particular who visits the shop each day to chat to someone as she doesn't have any family close by. Maybe I could look for local groups for the old people to meet up? Even have some details of local groups pinned on the display board near the entrance to the supermarket? I will give it some thought when I get home. We could probably all do that little bit more if we really think about it.

When Hannah switches her bedside lamp off, I decide to get some sleep too. I might need my rest if I am to go partying in Malia with Artemis. The very thought of it puts a smile on my face.

NINETEEN

It's a warm Saturday. In fact, the September sunshine feels warmer than ever today, the only clue to the gentle shift in season being the occasional leaf falling from a tree and twirling to the ground.

I'm just returning with a few of the dogs from a walk, along with Hannah, Doll and Michael, who are each walking several dogs too.

Tania is in the front garden, raking a tiny pile of mustard-coloured leaves into a mound in the middle of the lawn and I slow down as the others wish her a good morning, before they continue on to the rescue.

'Morning, Beth, how are things?' She puts down her rake and walks over to the fence.

'Good, thanks. How are you?'

'Great, thanks. I thought I'd make a start on the garden, whilst the weather is so pleasant.'

'Where are the dogs?' I look around but there is no sign of them.

'Oh, in the rear garden. They would have scattered all those leaves by now.' She laughs, pointing to the small pile. 'Nicos has gone into town today, then he's taking his son swimming after school. Actually, do you have time for a cuppa?' she offers.

'Sure. I'll get the dogs settled and be back in a minute.'

Inside, Lars and Doll are standing close together, and Lars seems to be whispering something in her ear. When I approach, they drift off in different directions.

I tell Judith I will be just across the road with Tania having a drink and she tells me to take as long as I like, as the morning chores have been done.

Tania invites me into her stylish, spacious kitchen that is simply furnished with white painted walls, wooden units and pots of fresh herbs at the windowsill. A beautiful sideboard dominates one wall, in a soft grey shade; a vibrant-blue glazed fruit bowl sits on the top.

'I upcycled that,' says Tania, when she notices me admiring it. 'It was dark wood originally, and a little project for me. I think it looks pretty good now.'

'I agree, in fact it looks amazing. You would probably pay a lot of money in a shop for that.'

'Thank you, and you most certainly would, especially in the city shops. I recently sold something to a shop in Heraklion, actually.'

Then scent of fresh coffee fills the air as she fills a cafetière and places it down alongside two glass mugs. She then fetches a tin, and when she opens it, a hit of zesty lemon fills the air.

'Lemon drizzle. Fancy a piece?'

'Ooh yes, please, it's my absolute favourite. It seems you are a woman of many talents,' I comment.

'Not really. And when it comes to baking, I just follow a recipe, you can't really go wrong then,' she says modestly, placing a generous slice of cake onto a plate beside me. 'I'll give you the recipe, if you like.'

'Thanks, but I'm not sure it would turn out like this.' I sink my teeth into the fluffy, moist sponge. 'Oh my goodness, that really is delicious.' I enjoy every mouthful of the lemon cake. 'And I am pleased things are working out for you with the upcycling.'

'Thanks. I have to earn a living, so thought why not give it a go? I emailed some photos to the shop, and they snapped it up and are even interested in purchasing more pieces I might have. It's nice to have the income, even if it is a little sporadic.'

'You're lucky you have a talent that you can use anywhere in the world.'

Thinking about it, I don't think I have a particular talent for anything. I can't draw, knit, bake or even play chess.

'I don't think I'm particularly talented, it's all about finding the thing you are really interested in.' She shrugs. 'And remember, necessity is the mother of invention. I had no choice but to find something that could earn me a little money, and as I don't speak Greek, the opportunities out here are limited.'

Talk turns to socialising and evenings out, and for a minute I think of how much fun it would be for Artemis and me to go out for the evening with Tania and Nicos. Before remembering that they have a history, that is. Even so, I tell her that I will be heading into Malia later with Artemis.

'That sounds like fun. I suggested it to Nicos once, but he definitely didn't fancy it,' she tells me. 'We compromised by going for lunch and spending the afternoon at the beach, which is really gorgeous. Malia is so much more than a party destination, though, there is a lot of history there if you look for it.'

'Sounds lovely, and I do love the beach. I might go for a swim as the weather is still so warm, although I'm sure Judith would be horrified.'

'Crete does stay warm late into the autumn usually. But I remember visiting Judith before at this time of year when I was younger, and she was worried about me catching a cold! I couldn't believe it, after the UK.'

Talking with Tania reminds me of when I discovered the

joy of the seaside with friends, the year we left school and spent a glorious summer – one of the warmest Augusts on record – swimming, having picnics and generally just mucking about. One of the lads from school had a tent, and we camped in the sand dunes overnight, before being chased in the morning by the council workers who were clearing the beaches and told us we shouldn't have stayed there all night.

I don't have any memories of trips to the beach with my parents, even though we were only a short bus ride away, but I push those thoughts away. Dad had a car once that fell to pieces after six months and I recall them arguing about it, Mum saying if he'd spent more on a decent car rather than down at the pub, then we might be okay. That was the evening she stuffed a few things in a bag, and we spent the evening at one of her friends' houses. She explained the bruise on her cheek to people by saying she had walked into a door, but it wasn't long after that that they finally broke up. I vowed that if I ever had children, I would be certain to spend the day at the beach with them, eating ice creams in the hot sun or flying kites on a breezy day, creating memories I hoped they would hold on to for the rest of their lives.

As we chat, I wonder whether Tania might mention the relationship between Artemis and Nicos, but she doesn't, so neither do I.

'Right, I must be going. Thanks for the coffee and that wonderful cake, Tania. Would you mind if I went and said hi to Annie and Smudge before I leave?'

'Of course I don't mind,' she says, leading me through the kitchen into the rear garden. I laugh at the sight of the dogs playing tug of war with a large tree branch, dropping it instantly and racing over when we enter the garden.

'Hello, you two.' I bend down and pet them both, before Annie runs around in circles and Smudge tries to leap into my arms. Tania tries unsuccessfully to calm him down before rolling her eyes and laughing.

'Oh gosh, it's like having a wayward child, but he is just irresistible and the two of them really are the best of friends. Plus, they keep each other occupied, which is good, otherwise I could never get anything done around here.'

I play for a little while, throwing the ball for the dogs and running along with them.

'Right, that's my daily exercise done,' I say, getting my breath back. 'I'd better get off. Bye, Tania.'

'I might bring the dogs on a walk with the other dogs tomorrow, and join you,' she says, when I head through the front gate. 'You can tell me all about your date.'

'I will do. See you later, thanks again.'

Back at the rescue, I shower and change. Artemis messages me just after one o'clock, telling me he is on his way. I feel a little surge of excitement as I think about swimming in the sea, maybe sipping a cocktail on the sandy beach that Tania described, or indulging in one of those massages.

'What are you going to do with your Saturday then?' I ask Hannah as I apply a little waterproof mascara. My skin has taken on a light glow, so mascara and a slick of pale pink lip gloss is all I need.

'Not sure.' She shrugs. 'I might go for a walk later, or do some reading. Maybe I will just hang out here with the animals. Eric seems to be in a good mood today.'

'I thought you might have headed to the bar?'

'No, Panos will be working anyway.' She dismisses the idea. 'Saturday can be busy with tourists to the church.' She smiles but it doesn't quite reach her eyes and I wonder whether all is okay between them. I don't have time to chat now, though, as I hear the sound of a car pulling up outside. It's Artemis.

'Have a nice day,' says Hannah as I grab my beach bag.

'You too.' I feel the urge to give her a hug and she gently pats my back.

I try not to think of it as a date, despite a physical attraction towards Artemis. We are definitely best to leave things as just friends.

'*Kalispera,*' says a sexy-looking Artemis, dressed in cream shorts and a black T-shirt, a day's stubble at his chin making him look even more attractive. 'And may I say you look amazing.' He tilts his head to one side and appraises my outfit, a short, bright green cotton dress. 'That colour looks good on you.'

'You may. Thank you.'

He opens the car door for me to climb inside.

The blue sky above is dotted with just a scattering of fluffy white clouds that drift by as we descend the mountain roads.

'How do you normally spend your weekend?' I ask, opening a window and taking in the smell of wild oregano as we drive past a cluster growing wild.

'You mean now that I am single?'

'I suppose so, yes.'

'Well, that depends on' – he turns to look at me – 'whether I am lucky enough to run into a beautiful woman.'

'Run over one, might be more accurate,' I remind him.

'I think maybe you will not let me forget that.'

'I'm joking. I'd say you have more than made up for it, by taking me to the restaurant near the monastery. And driving us into Malia, of course. I'm really looking forward to this.'

'Me, too. It's been a while since I've been here. Would you like to listen to some music as we drive?'

'Greek music?'

'No. Not unless you want to?'

'It's all Greek to me, but I really don't mind.'

The sound of 'Beyond the Sea' fills the car and has me smiling, especially when Artemis starts singing along. I'm singing along at the top of my voice too, moving in my seat along to the music, when Artemis brakes so suddenly, my head jolts forward. A trio of mountain goats are standing stubbornly blocking the road.

'Are you okay?' asks Artemis, after shouting out what I assume to be a swear word in Greek, as he beeps his horn at the goats.

'Yes.' I shake my hair out and rub the back of my neck.

'I think it was just a surprise as I was so lost in the music, really I'm fine,' I reassure him.

I don't add that maybe if he hadn't been driving like Lewis Hamilton I might not have jolted forward quite so much.

Artemis steps out of the car, talking loudly to the row of goats, who it seems like a challenge and are going nowhere. There is the drone of a moped behind us, and a couple riding it shave past one of the goats, which teeters to the side of the road, before zooming off.

'Maybe if you just start the engine, and drive slowly towards them they might move.'

'Run them over, you mean?' He raises an eyebrow.

'Not exactly. Maybe just encourage them to move out of the way.'

As it turns out, we never have to do anything as the goats decide it is time to move on, niftily scaling some rocks and disappearing off somewhere.

'I'd hate to see what would happen if you needed to get somewhere in a hurry,' I say, thinking about a casualty in an ambulance for example, heading to a hospital.

I think of back home then, and the endless stopping and starting at traffic lights, and how different things are here in the hills. It's such a beautiful, yet contrasting culture; it makes me think that Tania must truly love Nicos to make her home here, although she did tell me her home in the UK was a quiet canalside village, so maybe adapting here was not too difficult.

Driving on – me none the worse for the sudden braking – I

watch the soft sunlight shimmering through the trees. Glancing up, I spot a plane heading towards Heraklion Airport like a giant bird in the blue sky, bringing the last of the holidaymakers for this year. I can hardly believe I am travelling to Malia with someone I have known for such a short amount of time, yet it feels like, over here, anything is possible.

As we finally join the coast road, there are families walking along together, the children carrying inflatable swimming aids; an ice-cream kiosk has several people queuing outside. The sight of the sun beaming down on the sea, making it sparkle, has me almost wanting to stop the car and spend the rest of the afternoon here.

Further on, a few Greeks stroll by, wearing jeans and zipped-up jackets, clearly feeling the slight change in tempera-ture as autumn approaches, although I think it is still perfectly pleasant. Artemis also has a puffer jacket on the back seat of the car, I noticed.

'So what would your weekend look like back home?' asks Artemis as we drive along. 'Do you like to go out and party?'

'Not partying exactly, although the town where I live does have a few decent bars and restaurants. We have a train station into the city too, so sometimes I head there with my friends. Often, though, it's a takeaway and a movie,' I tell him. That is unless Jess succeeds in saving me from myself and dragging me out to socialise.

I don't tell him how I miss the weekends I spent with Marco, dining at the restaurant on a Saturday evening or taking long walks in the Lake District on a Monday when the restau-rant is closed. Sometimes, he would sneak off from work early on a Sunday if it was quiet, and we would take the hour drive to a hotel in the Lakes and spend the night there. The next morn-ing, we would take a long walk along our favourite lake, Ullswa-ter. Once we passed a rather grand country hotel, which I thought would make a perfect wedding venue, although clearly

I was alone with those thoughts. I wondered whether Marco might have suggested a wedding in Italy, had he shared my thoughts about marriage that is.

A short while later, the long stretch of the beach at Malia appears before us, hundreds of sunbeds with orange and white beach umbrellas stretched across the sand gently flapping in the sea breeze. The endless golden sand is flanked by snack bars and restaurants. It also looks pretty quiet.

We decide to park up near the old town and walk the streets full of sand-coloured buildings, the familiar grey broken flag-stones on the floors. A large restaurant has terracotta walls deco-rated with dozens of colourful plates and huge pots of flowers standing on a wooden terrace, beneath a huge lemon tree. The vibrant white walls of some of the buildings are contrasted by brown, weathered-looking village houses with stone arch door-ways and metal grids at the windows. At the end of one of the winding roads, two mopeds stand against a graffitied wall at the end of a row of houses. I notice a sign then on a rough stone wall that points us in the direction of the village centre. Walking on, we pass a fruit and vegetable van, loaded with melons, with several women queueing to buy one. A family walk out of a nearby supermarket loaded down with shopping; a young boy with black hair is bouncing a ball. Presently, the narrow streets give way to a large square surrounded by tavernas.

'I had no idea the old town looked like this,' I say as we walk. 'You kind of think places like Malia are just beaches and bars. You forget that people actually live here.'

'Malia was little more than a fishing harbour, and one of the first major settlements of the Minoan civilisation. These streets are literally thousands of years old,' Artemis tells me knowl-edgably.

Approaching the square, my eye is drawn to a particularly pretty-looking restaurant, its walls painted orange and the front filled with colourful flowers in blue pots.

'Would you like a drink? Maybe some lunch?' asks Artemis as we step onto the outside terrace that is set with white table-cloths and small vases holding a single flower at the centre of the table.

'A refreshing drink would be nice, but maybe we could have a swim before some food?' I suggest, something Hannah told me about to avoid cramping.

'Sure.'

I have some ice-cold freshly squeezed orange juice, whilst Artemis opts for a beer. He also orders some olives and snacks.

Sitting chatting, talk suddenly turns to our respective careers, and Artemis tells me he has been offered a promotion.

'To manage a sales team,' he tells me as he picks up a feta-stuffed olive.

'That sounds amazing. I take it it's something you are interested in, managing a sales team, I mean?'

'It's strange, but not particularly. Although it seems I am just good at it.'

It's not difficult to imagine. Especially if he is face to face with customers, charming them with his easy, engaging manner. Not to mention those looks.

'It sounds like an exciting opportunity I suppose, but I must say you don't sound very excited.' I pop a salty olive into my mouth.

'It is a good opportunity and there would be a substantial pay rise. There is only one problem.' He picks up a handful of nuts. 'The post is in Heraklion, over an hour's drive away.'

'And I take it you would not want the commute?'

'Not particularly. The city can be very busy in the morning. Besides, my mother is not getting any younger. Maybe I ought to stay a little closer,' he ponders as he takes a sip of his beer.

His comment makes me think about my own parents. Will my mother decide I need to look after her when she becomes old? Although, unfortunately, I don't think she will reach an old age if she continues to lead the lifestyle she does at present. Even so, I guess it's something we all have to think about in the future, our elderly parents. Once more, it saddens me to think of any old person not having a family.

'I can see what you mean. But I'm sure your mum would want what is best for you, and she has friends in the village, doesn't she? And according to Judith, your mother is as strong as an ox.'

'It's true. And maybe a fresh start is exactly what I need.'

'Maybe it is.' I smile.

We finish up our drinks and snacks and take the walk along the road to Malia Beach, passing bars pumping club music out, even though most of them are empty at this hour. The golden sand stretched out in front of us seems to go on forever, with the glittering blue sea beyond. I pay for two sunbeds before Artemis has a chance, and we settle down on our beds close to the water's edge. For a few minutes, I just lie there, listening to the soothing sounds of the waves crashing against the shore, watching swimmers in the water and people on jet skis. Glancing around the beach, I notice lots of young people sleeping, beach towels pulled up to their chins and probably sleeping off last night's partying. A couple of teenage girls run past then, giggling, before they tread into the water and start screaming.

'That's not as warm as I thought it would be!' says the English girl, racing out again onto the sand, her laughing friend running behind her.

'Maybe I will give the swimming a miss.' I turn to Artemis, who has his arms folded behind his head, stretched out just staring up at the sky.

'You cannot come to the beach and not swim. And I'm sure it isn't cold as the sun is so warm,' he argues.

'Go for it then.' I settle down onto my bed and remove my cotton dress over my head, to reveal my black and white bikini, before I apply sun cream. I know for a fact that the sun, although pleasant, is not hot enough for the sea to be warm; besides, I have just witnessed the young girls shrieking as they ran out of the sea.

Artemis smiles at me before removing his shorts and, beneath a huge beach towel, wriggles into some swimming shorts. He walks towards the water, and I take in his broad shoulders as he strides confidently. My eyes are still on him as he walks further out and dives beneath the water.

'Come on,' he shouts and waves to me as he resurfaces, but I sink further down onto my sunbed, enjoying the feeling of the warm sun on my face.

A while later, he strides out of the water, six-pack proudly on display, brushing his hair from his eyes and looking a bit like a Greek god. A young woman on an adjoining sun bed lowers her sunglasses to get a better look.

'That was refreshing,' he says, with a grin on his face, before he places his wet hands on my stomach and has me almost leaping off the sunbed.

'Come on.' He stretches his hand out and pulls me to my feet. 'You are accustomed to the temperature of the water now.'

Despite myself, I laugh and follow him into the sparkling clear water, before taking a breath and wading in. It doesn't feel cold after all and I swim out, lolling on my back and gazing up at the clear blue sky. It feels so wonderful, just lying here and listening to the drones of speedboats in the distance, and watching swimmers having fun, others soaking up the sun on the sand. I think of Hannah, and how she might enjoy swimming here, and resolve to return here with her and spend some time together. I also hope everything is alright with her and Panos, who she seemed to be getting along so well with, yet I got the impression she didn't really want to talk about him this morning.

Walking out of the water together, I suppose to a spectator we might look like a loved-up couple spending time together, but it couldn't be further from the truth. Even if I was in the right headspace to even consider a relationship, the news that Artemis may soon be moving away for work would make growing closer to him rather pointless. Then again, I guess I will soon be on my way back home too, even though with each day that passes, I fall a little more in love with Crete.

Settling down on the beds, I reapply some sun cream and Artemis offers to do my back.

'Sure, thanks,' I say, rolling over onto my stomach.

I hand him the lotion and he applies the cream with long, confident strokes, his strong hands almost sending me to sleep and I sink down onto the bed. He certainly knows what he is doing with those hands, and for a split second I fantasise about them running all over my body, before I sit bolt upright.

'That's great, thanks,' I mutter, hoping he doesn't know just how much my pulse rate seems to have gone through the roof as I slip my sun cream into my beach bag.

'No problem.'

He puts his sunglasses on and stretches out on the bed beside me, enjoying the warmth of the sun.

An hour or so later, Artemis sits up, stretching his arms, and asks, 'Are you ready for something to eat now?'

'I am, just about.'

We both take a quick beach shower, before drying off and going in search of a restaurant.

The main street in Malia has come to life a little now, with people drifting over from the beach in search of food. Restaurants and bars sit side by side, alongside games zones and flashing lights from children's rides. I follow Artemis down a side street, where we descend some steps and are soon standing outside a huge wooden gate. Artemis pushes it open, and it is as if we have entered a secret garden. Outdoor tables sit on a black and white tiled floor, with lemon trees dotted about, and diners sit at wooden tables.

TWENTY

'Wow. This is like a secret garden. I wouldn't even have known this was a restaurant as there doesn't seem to be a sign outside.'

'There is during low season. In high season it is not necessary,' Artemis explains. 'The locals eat here, and word of mouth is enough for the place to always be busy.'

Glancing around, I can see there is definitely no need to advertise, as the place is full. A friendly waiter scans the restaurant, before seating us at a table beneath a tree that has just become vacant. He quickly clears the table before reappearing with a menu.

'This is just gorgeous.' I take in the glazed pots of flowers, the lemon trees and the ambience; everyone seems to be enjoying the wonderful atmosphere.

Artemis speaks in Greek to the waiter, who takes our food orders, and orders a bottle of white wine.

'Don't forget about the drive home,' I remind him, thinking of how he enjoys getting behind the wheel, and giving those racing drivers a run for their money.

'If the car needs to stay here, we can take a taxi.' He shrugs. 'It is Saturday, after all. Let us see how the day plays out,' he says as the waiter appears with our drinks and he pours me a chilled glass of Pinot Grigio.

We dine on the most wonderful food. I enjoy the tastiest, melt-in-the-mouth lamb kleftiko and a colourful Greek salad. Artemis has a *fasolada*, which is a tasty-looking Greek bean stew, served with crusty bread. After a second glass of wine, I'm feeling mellow and more relaxed than I have in a long time. The food, the surroundings, the company, everything is adding to the day, making it all wonderful. We finish with a shot of ouzo, handed to us by a waiter, before we decide to hit the bars.

The streets are filling up now, music coming from the bars, and groups of people are dressed up and out to party, even though it is only just after six. A hen party passes by, the bride-to-be complete with veil and L-plates and a man in the doorway of a bar offers them all free shots, so they let out a whoop and follow him inside.

We sip a cocktail in a bar, and an hour later, the sun is slowly beginning to descend. The thought of heading back to the rescue is becoming further and further from my mind, as the smells, sights and sounds of the strip are so intoxicating that I find myself not wanting the evening to end.

'It is still so early. I didn't imagine it would be this busy,' I tell Artemis, as we stroll along the busy street.

'Maybe it is because the end of the holiday season is approaching. People want to make the most of every minute. So is Malia what you expected?'

'Kind of, yes. And it's probably quite tame at this hour. I'm not sure if I would like it a few hours from now.' I pull a face.

'Maybe not.' Artemis smiles. 'But as the night is still young, do you fancy a game of crazy golf?'

'That sounds like fun. Lead the way.'

We play the golf, laughing at my useless attempts as Artemis smoothly lands each shot in the holes.

'Have you had a lot of practice at this?' I ask him later as he thrashes me.

'Not really.' He shrugs before laughing. 'Okay then, yes, I have,' he admits.

Walking on, some noughties dance music is playing in one of the bars, evoking a load of memories.

'Come on.'

I drag Artemis to the bar that the hens have just descended on.

A barman offers us shots and, in one moment, I knock back an ouzo. Artemis refuses. As the music pumps louder, I give in to another one.

'Fancy a dance?' I gesture to a small dance floor, where the hens have just arrived and are going for it on the dance floor.

'No, but please, be my guest.' He smiles, pointing to the dance floor.

Emboldened by the drinks, I stroll towards the dance floor as my favourite song strikes up. The hens cheer in welcome, and start dancing with me and I laugh and enjoy myself, throwing my head back without a care in the world. Artemis is watching me from a bar stool, talking to the guy behind the bar. After a couple more dances and chatting to my friends, I join him.

'Oh, I really enjoyed that.' I ask the barman for another ouzo. 'I haven't let my hair down like that in a long time.'

'I would maybe be careful with the ouzo,' Artemis advises as he sips a beer. 'It isn't known as firewater for nothing.'

'Oh, I'm fine, really. I'm in the party mood,' I tell him, sipping my drink and singing along to the music. I notice the barman exchange a glance with Artemis, but I'm so loosened up it doesn't bother me in the slightest.

We spend another hour in the bar, and at times the floor feels like it is moving beneath my feet, but I put it down to the music and the neon lights. Suddenly, in the middle of a conversation when I sit back down, I don't feel too good and ask

Artemis if we can leave. When I stand, my legs feel a bit like jelly.

'Oh dear.' When the fresh air hits me outside, I want to be sick.

'Are you okay?' he asks, linking my arm through his to support me as we go.

'Truthfully? No. I feel ill.'

'Come on.' He walks slowly with me as I concentrate on my breathing.

I'm aware of the people around me, and flashing lights, and feel as though I am in a dream, as I grip tightly on to Artemis.

'Where are we going?' I mutter as the noise recedes away from the strip, the further we walk.

'My cousin has a bed and breakfast close by,' he tells me. 'Perhaps she has a room.'

I'm picturing a comfortable bed, cool, crisp cotton sheets and, at this moment in time, can think of nothing better.

A couple of minutes later, we arrive at a villa down a quieter street, and before long I'm in a room with white sheets on the bed and pine furniture. I am desperate to lie down. Maybe if I just rest my head for a moment...

TWENTY-ONE

I open one eye, slightly disorientated as the sound of ringing permeates my skull. It takes me a minute to realise it is a church bell ringing outside. When I'm fully awake, I stare at the shape in the bed next to me. Artemis.

I sit bolt upright, as my head rings as loudly as the church bell, and gulp down some water from a bottle on the bedside table. Artemis rubs his eyes and sits up too.

'Oh my goodness. What time is it? Where are we?' I glance around the room, wondering what on earth I have done.

'You don't remember? How insulting.' There is a smile playing around his mouth.

'No. Not really. Kind of. I remember walking,' I say, having little recollection of arriving at this place, that is what, a hotel? Apartment?

'I did warn you about the firewater.' He laughs, standing up and flicking on a kettle to make coffee.

'The ouzo. Oh my goodness, never again.' The thought of it makes me want to throw up. I have a vague recollection of doing just that last night, thankfully having made it to a bathroom. I think of the dog rescue then. Oh my goodness! Judith must be wondering where I have got to.

'I can't believe I stayed out overnight.' I put my head in my hands. 'What must Judith think of me?'

'Don't worry.' He hands me a coffee once the kettle has boiled. 'I phoned my mother. She was going to let Judith know what has happened. Your phone was out of battery, so I couldn't find the number to call Judith directly. We will head back when you feel ready.'

'Oh... Thanks. We didn't do anything, did we?' I ask, although it seems I am fully dressed, my green dress crumpled and my shoes on the floor.

'No. I am not in the habit of having sex with women who are barely conscious.' He raises an eyebrow.

I'm completely mortified.

'Oh, thank goodness for that.'

'Thank you.' He laughs.

'You know what I mean,' I say, feeling a little more human after a few sips of coffee.

'Indeed. And it would have been such a shame if you couldn't have remembered it.' He grins. 'I like to think it's something you would never forget.'

He's so cheesy I burst out laughing, but then my head hurts.

'I did think about us taking a taxi back to the rescue, but I didn't think you were up to the journey. This is my cousin's place. It was lucky she had a room available.'

I take a shower, then slip out of the small bed and breakfast and wait outside, while Artemis chats to his cousin, embarrassed by the whole experience.

'You must at least let me pay for the room,' I offer, but he tells me his cousin wouldn't let him pay as she has had a very profitable summer.

We walk towards the car park as the sun is still rising in the sky, a soft yellow ball hovering above a church in the distance.

The streets are eerily quiet now, the stillness broken only by the sound of a street cleaning machine making its way along the road, clearing up last night's debris. There is no sign of life, in complete contrast to the neon lights and pumping music of the previous evening. We walk silently to the car before making the journey back to the rescue. As we navigate the mountain roads, I begin to feel a little queasy and curse myself for drinking so much last night and not heeding Artemis's warning about the ouzo. Especially as there will be work to be done today, and no time for lounging around with a hangover.

It's just before nine when Artemis drops me off, telling me he will be in touch soon, before he drives up to pay a visit to his mother.

'I'm so sorry,' I say in my best apologetic voice to Judith, who is in the kitchen, emptying the dishwasher.

'Don't worry about it. You're not the first, and you won't be the last, to have indulged a little too much. It was Saturday night, after all.' She stacks some plates into the cupboard of the large dresser.

'I know. I got a bit carried away with the party atmosphere. Or should I say the ouzo,' I confess.

'I believe Malia has that effect.' She smiles. 'Not to worry. At least Artemis had the sense to call his mother and she was able to let me know you would be staying out for the evening. At least I wasn't worried about you. Well, not too much.'

'I was fine. At least I think I was.' I rub my temples. 'Right, I will just go and change, then I will start work,' I tell her.

'No rush,' she says kindly. 'And there are some paracetamol in there if you need any.' She points to a drawer.

'Thanks, Judith.'

'Did you have a good night then?' asks Hannah as we are out walking some of the dogs a while later. I'm feeling better having swallowed down some paracetamol and glugged two bottles of water.

'I think so. At least the bits I can remember. Oh gosh, never again. It was all going so well until I overindulged in the ouzo. Artemis did try and warn me.' I sigh. 'How did your evening go?' I ask as we arrive at the dog park and let the dogs off the lead.

'Okay.' She shrugs. 'Quiet. I read and then had a long phone chat with my folks back home.'

'How is the Greek going? Are you seeing Panos later?'

'I'm not sure.' She throws a ball and half a dozen dogs race after it.

'I don't mean to pry, but I thought you two were getting along well,' I ask, a little puzzled by her apparent sudden coolness towards Panos.

'We are. We still do the email thing but...' She pauses.

'But what?'

'Oh, I don't know. I'm not sure I need to spend every minute of my free time with him. I'll be going to back to England in a few weeks.'

'Have you got feelings for him?' I ask, as the penny drops.

'Oh, Beth, I'm not sure. I think I might have.'

She picks up a stick from the ground for the dogs to chase after, after they have lost interest in the ball.

'That night after Tania's party, you went in ahead of us,' she continues. 'Panos kissed me and I haven't been able to stop thinking about it since.'

'Are you completely against the idea of a holiday romance?' I ask.

'Yes.' She looks at me from under her glasses. 'I've never really had a proper boyfriend before, unless you count a guy from college, but that was nothing serious,' she admits. 'I usually have boys as friends, nothing else. I don't want to get hurt.'

'Oh, Hannah. I understand that but maybe you could still

enjoy time together while you're here? It seems a shame to back off so much, I can see how happy you look when you are with him.'

'But our worlds are so different. There can never be a future for us, so that's all there is to it,' she says, her mind made up.

'Does that mean you have to avoid him altogether, though? It seems such a shame.'

'I'm not. We are still helping each other with the language. I know quite a few Greek words now, and how to say them correctly, so I am grateful for that.'

'Well, if I might offer a little advice, I'd say it's best to tell him you would like to just be friends, or he might be wondering if he has done something wrong.'

'I suppose so.' She smiles. 'Thanks, Beth.'

Maybe I was right in thinking that the village is a place for romance. Or perhaps it's simply that there are so few residents in the village that visitors present an opportunity for it.

When we get back Judith tells us she is just nipping out to see her friend Yolanda, and I wonder whether Artemis is still there, and what he might have said about our evening out. I still cringe when I think of it and thank my lucky stars that Artemis has a relative who runs a bed and breakfast close by.

Later, as Hannah and I stop for a drink break, and Michael goes for a walk, Doll and Lars head into the kitchen and firmly close the door behind them. Not for the first time, I wonder what is going on.

TWENTY-TWO

The next morning, I'm just clearing away my breakfast things, when my phone rings. It's Artemis.

'How are you feeling today?'

'Other than exhausted, I'm fine.'

'Good. I had a nice time with you,' Artemis tells me.

'Me too, I'm sorry the evening ended the way it did,' I tell him. 'I'm afraid I cut your partying a little short.'

'Don't be sorry. It was a lot of fun, although I can't ever remember sharing a bed with an attractive woman in a platonic sense.' I can imagine him grinning.

'I bet you can't. Anyway, thanks for showing me around Malia. And for finding us a place to stay. Please apologise to your cousin the next time you see her.'

'There is no need. This is Malia, I am sure she has seen worse.' He laughs, making me feel a bit better.

'If you say so.'

'I do. Well, enjoy your day. I just called to see how you were feeling.'

'Thanks, I appreciate that. What are you up to today then?'

'I have the job interview for the new post. I don't mind telling you, I feel a little nervous.'

'Ooh, is that today? You never said. Well, good luck, although I'm sure you won't need it, especially if you were recommended for the post.'

'Perhaps. Will you have time for a coffee later today? I can tell you how the interview went. I am taking my mother to see a friend in Stalis who is very ill afterward, but I'll be near the rescue when I take her home.'

'You're a good son,' I tell him.

'Maybe I am just trying to be a better person all round. I am afraid I was rather selfish when I was younger.'

'Well, as I have said before, maybe wisdom comes with a little maturity. No one has led a blameless life, and hindsight is a wonderful thing.'

'Very true. I'll message you soon.'

'Oh, by the way, what did your mother think of you spending the night with me?'

'She said nothing. If I am completely honest, I don't think she minds who I see, as long as it is not my wife. She never did like her,' he lets slip.

Artemis texts me later to arrange to meet me at a coffee shop at six thirty, so when the day's work is done, I take a quick shower then get changed, before replying to a text from Jess, who asks me how Malia was. I suddenly remember Tania saying we might walk together today, but she hasn't been in touch. Tomorrow, I will ask her out for a walk and a catch-up.

As I walk towards the coffee shop in the early evening sunshine where Artemis has arranged to meet me, I think about how our friendship has blossomed over the past few weeks. And how Artemis has been a welcome distraction from my own thoughts, namely Marco. I think back to the first day we met and how my perception of him has changed since then. Although I am realistic enough to know that I have only heard one side of his story, especially regarding his marriage.

Artemis is already there when I arrive, sitting outside at a metal table with two chairs, glancing at his phone.

'*Kalispera*, how are you on this beautiful evening?' he asks, putting his phone away.

'I'm very well.' I smile brightly. 'You?'

'I am okay. Would you like a drink?' he offers.

'A latte, please.'

He heads inside for the drinks, and a few minutes later, we are sitting bathing in the weaker, but still warm, evening sunshine.

'I came here to say goodbye to you,' he says as he sips his coffee. 'Tomorrow morning, I am heading to Heraklion to begin a three-week training programme at the bank. I think you may have left by the time it is finished.'

'So you got the job? Although I don't think there was any doubt. Congratulations!' I tap my coffee cup against his. 'It does seem rather sudden. Did you know the training would start tomorrow?'

'I did actually. Maybe I was having second thoughts. Or maybe I just hate goodbyes.' He raises his coffee cup.

'Oh, Artemis, it's been so lovely hanging out with you these last few weeks, it really has,' I tell him, reaching across the table and hugging him.

'I think so too. Hanging out with you, I mean.' He smiles.

'And who knows what might have been, given different circumstances,' I say.

'Another time or place, or another lifetime as they say,' he says philosophically.

'Something like that. What did your mother think about you moving so far away?' I ask.

'She was very pleased for me. Maybe she is happy I am

getting away from my ex,' he says. 'I am relieved she is seeing a lot more of Judith now too, they were such good friends. It hurts when friendships break down.'

'Like between you and Nicos?'

'Get straight to the point, why don't you? Although I have learned you are one who always gets to the heart of the matter.'

'There is no other way. If people communicated their feelings a bit more, there wouldn't be half the breakdown in relationships.' I unwrap my little caramel biscuit that arrived with my coffee, and pop it into my mouth.

'And, yes, maybe you are right. I messed up when I was young, I was selfish. But getting with the fiancée of my friend was the worst thing I could have done.'

'Have you ever told him that?'

'Never. I couldn't bring myself to reach out while we were still together. I also probably stayed with my wife for too many years, as I felt bad about leaving her. Maybe I thought to myself that I had better make it work to justify my actions, I don't know.'

'I can understand that, I suppose. But it's never too late. Who knows? You might even make friends again with Nicos one day.'

'I do not think so. He would never forgive me, and why should he? I have never had a friend like that, though, ever since, but it is a regret I have to live with.'

He looks at me with his gorgeous eyes, and slowly leans across the table and kisses me lightly on the lips. And there's nothing. It's like kissing a good friend. I wonder if Artemis feels the same.

'Did that feel a bit weird?' I ask.

'Not weird exactly, but not what I expected,' he admits.

'So that's it. Firmly friends.'

'So it seems. And when I think about it, maybe I need more female friends in my life.'

'Maybe you do. I won't lie, your looks obviously attract women, but take time out and figure out what you really want before you jump into another relationship.'

'Wise words. My mother once told me my looks are a curse. Can you believe that?' He shakes his head and laughs. 'But perhaps you are right. I must focus on my career, and maybe really get to know the next person I become involved with. But there is no hurry. Unless my looks disappear overnight.' He winks and I tell him not to be so shallow.

Artemis drops me off at the rescue, and I say goodbye to him once more, wrapping him in a lingering hug. Nicos is across the road watering the plants in the garden with a hose before the light fades, and glances in our direction. I think it's so sad that their childhood friendship remains in ruins, even though Artemis's marriage to Nicos's one-time fiancée is over. I also think that if she was so easily seduced by Artemis, she could not have been truly in love with Nicos, so perhaps he had a lucky escape. Not that I would ever say that, of course.

'Good luck. And keep in touch.'

'Of course. Goodbye, Beth.'

There was real affection in our farewell hug, and I get the feeling I may see Artemis again one day. Only as friends, of course. As his car roars off into the distance, I can't help hoping that whatever he does in the future it all works out for him.

TWENTY-THREE

I'm with Tania and the dogs the following afternoon, strolling the forest paths. She has brought Annie and Smudge out today and I am walking four dogs, two either side of me on leads, that are walking really nicely. There had been plenty of volunteers out this morning walking the dogs, but there were a couple of stragglers who needed a walk, so I have taken those.

'Tell me all about your date with Artemis?' asks Tania as we walk along the road, the sun shining brightly above us, and the sound of crickets in the hedgerows.

I do so, describing the lovely time we had in Malia, until I went overboard with the ouzo and she laughs.

'Oh dear. I must admit, I learned that lesson years ago in Greece. Ouzo is wonderful in moderation.'

I tell her all about how Artemis looked after me, and found a room at his cousin's place. I also tentatively question whether she knows Nicos and Artemis were once friends and grew up together.

'Yes, I knew they were friends when they were young, but he doesn't talk about him now. Hardly surprising given the circumstances. Did Artemis mention he married Nicos's fiancée?'

'He did. Artemis told me he regrets losing the friendship because of a woman,' I tell her as we turn a corner and for a moment I wonder whether or not I should have said anything. 'Especially as the marriage didn't last.'

'He said that?' She turns to look at me.

'He did. He said he is nothing like his younger self,' I tell her. 'He told me he was selfish and that he has grown up a lot since then, regretting some of the things he did in the past. I got the impression he had fond memories of his childhood here with Nicos and the other boys.'

'Maybe we all look back on life and wonder whether we might have done things differently, if we had our time again. It's human nature,' says Tania, as we make our way through a sandy path that leads towards a forest of pine trees at the top of the hill that gives a wonderful view of the sea below.

'Shall we walk up?' Tania gestures to the hill that has a marked footpath and I nod and follow her lead. We sit for a few seconds when we reach the top, just gazing into the far distance. The dogs are sitting patiently, lapping at some water from a large bottle Tania has pulled from her rucksack and poured into a plastic bowl.

We make our descent and continue past the nature reserve; Tania tells me all about how some of the dogs took ill in the summer after they had been in the water. She tells me how Judith was worried about vet bills, until a generous donation was made by someone who hooked up with one of the previous volunteers. Such incidences highlight the need for constant fundraising.

'Now I definitely think there is something in the water around here, and I don't mean bugs. Apart from maybe a love bug,' I say and she laughs.

The sunshine shimmers on the lake, casting ripples of light, and a duck emerges from some long grasses that has the dogs going crazy, barking and straining at their leads. We continue our walk in a complete loop until we are back near the rescue.

'Are you looking forward to Judith's wedding?' I ask Tania.

'Oh, I am. It feels so wonderful to be a part of it, I am so happy for her. And, of course, the hen party at the bar on Friday. It's been so long since I have had a girls' night out, I am really looking forward to it. You are coming, aren't you?'

'I wouldn't miss it.'

At home later that evening, I think about Tania's comment and it goes round and round in my head. Maybe we could have all done things differently when we were younger. Perhaps if I wasn't so fixated on marriage, I would still be with Marco. I plug my earbuds in and listen to a podcast before I drift off to sleep. Anything to stop those thoughts persisting in my head.

'I hope I have done nothing to upset her.'

Panos looks concerned the next morning, after calling me over when I take a walk past the bar with several of the dogs, asking after Hannah.

'Hi, Panos. No, I don't think so. Although maybe you should talk to her,' I tell him. 'Other than via email, I mean.'

'Okay. I will. She is at the rescue now?'

'Yes, for a little while I think. She will be out walking some of the dogs this afternoon.'

'Okay. I will finish clearing up here first but maybe you tell her, I ask about her?'

'Of course I will.'

He carries on sweeping some fallen leaves from the stone floor of the terrace, a hose at his feet ready to rinse the path down later. Just then, Helena approaches.

'Beth, do you have a minute?'

'Yes, is everything okay?'

'It is. I was just thinking about the hens party on Saturday.'
She beams. 'Are you coming?'

'Yes, I wouldn't miss it.'

My stay here has gone so quickly, it's hard to believe Judith
and Lars's wedding will be in just over a week's time.

'Great. Is Hannah coming too?'

'I'm pretty sure she is, yes.'

'Oh good. I am excited, because my mother is also coming.
She has been out a little more since the BBQ. After my father
died she locked herself away at home.' She frowns a little when
she thinks of it.

'Oh, Helena, that's wonderful. I'm so happy she is slowly
getting back out there; it can't have been easy for her.'

'It was not easy for any of us. My father was only forty-eight
years old. It was a sudden heart attack.'

'I am so sorry to hear that,' I say, my heart breaking for the
family. 'But I'm pleased your mum is getting out a little more,' I
say, and she smiles.

'Me too. Enjoy the rest of your walk, see you soon.' She
heads back behind the bar, as the sound of a beer truck bleeping
slowly makes its way up the road towards the bar.

I have six dogs this morning, three on each lead and all
perfectly well behaved. A few of the volunteers are up ahead
somewhere, walking two dogs each. As I head back towards the
rescue, I notice Doll and Lars emerging from a clearing in the
forest.

'Fancy meeting you here,' I say, unable to hide my surprise.
'Are you out walking without the dogs?' I ask as if it's any of my
business. 'I can't see any.'

'No,' says Lars, shifting a little uncomfortably on his feet.

'Oh,' I say, unable to hide my surprise.

Doll and Lars exchange a glance then, and Doll shrugs.

'Look, can you keep a secret?' asks Doll.

'Well, it depends what the secret is,' I reply, feeling a loyalty towards Judith and wondering, not for the first time, what exactly is going on.

'Well, the thing is,' says Lars in a low voice, as if Judith was within earshot. 'Not a word to Judith, but Doll is teaching me how to dance.'

'She's teaching you to dance?' I glance at Doll in surprise.

'Yes. Judith knows I have two left feet, but she once told me how she loved to dance,' explains Lars. 'I felt like she was missing out on something she once enjoyed, especially as it seems her husband was a wonderful dancer. I am going to surprise her by dancing a waltz with her at our wedding.'

'Oh, Lars, that is wonderful. Judith will be thrilled,' I say, relief flooding through me.

'I hope so.' He grins.

'So, how's he shaping up?' I turn to Doll.

'Really good, actually. I can't believe he hasn't danced before. Come on.' She guides us through the forest to a clearing.

'If you have the time, we will give you a sneak preview. Remember, Lars, shoulders back,' she instructs. 'Stand tall.'

I take a seat on a tree stump, the dogs sitting on the floor beside me.

Even on the uneven grassy floor, they dance an elegant waltz with no hint that Lars was a terrible dancer, as he claimed he was. I gasp at how good he actually is. I find myself breaking into applause as the dance finishes and even the dogs bark in appreciation.

'That was really good.' I clap my hands together. 'Lars, you were either being modest about your dancing skills or Doll, you are a very talented teacher.'

'Maybe a bit of both.' She winks.

'I won't lie, I was wondering what all the sneaking off was about. I hope Judith hasn't noticed anything,' I inform them both.

'I was a little worried about that, but you can understand

why I need to keep it secret. I want it to be a real surprise at the wedding,' says Lars.

'And I am sure it will be.' I smile. 'Are you heading back now?'

'Yes, we slipped out when Judith went to the village shop. Maybe we ought to take one of the dogs each and make it look authentic,' suggests Doll, so I hand over a couple of the small ones I am walking.

'Oh, how I hate all this secrecy. But I hope your dancing will make it a wedding to remember,' says Doll as we walk. 'You really are a good dancer, Lars, despite you thinking you would be useless. You clearly just needed a little tuition.'

'More than a little, I'd say.'

'So is Michael in on this too?' I ask as we walk.

'He is,' admits Doll. Which makes sense now as, thinking about it, he has seemed completely unfazed by Doll's frequent disappearances of late.

TWENTY-FOUR

Judith has just returned from the shop when we arrive at the rescue, and once the dogs are settled I follow her into the kitchen, where she is unpacking some dried pasta and a bottle of olive oil.

'There you all are.' She smiles. 'There is some lemon iced tea in the fridge if anyone would like some. Oh and, Beth, I had a call earlier for you. Someone who has been trying to get in touch with you apparently.'

'My phone is charging up in my bedroom. Did they leave a message?' I say, reaching into the fridge for a drink.

'They did,' she says, placing the last of the shopping into a cupboard. 'He asked if you could give him a call when you get the chance.'

I immediately think of Artemis, who has only been gone five minutes. Maybe he is missing me, although I highly doubt it. He is doing his training at the bank, and we parted as nothing more than friends.

'He was very charming,' she says as she unpacks the last of her shopping.

'Did this person have a name?' I ask.

'Oh goodness, sorry. I thought I had already said it. His name was Marco.'

'Marco called here?' I'm almost too stunned to speak.

'Well, he did say he had tried your mobile several times. I think he just wanted to make sure you were okay. I told him you were fine, and out walking the dogs.' She closes a kitchen cupboard. 'Although I didn't know initially if I should tell him whether or not you were here. You can't be too careful these days.'

'Of course, I understand that.'

I wonder what on earth can be so important that he had to phone the rescue? And how did he know I was here?

Judith sits down to have a cup of iced tea with me and I find myself telling her all about Marco.

'And did it work? Coming here to try and forget about him,' she asks as she sips her tea.

'Not really. Well, a little bit, especially the first couple of weeks,' I admit.

'In the company of a certain gentleman?' She smiles knowingly.

'Yes, and being with the animals really helped too, I adore them. Although it did feel good being in the company of the delightful Artemis, even though there wasn't really a spark between us,' I tell her truthfully. 'I admired his looks, who wouldn't? Even, dare I say, imagined what it would be like to kiss him.' I leave out the bit about being at the beach, and briefly picturing him running his hands all over me, giving me a deep massage. 'And when we did kiss... Nothing. It seems we were meant to be just friends. Maybe we were just helping each other get over our relationship breakdowns,' I tell her truthfully.

'Well, no one could blame you for going out with Artemis. If I was twenty years younger.' She winks. 'Oh, actually, no, make that forty,' she says and we both roar with laughter.

'Oh, Judith, it's so good to talk to you.'

'And you too. In the meantime, are you going to call Marco?'

'Yes, I will,' I tell her, realising the thought of hearing his voice has given me a fuzzy feeling inside. I should at least find out what he has to say.

But when I ring his number it just goes to voicemail and I don't leave a message.

TWENTY-FIVE

'Are you sure the music is sorted? Ooh, I don't why, but I feel as nervous as if I were dancing for our first world championship,' says Doll. 'I wish I still smoked.'

'No, you don't,' says Michael. 'It's bad for your health, and I want you to live to be a hundred years old.'

'Says the man who regularly puffs on a cigar after dinner,' she points out, but she laughs.

'Only occasionally, my love. Anyway, what are you nervous about?' Michael places his arms around his wife and kisses her on the cheek. 'You look wonderful and your dancing is as good as it has ever been.'

'I know it's silly, isn't it? I've been watched by world-class judges, yet I'm worried about dancing in front of some diners in a Greek village square.'

Doll looks sensational in a shimmering pink sequinned gown that she picked up in the town, and Michael handsome in a dark-grey suit, complete with waistcoat and a pale pink shirt beneath. Tonight, we are all heading into the next village for the fundraiser to watch them perform outside the restaurants in the square.

'Well, I for one can't wait. Good food and a marvellous dance show, what a combination,' says Judith.

With the animals settled after their evening feed, we get ready too, and Hannah and I accept a lift from Lars and Judith, whilst Doll and Michael travel in the car that they have hired for the duration of their time here. I thought it might be fun if Tania and Nicos joined us this evening, but when I mentioned it to Tania she told me they already had plans that evening.

'Your carriage awaits.' Michael opens the door of the car for Doll and she carefully folds her dress as she steps inside and thanks him.

We chat as we drive, glancing at the outside scenery that still manages to make me gasp at its beauty. Around fifteen minutes later, we pull into the village and drive through some narrow streets until we arrive at the village square, surrounded by several restaurants and a couple of gift shops. The tables outside the restaurants sit beneath lemon trees and I imagine the scene on a fine summer's day, with the scent of thyme and rosemary from bushes dotted along the village road filling the air.

The square is dominated by one particular sprawling, white restaurant that has indoor and outdoor seating, blue painted chairs, and blue and white checked tablecloths are set on tables with some diners already seated. A stone church overlooks the square at the far side, its bell pealing gently into the evening.

Doll and Michael slip inside the restaurant with us, and people glance around excitedly as they thread through tables and head to a quiet corner table. I notice a board outside announcing the dancing this evening, which may explain why it is already half full. I hope Doll isn't feeling too nervous.

'I think I will have an ouzo, loosen me up a bit,' says Doll, tapping into my thoughts.

'Good idea, but just the one,' says Michael. The thought of ouzo makes me blanch so I order a soft drink, thinking I will save myself for a glass of wine with dinner later. The interior of the restaurant has a large wooden ship's wheel displayed on its white walls and fishing nets draped along, a nod to the village's fishing history.

Finishing our drinks, it's almost eight o clock when the Greek restaurant owner announces the dancers, and the restaurant bursts into applause as they make their way outside.

Doll and Michael give a little bow as some Cuban music strikes up. Already the diners are clapping their hands together in anticipation.

'Oh, how exciting,' I say to Hannah as I sip a drink. 'I can't wait to see how much money they make for the rescue. I hope people don't mind me passing a hat around.'

'I think that's perfectly acceptable. They are going to get quite a show. In fact, I'll do it,' says Hannah as she sips her cola.

'You will?' I'm stunned.

'Sure. Maybe we could join forces. You do the inside tables, I will do the outside,' she suggests. 'We have two hats after all.' She laughs, removing her straw fedora that she is wearing this evening with a long, black broderie anglaise dress, a pink cardigan thrown over the top.

Michael and Doll work their way through a set of fast-moving songs, as Judith shakes her head in awe and wonders where they get their energy from.

'Aren't they just wonderful.' She claps her hands together. 'I love watching people dance. I used to enjoy a bit of a dance myself, you know, especially a waltz,' she says with a faraway look in her eyes. I exchange a glance with Lars then, and he winks.

When Doll and Michael finish their last energetic dance, everyone is on their feet. The diners from surrounding restaurants also had a view as they danced in the middle of the square and the applause rings around the centre of the village. Even the church bell, right on cue, rings its hourly bell, as if in appreciation of the show. Michael and Doll take a bow before they embrace each other in a lingering hug.

Hannah and I are on our feet, whilst the crowd are giddy with excitement, and work the tables, proffering our hats. Notes and coins are happily dropped in, with expressions of gratitude.

A while later, Doll and Michael emerge, having slipped into the restaurant bathroom and changed into some comfortable clothes that they brought with them.

'I propose a toast,' says Judith, raising a glass. 'Good health to us all, and I hope you two dazzle people with your dancing for many years to come. To Michael and Doll.'

'To Michael and Doll,' we all say as we raise a glass. Just then, the owner of the taverna approaches.

'Are you here next week? I think maybe you are good for my business.' He smiles, glancing around the packed-out restaurant.

'Oh, I'm sure your food is the real crowd-pleaser,' says Doll modestly. 'At least I hope it is, I'm starved.' She laughs.

At that moment a waiter appears with a meze of starters that includes a selection of mouth-watering looking food. Platters of stuffed vine leaves, meatballs in a tomato sauce, pork ribs, soft pitta breads and a selection of creamy dips look wonderful. Deep-fried calamari and whitebait are set on the table with lemon slices and a huge Greek salad.

'Mmm. Why does food taste so good when someone else makes it?' I scoop some hummus into a soft, warm pitta and devour it.

'And that it happens to be Greek food. The fruit and veg is so much nicer here, grown under the sun,' Judith reminds me.

'I suppose so.'

The conversation halts a little as we all dive into the wonderful food, as plate after plate arrives at the table. I'm already stuffed, but as everything is so delicious, I manage a bit of everything.

'It's a pity I can't dance. I think I need to work off the

million calories I have consumed this evening. Maybe I'll have a super long walk in the forest tomorrow,' I say, although I don't regret eating a single mouthful.

'All the food you have eaten is healthy,' says Lars, just as a waiter arrives and asks if we would like some dessert, which we all politely decline, the table piled high with almost empty plates.

'I really cannot thank you enough.' Judith turns to our marvellous dancers. 'And I am so excited to count the money from this evening,' she says, which is safely tucked inside her large handbag. 'It seems people were very generous.'

It's easy to see why Michael is so keen to dance; I imagine the reaction from an appreciative audience is quite addictive.

'Hardly surprising,' says Hannah, finishing off the last of some lemon and oregano potatoes. 'Everyone commented when I passed the hat around on how fantastic you both were.'

As I watched Hannah earlier, chatting confidently to the customers, I felt a sudden surge of pride towards her.

'Right. Are we ready to leave?' asks Judith. 'Although, of course, you may prefer to travel back together,' she says to us all. 'But I have an early start tomorrow, and I'm a little tired. It's been quite a long day.'

'Maybe another drink then we'll follow?' suggests Michael, and Hannah and I agree.

'As you are not the one driving,' says Doll, when Michael orders another glass of wine.

'I haven't drunk any alcohol this evening,' says Hannah. 'I will drive if you like,' she surprises us all by offering.

'Oh, it's sweet of you to offer, Hannah, but I'm joking.' Doll smiles. 'I'm far too tired to drink any more alcohol, and I only had a tiny one earlier when Judith made a toast. I'll have a bottle of water, though, that dancing is thirsty work.'

Just after ten, we stand to leave and the restaurant owner

escorts us to the door, where he shakes us all warmly by the hand.

'*Efcharisto.* Have a good journey home. And you are welcome to dance here anytime.' He smiles at Doll and Michael. 'Now I am certain you are good for my business.'

'I've told you, you don't need us for that,' says Doll kindly. 'Your food really is wonderful.'

'I like to think we did add a little something extra, though,' says Michael as he links arms with Doll and we all head to the car. 'I bet they haven't had a night like that in years,' he says proudly.

'Of course,' says Doll, casting us a knowing glance.

TWENTY-SIX

'What a wonderful night,' Hannah says with a deep sigh.

'It was, wasn't it?'

Hannah and I are in our shared bedroom, speaking in low voices as Judith and Lars have already gone to bed. I can't wait to see how much money was raised for the shelter. I imagine it's been a real godsend having Doll and Michael here. I think of the amount of money the diners were happy to contribute after watching the dance show.

'Imagine having a talent like that, that can take you around the world, not to mention winning championships.' I sigh, thinking how glamorous their life must be compared to most people's.

'I know. I'm quite surprised they chose to stay somewhere like this, to be honest,' says Hannah.

'I know what you mean, but they are both dog lovers and I suppose this setting is a real antidote to crowded dance halls,' I suggest. 'They really seem to enjoy each other's company too, aside from the dancing. I like how they still have fun together.'

'I know. Still being friends after all those years together must be lovely,' she says as she heads towards the bathroom to brush her teeth. When she returns, I do the same, then use the loo, wishing the old building had a quieter flush as I tiptoe back to my room.

As I settle down to sleep, I can't believe I have just over a week left here, and Judith and Lars's wedding is looming. I'm really looking forward to the hen party at the bar on Saturday too, in a few days' time. I also think of how wrong I was to think that something untoward was taking place between Lars and Doll, although they were acting suspiciously, so I guess it was an easy assumption to make. I feel lucky to have met such lovely people here, and think of my own friends back home, especially Jess, and count my blessings before I drift off. I have a job I can return to, and a cosy place to live. Maybe not everything in my life is perfect, but no one's is I suppose.

'I don't believe it.'

Judith tells us over breakfast the next morning that over one thousand euros has been collected for the charity.

'Well, I can believe it, that restaurant was huge and it was packed out,' I say and Michael agrees.

'I simply must give you a cut of the money,' Judith offers Doll and Michael. 'I never imagined we would raise anything like this for the rescue, especially at this time of the year. Most of our fundraising is done in the summer months.'

Doll and Michael tell Judith that they wouldn't hear of taking a fee, so she insists on taking them out for a special meal before they head home.

'You have invited us to your wedding, remember, that's more than enough,' says Michael kindly. 'The rescue relies on charity, and we are only too happy to have been able to give it a little cash injection.'

'Well, it's marvellous. We can't thank you enough, can we, Lars?'

'We really can't. For everything.' He catches Doll's gaze and she smiles.

As we are just finishing breakfast, having already fed the animals, Tania calls over.

'Morning, love. How are you?' asks Judith.

'I'm good, thanks. How was the fundraising?'

'Oh, it was wonderful,' says Judith. 'It's a shame you couldn't come, it was a night to remember. And we raised so much, I still can't quite believe it. It will give a real boost to the money for the animals.'

'That is wonderful.' She smiles.

'How did your evening go?' I ask as I make my way to the animal food storage and Tania walks with me.

'Really good. We invited some of Nicos's friends over for a meal, so I could meet them properly, and they were just lovely. I also had an unexpected visitor.'

'Really?'

'Yes, they had called at the rescue, but there was no one home, so they came to my house to leave a message.'

'Oh. Where they looking for Judith?'

'No, actually,' says Tania, as I fill a bucket with dried dog food. 'They were looking for you. I offered to put them up for the night as I wasn't sure what time you would be home. Perhaps you would like to call over and say hello.'

'Does your unexpected visitor have a name?' I can feel my heart hammering in my chest.

'Yes. His name is Marco,' she tells me and I drop my bucket in shock.

'Marco is here? He's at your house? I don't understand.' I'm babbling as I try to process the fact that Marco has travelled here to Crete.

'He sure is. And I can see why you might have had a little trouble forgetting him. He's an absolute dream.'

'Don't let Nicos hear you say that,' I reply, as I try to gather my thoughts.

'Just honest facts. I'm not saying that he could compare to Nicos, simply admiring his looks,' she teases.

'Oh my goodness! Look at the state of me.' I look down at my old jeans and T-shirt, and messed-up hair beneath a cap, not to mention make-up-free face.

'I'm sure he knows what you look like,' she says kindly. 'And I got the impression he couldn't wait to see you.'

'You did? But why come all this way? I'm going home next week.' My head is whirring.

'Maybe he was unaware of that. Or he couldn't wait that long to see you. Look, I came to say that Nicos and I are heading out shortly, if you would like to come and have a private chat with Marco. I'll brew some coffee, in say, half an hour?' She glances at her watch.

'Yes, yes. If it's okay with Judith. Thank you, Tania.'

'I'll square it with her,' she says, heading into the kitchen, where Judith is busy sorting our lunch.

Upstairs, I run a brush through my hair and apply a slick of mascara, as well as a quick spritz of my perfume. I realise then that it's the perfume Marco bought me, and one I always wore when we went out together. I think about trying to wash it off and hope he doesn't think I am wearing it especially for him. But maybe I do want him to think that. I suddenly don't know what I want, or how I feel. Marco is here in Crete. But why?

I notice Nicos and Tania's car has gone, and I'm a bundle of nerves as I approach their house half an hour later, as planned. Marco is sitting on the porch, with his back to me. As I walk closer, he turns and smiles and I get that funny, familiar feeling that makes my heart soar.

'Hello, Beth,' he says, as he stands and walks to greet me.

'Hi, Marco.'

Before I can ask him why he is here, he has taken me in his

arms and crushed me in his strong embrace. I take in his familiar scent, the smell, every familiar curve in his body, his strong chest. When he finally releases me, he looks at me from arm's length.

'I've missed you,' he says in a breathless whisper. And, all at once, I realise I have missed him dreadfully too. The days out, the animals, even the wonderful days with Artemis have done nothing to quell my feelings for Marco, I realise that now.

'Me, too,' I say, and when his lips meet mine, there is nothing I can do but kiss him back and feel a million fireworks go off inside my body.

TWENTY-SEVEN

'I still can't believe you are here.'

We are holding hands and sipping coffee on the terrace, both of us grinning from ear to ear.

'I had to come and see you. I missed seeing you around town, which I enjoyed doing, even though we had parted.'

'I found it difficult at times,' I tell him honestly.

'Is that why you came out here?'

'Maybe.'

I don't want to give too much away, until I am clear of his intentions.

'Anyway, you still haven't told me exactly why you are here?'

'I told you I missed you.' He sips his strong black coffee. 'I mean, I know we had parted, but I always caught a glimpse of you, almost every day. When you weren't around, I felt empty. I noticed you sometimes, walking along, your tumbling hair bouncing and wished things were different,' he says, baring his soul. 'I began to wonder how I would feel if I ever saw you out and about with another man.' His eyes reach mine, and I take in his handsome face. The thick, stylish dark hair and olive skin, strong jawline and striking blue eyes that seem to look straight into my soul. 'I wasn't sure I could bear it. For some reason, I never thought it was a permanent split. I always imagined us getting back together.'

'I'm not sure how that could happen, given our differing viewpoints about certain things,' I say, and he goes a little quiet.

'So what happens now?' I ask, drinking him in.

'Well, that rather depends on you.' He stirs his coffee.

'On me?'

'Yes. Look, Nicos and Tania will be home in around an hour, but can I take you to dinner this evening?'

'Yes, I would love that. Have you booked somewhere to stay?' I ask, unaware of any hotels in the immediate vicinity.

'Yes, an Airbnb a couple of miles from here, on the road towards Koutouloufari. I've already discovered a cute restaurant there on Google.'

'It's not Italian, is it?'

'No. I would be far too critical, I know that.' He smiles.

The restaurant he works at back home, Little Italy Trattoria, was founded by his grandfather and *nonna*, before his parents took the reins. It is authentically Italian and many of the old family recipes are still used in the restaurant today.

'I really must get back to work now, Marco, but I can't wait to see you tonight.'

'Me neither.' We stand and he circles his arms around my waist as he moves in for another kiss. I feel like I'm drifting along on a floor of cotton candy, when he waves goodbye, telling me he will collect me at seven this evening. Even though a part of me wonders what we could possibly have to say to each other that hasn't already been said, I can't wait to feel him in my arms again.

'How did it go with Marco?'

Hannah and I are walking the dogs in the late afternoon, as the sun is filtering through the trees on the footpath.

'Confusing,' I tell her truthfully. 'It was wonderful to see him. Don't get me wrong, he can still make my pulse race. And we shared some wonderful kisses.' I find myself smiling, as I relive that first kiss.

'Yet it was confusing?' She looks puzzled.

'I know that sounds crazy, but I am just wondering what has changed, although I guess I will find out this evening. He's taking me out for dinner.'

'I'm sure all will become clear. He's flown all this way to see you, after all.'

'I guess so. He told me that even though we had parted, he missed seeing me around. Maybe he's been harbouring thoughts of us getting back together, and me coming around to the idea of not getting married.'

'And you?'

'I have absolutely not changed my mind about that.'

'Well, I hope everything goes well at dinner this evening. As I said, I'm sure he hasn't come all the way out here for nothing.'

We climb uphill a little until the distant sea view captures my heart once more. The scent of pine seems stronger now that autumn is almost well under way, and I breathe deeply, thinking this place really is good for the soul.

'Did you know, pine trees emit a scent that is proven to give us a feeling of well-being,' says Hannah as we walk. 'I heard about that in a nature programme.'

'I can imagine. I always feel good after a romp through the forest. I joined a women's walking group once, but I never kept it up. I think I was too tired after my long days in the supermarket. People are even guiding groups of people through the forest these days, to sit and breathe. Forest bathing, they call it.'

'Seems crazy to need a guide for a forest walk, but I think it's designed to remind people to stay in touch with nature,' says

Hannah. 'Maybe you ought to give your walking group another go. Sometimes when we are feeling tired, it's the exact time to get outdoors and reenergise.'

'Maybe. But having to climb in the car to get somewhere like that puts me off a little. My town isn't exactly filled with hills like this.'

'Perhaps it's worth making the effort. You did tell me you could do with some hobbies,' advises Hannah.

I turn to face her. 'You are so right. Walking was a hobby, and so was gardening once upon a time. Maybe my work has gotten a little bit in the way of my own self-care.'

'It can happen to us all if we let it, but we must make the time.' Hannah smiles. 'We have to make certain things a priority. Sorry, I sound like I am lecturing you.'

'Don't be sorry.'

Talking of being outdoors and gardening stabs at my heart a little. I think about the little two-bedroomed house my mum and I moved to, after the brief stay at an apartment that was entirely unsuitable for us, after Dad became violent. It had a small back garden that Mum filled with flowers in pots. We even grew potatoes in sacks and lettuce and cucumber in a frame that was already there when we moved in. I helped her to dig up the weeds from the overgrown lawn, and the kindly neighbour next door let us borrow his lawnmower. On sunny days, we would sit outside with cold drinks eating our lunch. Sometimes she would invite our widowed neighbour, who was sad to see us leave when we eventually moved on. I was thirteen at the time and he pushed a twenty-pound note into my hand with a tear in his eye and wished me well in my future. Mum was happy in that house, I know she was, despite her once telling me in a drunken ramble that she had never known any joy in her life.

'Anyway, talking of romance.' I turn to Hannah when we stop at a bench for a minute. 'How are things going with Panos?

Did he come and see you the other day?' I ask, recalling him saying that he would.

'Yes.'

'And are you still friends?'

'We are.' She tosses a ball and several dogs chase after it.

'You're not giving much away, are you?' I raise an eyebrow.

'I'm sorry, Beth.' She sighs as she takes a seat on a nearby tree stump. 'Maybe I am just trying to protect my heart. I'm sure you of all people can understand that.'

'Of course I can,' I say gently. 'I also know that if we never take chances in life, then we are not really living. I'm sure you must have come across that quote about better to have loved and lost, in all those books you read.'

I pick the ball up and throw it once more, when a black Labrador drops it at my feet.

'Alfred Lord Tennyson: "Better to have loved and lost, than never loved at all." It was in a book about Britain's favourite love poets. I'm not sure I agree with it, though.' She frowns. 'How can anything be worse than losing the one you love?'

'Well, you'll never know if you refuse to give it a chance.'

'Perhaps. But I'm heading home in a few weeks. There can never be a future for us, our lives are so completely different.'

'You can think about it practically, but maybe you ought to relax and just let things happen naturally. Life isn't all neatly wrapped up like it is in stories,' I find myself saying, then hope that didn't sound too harsh. 'Sorry, that came out a little clumsily, I just meant that we can't shield our hearts from everything, what is meant to be, will be.'

She doesn't answer, and we round the dogs up and carry on with our walk, enjoying an unexpected blast of sunshine that has appeared from behind a cloud, and a warm glow is cast all over our arms. I remove my hooded jacket and tie it around my waist, enjoying the warmth on my face as we walk.

Turning a corner, I hear the sound of a moped, and

suddenly Yolanda appears in the road. She comes to a stop and removes her helmet.

'*Kalispera*, Beth. How are you?'

'I'm good, thanks. How are you?'

'Very good. Better now that my son has got rid of that gold-digging wife. Thank you for making him smile again.'

'He made me smile too,' I tell her.

'Happy to hear that.' She gives a cheeky smile.

'Not in an intimate sense,' I quickly add. 'Neither of us were ready for anything else. In fact,' I tell her, knowing that Judith will probably mention it anyway, 'my ex-fiancé has arrived here to see me.'

'Here in the village?'

'Yes. I am going out with him this evening to talk.'

'To talk, huh?' She smiles and for some reason I can feel the heat rising in my cheeks. 'Well, *kali tychi* to you. It means good luck,' she says, before zooming off down the hill to no doubt have a good gossip with Judith.

Soon, we arrive at the section of the road near the bend, where Artemis almost knocked us over, and I recall Hannah flying into a panic when I strode off ready to give him a piece of my mind. I'm not sure she would do quite the same thing now. In fact, maybe she would be the one to give him a dressing down.

'Remember when Artemis almost mowed us down,' she says then, guessing my thoughts as she frequently seems to do.

'How could I forget? Who would have thought he would turn out to be a good friend? I'm glad we ran into each other, even if it was almost literally.'

'Well, as you say, life does present us with unexpected opportunities, doesn't it? And maybe you're right in saying that we ought to be a little more open to them.'

'We're all different, and I get that. But at times, it's no bad thing to take a leap into the unknown.'

TWENTY-EIGHT

Lars is in the pool and the rest of us are sitting around, Hannah lying in the sun, drying off having already had a swim. Lars does numerous lengths as usual, and Judith says she wonders where he gets his energy from.

'I wish I could do half of what he does,' she says, smiling as she watches him.

She sips a glass of home-made lemonade, before diving into a slice of home-made carrot cake.

'Maybe he is getting himself fit for the wedding night,' says Yolanda with a wink and Judith slaps her on the arm. Hannah and I can't help laughing.

'He's been missing half the morning,' Judith lets slip. 'Then Doll disappeared, saying something about having to nip out and see someone. I don't know if it's my imagination, but they seem to be spending rather a lot of time together. Not that Michael seems to notice.' She takes a sip of her lemonade.

I'll be glad when Lars dances at the wedding and is able to reveal the reason for his frequent disappearances. I hate Judith having any unfounded suspicions.

We carry on drinking lemonade and eating cake, and

Yolanda tells us how much she is looking forward to the hen party at the village bar on Saturday.

'Last year I bought dancing shoes. They have not been out of the box yet. And now, I will wear them twice.' She holds up two of her fingers. 'For the hen's night and the wedding,' she says with satisfaction.

'Sometimes I can hardly believe I am marrying again at my age. Life can really take us by surprise at times.' Judith sighs, and I glance sideways at Hannah. 'I suppose we ought to be open to opportunities life presents us.' She smiles. 'And really, I shouldn't be eating cake.' She places the half-eaten piece back onto a plate. 'I have a wedding dress I want to fit into next week.'

'You not worry.' Yolanda bats her hand away at the very suggestion. 'You have the nice figure. Lars is a lucky man. I hope you have saved yourself for the wedding night.' She laughs loudly.

Judith gave us girls a sneak peek at her wedding dress the other day and it is absolutely beautiful. It's a gorgeous oyster-coloured shift dress, embellished with pearls and jewels at the hemline and a sheer bolero-style cover up. The visitors from the holiday cottage will be flying in two days before the wedding, having been invited. Monica is a hairdresser who will pin Judith's hair up into a glorious topknot that she looked so beautiful with when they did a trial the last time she was here.

Once more, Judith taps her friend on the arm, slightly embarrassed in front of me and Hannah, as though we were her daughters.

Lars climbs out of the water then, and passing the table we are sitting at takes a piece of cake and pops it into his mouth. 'Delicious. And I think maybe I have burned enough calories to have it.' He winks before he heads off to get dressed.

'I joke,' says Yolanda, with a mischievous grin, once Lars has left.

It really is lovely to see how she interacts with Judith. When we were out walking and talking of Artemis one day, Tania told me that Yolanda has been like a new woman since she got her moped, and began seeing Judith a little more. I suppose it's easy to isolate yourself as you get older, which is probably the worst thing you can do. Although I was slightly surprised it could happen in a small village, but Yolanda's house is at the top of the hill I suppose. Yolanda has neighbours who I met at the party, but their English isn't quite as good as Yolanda's, and they seemed to be on good terms, but maybe they just weren't close before.

As the afternoon draws to a close, my tummy is turning over in anticipation of my meeting with Marco this evening. Should I call it a date? Is it a date? I was so thrilled to see him. And his kisses had the same effect they always did. Gosh, I've missed him so much.

Heading upstairs to my room to get ready later, I see Doll and Lars chatting at the donkey area, under the watchful eyes of Judith, who is picking some rosemary from a pot growing in the garden. I wish I could tell her what is happening between them, especially as she mentioned things to Yolanda earlier, but I don't want to ruin the surprise. I can just imagine Judith's face when he takes her in his arms for a waltz, although maybe I ought to suggest Lars show a little more discretion.

I shower and try several outfits on, before I finally settle on a white knee-length dress that shows off my light tan. I pull my pink denim jacket from my wardrobe, as it is getting a little cooler in the evenings now. Standing in front of the mirror, looking at my reflection, my hair long and loosely curled, I feel those butterflies once more.

'You look really lovely,' says Hannah as she enters the room, carrying a book.

'Thank you. So what are you up to this evening?' I ask.

'Take a guess.' She smiles, holding up the book. 'This is a

real page-turner. As soon as dinner is over, I'm going to take a shower and settle down with it. Are you looking forward to seeing Marco?'

'I am, yet I feel inexplicably nervous. Silly, I know, I was with him for years, yet it feels like I am going on a first date.'

'I suppose you are in a way. Well, it's the first date since you broke up. I hope it goes well.'

'Thanks, Hannah, me too.'

I spray some perfume onto my wrists and behind my neck and, taking a glance at my watch, which shows almost seven, I head downstairs.

Judith is putting the finishing touches to the dinner table outside, a fire pit gently glowing warm in the cooling evening air. Michael and Doll are laughing at something together and Lars lights a candle before giving Judith a kiss on the cheek. Judith smiles at Lars fondly, but I can't help noticing the smile doesn't quite reach her eyes.

TWENTY-NINE

Marco is pulling up in his car as I make my way to the gate.

'Perfect timing,' he says, climbing out of the car and kissing me on the cheek.

'You look lovely,' he says. 'And you smell gorgeous too.'

'You recognise it?' I ask, thinking of the first time he bought me the scent, after I'd commented on it when spraying samples in a department store. He'd surprised me with it on our next date.

'Of course I do.'

'You look nice too.' I smile, taking in his fashionable shirt, and navy jeans.

'Have you been to a hairdresser?' I say, eyeing his freshly cut and styled hair.

'Thought I'd make an effort.' He grins. 'I drove into Malia earlier and found a barbers. We should go there, the beach looks great.'

Marco has always been proud of his thick head of hair, and often frequents a Turkish barber's back home so it always looks its best.

'So how long are you staying around here?' I don't tell him about my drunken escapade in Malia with Artemis.

'I thought I would stay for a few days. It's a long way to come just for dinner.'

'So where are we going?' I pray it isn't the restaurant at the beach that Artemis took me to.

'Not too far. Somewhere that was recommended to me in Hersonissos,' he says, and I breathe a sigh of relief. 'It's down a side street, close to the harbour. The food, I'm told, is outstanding.'

'Who told you that?'

'Tripadvisor. It's got a rating of four point nine.'

Marco always consults public opinion before he visits restaurants, saying there is no sense shelling out a load of money for a bad experience. Maybe it comes from working in the family restaurant. I remember going to a fancy restaurant with him once, with a menu that declared foraged mushrooms and hand-selected onions. I laughed all evening after a woman at the next table asked what other way could you select an onion, other than by hand – pick them with your feet? Marco told me that anything hand selected usually meant it was home-grown, and not collected by machinery, but it was too late. I kept visualising farm workers picking onions up with their feet. We both laughed about it on the way home, and it was one of the things I really missed. The sound of his big laugh.

As we drive down the hill, I still can't believe Marco is here, and find myself glancing at his handsome profile. I also catch him keep glancing at me and smiling.

Soon enough, we are pulling into the harbour at Hersonissos and I climb out of the car and close the door. For a second, I think of how Artemis always held the door open for me, something considered old-fashioned in the UK, at least amongst the younger generation.

The sun is setting, an orange orb floating above the water, as boat owners secure their vessels for the evening. A trio of old men wearing flat caps are playing cards at a fold-up table near a fishing boat, sipping an ouzo, others sitting at a bench overlooking the water, and chatting. I notice they are all wearing thick jumpers now as the evening temperature cools a little, although a light jacket is enough for me, as it still feels like a spring evening. As we walk, we pass many locals out for the evening, families and couples alike walking along the harbourfront, an occasional English or German accent as holidaymakers make the last trips here for the season.

We walk past a bar with a neon sign outside, and Marco asks me if I fancy a pre-dinner cocktail.

'Sure, why not?'

'Do you still enjoy sex on the beach?' he asks with a twinkle in his eye.

'No, actually, my taste is far more sophisticated these days. I'll have a Cosmopolitan.'

'I'm going old school and having a Harvey Wallbanger,' says Marco, as a waiter approaches and takes our order. Sitting here with a cocktail, in the early evening, the sun shimmering on the water, I feel wonderful, yet wonder where this is all going. Still, I try and relax into the evening, as I am sure all will become clear as the evening progresses.

'I can't believe I've never been to Greece before,' says Marco, taking in his surroundings.

'It's gorgeous, isn't it? I remember coming to Corfu years ago, although I can't say I saw very much of it, to be honest. It was only a few days in Kavos to celebrate a friend's twenty-first birthday.'

'Crete is gorgeous, what I have seen of it at least,' Marco says, as he takes a sip of his cocktail. 'Are you enjoying being at the dog rescue?'

'I love it. I have always loved dogs, but living in a first-floor apartment, it wasn't really possible to keep one.'

We finish our drinks, and head down a side street, before arriving at a restaurant with a dark-brown wooden door, set in a stone archway. Small windows with metal grids are set into the thick, sandstone walls, giving it an almost medieval feel. A metal sign bearing the name Apollo Taverna hangs outside, reminding me of an old inn.

Marco pushes open the heavy door, and at once the smell of garlic hits my nostrils. Inside, the thick stone-walled room has dark beams, and wooden tables set with red tablecloths and chunky cream candles at the centre. It's cosy inside, and buzzing with atmosphere, as chatter rings from every table that is full of diners.

'These smells are almost as good as a little Italian restaurant I know back home,' says Marco, once we have been shown to our seats and he orders a bottle of red wine and some water.

'What do you recommend, now that you have had a chance to sample some Greek food?' he asks as he peruses the menu.

'I don't think you can beat a good moussaka, although I know you like beef. So perhaps a beef stifado? Then again, the mixed mezes look good,' I say, glancing at the menu. 'I don't know, really I love all of the food, and it certainly smells good here.'

'I like the sound of the beef stifado,' he says, snapping his menu shut and pouring us each a glass of red wine that a waiter has just set down on the table. I opt for a baked chicken dish with aubergines and a béchamel sauce that sounds like a twist on a moussaka.

'How's the restaurant back home?' I ask Marco as another waiter arrives with a basket of bread.

'Good. Busy, as always. I worry my parents are working too hard, though, as they are both approaching retirement age.' He picks up a piece of warm crusty bread and butters it.

'I'm surprised you were allowed the time off,' I remark.

'It has been a long time since I took a break, and the other staff are more than capable without me, as long as good food is coming out of the kitchen.'

Marco works front of house in the busy high street restaurant in the town, which is often the venue for people's celebrations and milestones. He is also a trained sommelier. His mother and father prepare the food in the kitchen, along with an apprentice, with one or two locals working as waiting staff with Marco.

'Do you think you could find a good chef to maybe take the reins in the kitchen from time to time?' I ask, as I take a sip of my delicious wine. Marco has a sister who works as a nurse and has no interest in being involved in the restaurant business.

'Not while my parents still have breath in their body, you know what they are like. It helps that they have an apprentice from a local catering college, though, as he is a talented young chef. I am sure he will learn a lot from my parents.'

Our food arrives then, and Marco makes appreciative noises as he devours his tasty-looking beef stifado, presented in a glazed terracotta pot, as is my chicken dish. When he finally pushes his plate back, and dabs at his mouth with a napkin, he is nodding and smiling.

'That was fantastic. I'm stuffed,' he says, taking a sip of water.

'Mine was gorgeous too.'

I made short work of the chicken and aubergine dish, rich with herbs and a delicious tomato sauce with a hint of cinnamon.

'It's a shame, as I was looking forward to a dessert. I think I spied some sort of custard pie on the dessert menu.'

'You could have some ice cream. Or maybe a coffee?' I suggest.

'You suggest ice cream in Greece to an Italian?' He grins. 'Surely nothing can beat a gelato.'

Marco has told me many times of his first trip to Italy, when he sampled every flavour of gelato known to man and almost made himself sick.

'Perhaps I will just have a shot of ouzo to finish off. Would you like one?'

'No, thanks, I'm not really a fan,' I confess, or more accurately I have been unable to touch the stuff since the evening in Malia.

We are debating our choices, when a waiter appears and places a small piece of baklava down in front of us, topped with crumbled pistachio.

'Compliments of the house,' he says, and it's a perfect size to round off the meal just nicely. Marco orders a Greek coffee then, and I finish off with a cappuccino.

'What a great choice of restaurant,' I say, when we head outside into the now dark cobbled street, a street lamp leading the way as we walk. There's an alleyway that leads towards the harbour, and suddenly Marco takes me by the hand, and pulls me into it.

'I've been dying to do this all evening,' he says, as he presses his lips against mine, and I lose myself in his kiss. The sound of a group of people heading our way has us pull apart and walk on, holding hands. As I look up at his handsome face, I think I feel happier than I have in a long time.

THIRTY

'So where to now?'

'A walk along the harbour might be nice,' suggests Marco.

'It's so wonderful here, isn't it?' I glance at Marco as we walk, our hands entwined.

'Really lovely. I can understand why you like coming over here.'

I don't tell him that the main reason for my visit this time was to try and put some space between us.

We have reached the end of the harbour and are glancing out across the water, the sound of distant music coming from a bar.

'But I must ask you, Marco, what happens now?'

'That rather depends on you.' Marco moves closer and kisses my neck, sending thrills through my body.

'It does?'

'Hmm.' He kisses my lips, then my face with feather stokes that send me into a spin.

'I could drive you home, but maybe I am a little over the limit,' he says.

'What did you have in mind?' I can feel my pulse racing,

just standing here next to him, lost in the moment. Maybe any deeper chats can wait.

'I could leave the car here and drive you back in the morning? My Airbnb is a short walk from here.'

His eyes are fixed on mine as he waits for an answer.

'Lead the way,' I tell him as he takes my hands in his and we set off, the street lamps dotted along the road leading the way.

It feels like déjà vu when I message Judith and tell her I will arrive back tomorrow morning, although this time I am able to deliver the message myself.

When Marco leads me to the bedroom of his stylish accommodation, and we slide into bed together, I sink into his arms and feel like I have come home.

THIRTY-ONE

'Good morning, beautiful.'

Marco kisses me on the top of the head as he places a coffee on the bedside table. I'm still tangled in the expensive cotton sheets, reliving the wonderful time we had together last night. I stretch out my arms and sit up and take a sip of the delicious coffee that really hits the spot.

'It's a pity you have to work today,' he says, sitting on the edge of the bed and sipping his coffee. 'We could have gone into Malia, maybe have taken a boat trip before they finish for the season and had some lunch. I bet you haven't had a chance to go there, have you?'

'Actually, yes, I have. I went with a friend. It wasn't for a boat trip, though, we just stayed in the town.'

I cross my fingers and ask for forgiveness for avoiding the topic. We didn't do anything, and Artemis was no more than a friend. I am not sure why I am being so secretive about it, but maybe I don't want to ruin the mood.

'What was it like?' he asks before he heads into the shower.

'A typical tourist destination, if I'm honest, although the beach was beautiful.'

I recall stretching out on a bed beneath the sun and watching the waves gently roll onto the shore. I try not to think about the evening at the bar, where I knocked back the ouzo.

When Marco is in the bathroom, Judith calls me.

'Judith, hi. I will be back in half an hour, if that's okay?'

'That's why I've called you.' She surprises me by telling me to take my time, and at least have breakfast. 'I imagine you have a lot to talk about this morning. I hope everything is okay between you both, but maybe you can't talk now.'

'Marco has just stepped into the shower, so I'm okay to talk for a moment. Oh, Judith, we had a lovely evening, I hadn't realised quite how much I missed him.'

'It was plain to see,' she says honestly. 'I could tell by the way you spoke about him that you still loved him.'

I hear the sound of the shower turning off, and thank Judith, telling her I will be back after breakfast.

'It seems I have been given at least another hour from work,' I tell Marco as he emerges from the shower, a white towel around his waist. 'I've just been talking to Judith, who tells me there is no rush, and that maybe I want to get breakfast somewhere.'

'Is that right?' Marco strides towards the bed. 'At least an hour, you say?'

'Marco, I need a shower,' I say, throwing the covers back, and racing to the bathroom.

'Mind if I join you?'

'But you've just showered.'

I don't regret anything about last night, despite Marco not really discussing the real reason he is here. But I want a little thinking time.

'Who said anything about showering,' he says, before following me into the bathroom.

'Please, Marco.' I gently push him out of the door. 'I'm taking a leisurely shower. With no distractions.'

THIRTY-TWO

We have stopped at the café not far from the rescue in the forest, eating pancakes and drinking coffee.

'What will you do with yourself this evening?' I ask Marco, as I pop a strawberry into my mouth.

It's the evening of the hen party and I am really looking forward to it. I still haven't asked Marco why he is really here, but thinking about it, maybe I wanted to confirm my feelings for him, which may or may not be a foolish thing to do. So much for coming here to get over him.

'I was going to tell you that.' Marco dives into his pancakes, which are drizzled with honey and berries, and makes appreciative noises. 'Nicos has invited me to go night fishing with him and Lars. They have invited Michael too, I think his name is, the dancer?'

'Yes. That's right.'

'Nicos and Tania are such a great couple, aren't they? It was so kind of them to let me stay the night I turned up,' he tells me.

'They really are lovely. And only you could come over to a place where you don't know anyone and you've never visited, and be invited to a stag party immediately.'

'I wouldn't call it that exactly, going sea fishing. I can't imagine there will be any visits to lap-dancing clubs, or the groom being tied naked to a lamp post.' He laughs.

'It says a lot about the stag nights you have been on.'

I wonder then if he will ever have one of his own. Probably not, if he still feels the same way about marriage.

'Tania and Nicos are a lovely couple,' I say, returning to the conversation about them. 'I quickly became friends with Tania. And she makes the best lemon drizzle cake.' I almost salivate, just thinking about it.

'Even nicer than my mother's?' He winks. 'I promise I won't tell her.'

'On a par, I would say,' I tell him diplomatically, although I think Tania's just had the edge.

I think of Marco senior then, and his wife, Luisa, the loveliest, warmest people who quickly welcomed me into their family when we started dating. I missed them when I split with Marco. I always imagined being in their lives for as long as they lived, as their daughter-in-law. I know Marco's father was disappointed that Marco and I never got married, but he loved me like a daughter-in-law all the same.

'So, are you going with them later? I didn't realise you liked fishing.' I drain the last of my latte.

'I don't particularly, although I have never tried sea fishing. Me and my sister used to go with my grandfather occasionally, sitting on a riverbank with him, but he never usually caught a thing. We went along for the picnic, as he always brought a basket filled with goodies.' He laughs. 'I think my parents appreciated him taking me and my sister out from under their feet when they were busy with the restaurant, especially during the school holidays.'

'Probably,' I say, glancing at my watch and standing up. 'Right, I really must get a move on and make up for the time I have missed this morning.'

Marco settles the bill and takes the short drive to the rescue, where he drops me off.

'Have a lovely evening.' He kisses me once more before I head inside. 'I will call you tomorrow.'

'Thank you. Enjoy your sea fishing trip.'

Inside the rescue, the animals have all been fed and most of the chores already done, even though it's only nine thirty.

I run upstairs to change before I round up some of the dogs to take out for a walk. Back downstairs, I run into Judith in the kitchen.

'Hi, Beth.' She gestures to a chair and I sit down, declining some coffee after not long having had one.

'So are you two getting back together?' she asks, sounding excited for me.

'Well, that's the thing, Judith, I'm really not sure.'

'Not sure? I thought you said this morning that you had enjoyed a wonderful evening together.'

'Oh, we did, I can't deny that. It's just we haven't really discussed what happens next. I think we both just enjoyed spending time together again.'

'Well, there is plenty of time to figure that out, I'm sure, although I am surprised you haven't come right out and asked him.'

'Maybe I selfishly needed to find out how I feel about him. But there's no doubting it, I'm afraid. He still makes my heart thump, every time I see him,' I tell her.

'The main thing is he came all the way out here, to see you. Surely that tells you a lot. Maybe after the hen party, you can sit down and discuss what it is you really want.'

'Hmm, maybe.'

'I'd love to meet him. Maybe you could invite him for dinner here tomorrow evening?'

'That sounds lovely, if you're sure. Thanks, Judith. So, are you looking forward to your hen party later?'

'I am. Helena is laying on some nibbles and a little music. She called me last night and told me her mother might come, which will be lovely. I never got much of a chance to chat to her at Tania's BBQ. It's lovely to see her venturing out again.'

'It is. And maybe someone else you could go shopping with, along with Yolanda.'

'You know, that isn't a bad idea. I might offer to drive us to a market next time there is one nearby. City shopping might still be a bit much for her at the moment. Yolanda could come too, we could grab some lunch somewhere.'

'That sounds lovely.'

As I walk the dogs with Hannah, I daydream about last night, reliving those intimate moments and long, thrilling kisses.

'Are we walking past the bar?'

I'm thinking about the shower we took with a huge grin on my face.

'Beth! Are we walking past the bar?' asks Hannah, jolting me from my daydream. 'That's the second time I've asked. I daren't ask what you are thinking about.' She grins.

'Oh, sorry, Hannah. Yes, sure we can walk past the bar. I take it you aren't avoiding Panos anymore then?'

'I wasn't exactly avoiding him. Okay, yes. Well, maybe a little,' she admits. 'But I want to ask Helena if there is anything I can do to help with Judith's get-together this evening.'

'I've already offered, and she told me everything is already sorted. But we can still swing by, if you like.'

Panos is loading a fridge with bottled beer when we arrive, and he smiles politely at us before disappearing behind the bar. His grandmother is busy folding coloured paper, which I realise are paper chains.

'*Kalimera.*' She nods as we approach the bar, bending down to pet one of the smaller dogs. 'Please. Wait.'

She heads inside, before reappearing with some slices of leftover lamb and feeds titbits to the dogs.

'Shh, no tell.' She winks, before wiping her hands on a napkin and continuing with her paper chains.

'I make for her,' she says, pointing to the bar, where I imagine the chains draped along for this evening's gathering.

'*Poly oraia*,' says Hannah, and Panos's grandmother grins. '*Efcharisto!*'

'Ladies, good morning.' Helena appears then, but Panos is chatting to the delivery driver, who has just delivered the cases of bottled beer, seemingly in no hurry to say hello to us.

We chat to Helena for a few minutes, asking if we can offer any help, but once more she tells us everything is sorted for this evening.

'What did you say to Gran?' I ask Hannah as we walk on.

'"*Poly oraia*". It means "very nice",' she says. I can't help noticing that she sounds a little flat.

'So you are remembering some Greek words. Are you still exchanging emails with Panos?'

'Not as much,' she tells me. 'I have been studying online a little.'

'Have you fallen out with him?' I ask, as we approach a bench in the forest that overlooks a stream.

'Not exactly. Well, at least I didn't think so, but he wasn't exactly in a rush to say hello this morning, was he?'

'I did notice. Although he was taking delivery of some drinks,' I remind her, even though they had finished up, and were clearly just having a chat.

'I suppose so. Anyway. I wouldn't blame him if he has cooled off, I have kind of been giving him mixed messages.' She sighs. 'I was so keen not to fall for him, I'm worried I might have come off as a little rude.'

I wonder whether he will be here this evening, tending the bar, or whether has been invited out on the fishing trip.

'Then maybe honesty is the best policy. Tell him the truth.'

'What? That I decided to cool things as I was falling for him?' She looks horrified.

'Would you like me to tell him?'

'NO. Beth, really, promise you won't say anything, he will think I am a right idiot. Besides, I am over it now. I'll be home before you know it.'

'If you say so.'

'I do,' she says firmly, although her eyes tell a different story.

Back at the rescue, my phone signal comes back to life and I hear a beep in my pocket. It's Marco sending me a row of hearts in a text message. I send a red lips emoji back and slide the phone back into my pocket.

Doll is in the kitchen glugging down some cold water, before fanning herself with a hand fan, as Judith has turned the air conditioning off now as autumn approaches.

'Hi, Doll, are you okay?'

'Hello, Beth, I'm just a bit hot. I'll be alright, though.' She plasters a smile on her face.

'You're not ill, are you?' I ask, thinking she might have a temperature.

'Ill? Oh no.' She smiles. 'At least not in the way you think. It's the bloody menopause,' she confides.

She looks far too young to be going through it, although I read in *Women's Health* magazine at the shop back home that perimenopause can start in your forties.

'I'll be fifty next month,' she tells me, much to my surprise. 'Fifty. I'm absolutely bloody dreading it.'

'Well, you don't look it, and why are you dreading turning fifty? Isn't age just a number?'

'Don't you believe it. Everything starts falling to bits during menopause. It's already started. Oh, I'm still fit, but I have to take joint supplements for my knees, and evening primrose oil for hot flushes. They aren't working yet, though, obviously, as it takes a month or two apparently, if they work at all.' She sighs. 'And don't even get me started on hormonal migraines. And then I read that my two favourite things, wine and cheese, can bring them on. The menopause is designed to suck every bit of joy out of life, I can tell you.'

I'm about to say that most women come through the other side of menopause with the right support but she hasn't finished yet. 'And then there's the brain fog. I literally stop mid-sentence sometimes, and wonder what the hell I am talking about. Men have it easy, I tell you. Apart from having to share a bed with someone who soaks the sheets with sweat every night, that is. Poor Michael almost froze to death last winter when I insisted on having the bedroom windows flung open, even in January.'

'You should see a doctor if things are that bad. Especially as you still tour.'

'I might do. I don't want to stop dancing yet, why should I?'

'Absolutely, why should you?'

'Thanks, Beth. I don't really talk about it as I don't want to bore people. At the end of the day, it's something women have to go through, although some women seem to breeze through it. Where is the justice in that?'

'You are not boring me, I am always here to talk to, if you feel like offloading. Or screaming. Or having a glass of wine with,' I offer. 'And you know, I'm sure Judith has been through at least some of what you mention. She might be good to talk to sometime.'

'That's not a bad idea. And I'll definitely be up for a glass of wine, despite what the doctors say about it.' She smiles. 'I'm really looking forward to this evening at the bar.' She squeezes my hand before she heads back outside and I make my way upstairs to sort some laundry out in my bedroom.

As I glance out of my bedroom window that has a good view of the pool, even though, just yesterday, Lars pulled the pool cover over for the approaching autumn, I see Lars and Doll hanging around the pool area, practising some dance steps. Judith's room is on the opposite side of the house, and doesn't give the same outlook. I'm not sure if that's a good thing or not; maybe it would put her mind at rest if she noticed them simply dancing together.

'Are you looking forward to the fishing trip?' I ask Lars as I pass him later, carrying some bags of food to a storage area.

'I am. I used to enjoy sea fishing. And it is a long time since I had time at sea with a bunch of men. It will give me a chance to get to know Nicos a little more too,' he tells me. 'Judith is thrilled that Tania has settled down here in the village.'

'I can imagine.'

'She also tells me your fiancé is joining us. Or should I say ex-fiancé.'

'It's complicated.' I sigh. 'But I think we are trying to work things out.'

'Well, I hope you manage to do just that,' says Lars kindly, and I thank him.

'Oh, Lars, while you're here, how is the dancing coming along?' I ask him.

'Absolutely brilliantly, if I say so myself. Doll is such a great teacher.'

'I'm glad to hear it. And I hope you don't mind me saying, but perhaps you could be a tiny bit more discreet,' I tentatively suggest.

'I thought we were.' He looks surprised. 'What makes you say that?'

'Well, to be truthful, it hasn't gone unnoticed by Judith that the two of you seem to disappear together. I heard her mentioning it to Yolanda.'

'You did?' Lars looks horrified. 'Surely she doesn't think there is anything untoward going on between us, does she? I love Judith more than anything,' he says, a worried expression on his face. 'Besides, Doll and Michael are completely happy together. I would never dream of doing anything like that under his nose.'

'I know you wouldn't, and I know how much you love Judith. But you can see how it might look. I once spotted you both entering the rescue at different times, having seen you get out of your car together.'

'Oh dear.' Lars runs his hand over his head and sighs. 'I don't know what to do now. The wedding is in a few days' time. Do I come clean and ruin the surprise? I hate the thought of Judith worrying over nothing,' he says, genuinely concerned.

'I don't think there is any need for that. Maybe just be a little more careful when you practise together,' I gently advise.

'Thank you, Beth. And maybe I ought to make an extra special fuss of Judith.'

'Then you might arouse even more suspicion. You are loving enough towards Judith. Just be aware, that's all I am saying.'

THIRTY-THREE

We feed the animals a little earlier than usual, around five, as we prepare for the hen night at the bar. It's six o'clock by the time we are gathered in the kitchen, and Judith offers us an ouzo cocktail before we head out. Lars came over and said goodbye before he left, kissing Judith on the cheek before he departed.

'What exactly is in it?' I ask, still thinking about the night I overdid it on the stuff.

'Well, there are various recipes out there, but I have discovered my favourite cocktail is an ouzotini.'

'An ouzotini? That sounds interesting, what's in it?' asks Hannah.

'Pineapple juice, ouzo, vodka and fresh lime juice. Poured over ice.'

'That sounds wonderful,' says Doll, who is looking lovely in a white jumpsuit, and a bunch of silver bangles on her arms.

'Sounds lethal, more like,' says Hannah.

I feel so blessed to be sitting here with my new friends, and being at a hen party makes me wonder whether I would have one myself, and if so, what would it be like? Not that we have actually discussed wedding plans yet, or any future plans really. But I think I would quite fancy doing something adventurous, like a zip wire over the Welsh mountains. Maybe.

As I do love a cocktail, and I figure the pineapple and lime juice will make it delicious, I agree to a glass of ouzotini that has already been prepared and is in a pitcher, filled with ice. As I expected, it is delicious, although I do limit myself to one small glass.

'Did Nicos get away okay?' I ask Tania, as I sip my cocktail through a straw. 'Are they ready for Lars to arrive? By the way, it was really kind of him to invite Marco to join them.'

'Yes, they were all quite excited, I think. They are meeting Marco at the harbour as it's not far from where he is staying. I kind of thought he might appreciate being asked, as you would be joining us for Judith's hen party.'

'Are we ready then?' Judith is the first to stand, and we link arms and take the walk slowly uphill to the bar.

'At least it will be easier coming down,' Judith says with a laugh as we climb a little higher.

'Any more cocktails like that, and we will be rolling down the hill,' says Doll, and we all laugh.

'The others ought to be there by now,' says Judith, glancing at her watch, the others being Yolanda and her close female neighbours, as well as Helena from the bar, her mother and grandmother.

Stepping onto the terrace to the bar, I notice the remembrance tree on the flagged area at the foot of the church. Coloured ribbons are tied around the branches in memory of loved ones, messages written on them and on little ceramic hearts.

Judith gasps when she sees the bar area; the pretty paper chains that had been painstakingly made are threaded along the bar with pastel-coloured balloons. There is a huge banner saying 'Good luck Judith' in the middle of the bar, all hand-painted, little splashes of glitter here and there, and red hearts made from fabric have been stuck on. Several tables have been pushed together, and set with tablecloths and candles, and several bottles of wine sitting in wine buckets.

'Oh my goodness, you did all this?' She hugs Helena, as she takes everything in.

'We all did.' Helena gestures to her mother and grandmother. 'We wanted to make it special for you.'

'Well, you have certainly done that.' Judith looks a little teary as she takes everything in. 'I'm sure I don't deserve all of this.'

'Of course you do. And I am sure all of the animals would agree,' says Helena firmly.

There are large platters of food sitting on the bar, covered with clear domes, and when I spy some delicious-looking filo pastry tarts, my stomach gives a little rumble.

'Please, please. Everyone sit down. I make a toast,' instructs Helena, as she offers around a bottle of champagne and fills some flutes.

'Judith, I hope you and Lars have your happy ever after. You definitely deserve it. Congratulations. I hope you enjoy your special evening.'

She pops the cork on a champagne bottle, dropping a little into our glasses, which we all raise to Judith and Lars.

'Oh this is just wonderful,' says Judith. 'But who paid for all this? I didn't want people going to any expense,' she continues, as we take our seats at the long table.

As the sun begins to set, Helena quickly lights some chunky candles in storm jars, which are lined along the broken flagged floor.

'We all chipped in with the food, and I have done some of the baking,' says Tania. 'Helena, her mum and grandmother have been busy decorating the bar. Oh and Lars paid for the champagne and wine, as well as putting some money behind the bar. Helena, make sure you let me know when it runs out,' Tania tells her.

'For sure.' She smiles.

Panos appears then and sets down the platters of food on the table, assisted by Helena and her mother. I notice Hannah glance at Panos, and he smiles at her.

'Is Panos staying?' I ask Helena as I chew on one of the tasty feta and red pepper filled tarts.

'I think so, yes. He was invited on the fishing trip, but he has never really been one for the water. He gets seasick,' she reveals.

I'm sure Hannah will be pleased that he is sticking around this evening, and I hope that maybe they will get the chance to talk to each other.

The drink is flowing, and the sound of laughter rings around the forest as we eat and chat and have a wonderful time. When we have had our fill of savoury dishes, including meatballs, chicken with rice and tasty pies, Panos brings out a show-stopper of a cheesecake loaded with red berries and places it at the centre of the table before going to get cutlery.

'That looks exactly like the one I brought to your BBQ,' Doll says to Tania, as she takes a slug of white wine.

'It does, doesn't it?' Tania says innocently.

'It certainly does. The one Smudge gobbled up.' Doll smiles as she refills her glass.

'You knew about that?' Tania's mouth falls open.

'Of course I knew.' She grins. 'Every time someone mentioned it, you kind of took them to one side. I figured it out when I tossed something into the bin in the kitchen, and there was my cheesecake. Well, what was left of it anyway.' She raises an eyebrow. 'And don't think I didn't notice when Nicos kept topping up my wine glass. Not that I minded that! But don't worry, I forgive you.'

'Oh, Doll, I'm so sorry. I'm afraid dogs will be dogs, especially the big daft Vizsla. And that is kind of why I made this, to try and make up for it. I will admit, yours looked even better, though.'

'I don't know about that, but thank you,' says Doll.

'I know someone who was devastated to have missed out on your cheesecake,' says Hannah. 'I bet he can't wait to sink his teeth into that.'

'You are right about that,' says Panos, who appears at that very moment to clear away some plates.

'Maybe we have some together,' he says to Hannah, who visibly brightens.

The drinks flow and the night progresses and I notice Helena's mum slowly come out of her shell, joining in the conversation and singing along to some music that is playing in the background. Soon enough, talk turns to Judith's upcoming nuptials.

'Did you ever think you would marry again?' asks Doll, moving away from the patio heater Helena has lit.

'Never. I thought Ray was my one and only, but it seems fate had other ideas.'

'And we are so happy for you,' says Yolanda, raising her glass. 'But now, can we have a little lively dance music.' She stands up and points to her feet. 'Especially as the dance shoes have finally come out this evening.'

Everyone laughs, and when Helena selects some songs guaranteed to get the party started, everyone is on their feet. We dance and laugh, stopping occasionally to have a drink and draw breath, and I marvel at the scene. Woman of all ages and backgrounds, some with limited English, are having the time of their life dancing and listening to the music, despite any language barrier.

'How about a little hokey pokey!' says Yolanda, raising her glass in the air.

'Do you mean the hokey-cokey?' asks Tania, bursting out into laughter.

'Okey cokey, hokey pokey, what does it matter?' says Yolanda. 'As long as we go in and out, like this.' She moves backwards and forwards, holding on to the glass of ouzo in her hand for dear life as she moves.

There's a flurry of movement, and after placing our drinks safely on the table out of the way, we are all doing as Yolanda suggested, putting our left foot in, left foot out before rushing to the centre of the circle, singing at the tops of our voices, to hilarious effect. When we finally sit down, I struggle to remember an evening when I have had so much fun. Not like this – throwing our heads back and feeling like a child. It's a far cry from doing a bit of a dance at a bar back home, shuffling around a tiny dance floor.

'I can't cope, I think I might spontaneously combust,' says Doll, flopping down onto a chair and gulping down some iced water, followed by a long swig of wine.

As we all get our breath back, Panos approaches Hannah with two helpings of cheesecake on blue plates, and I watch them drift off together to sit at a small table beneath a lemon tree.

'Oh, what a night,' says Judith, taking her shoes off, and rubbing her feet.

Taking our cue from Panos, the rest of us dive into the wonderful cheesecake, and a brief silence descends on the group.

'Tania, that was amazing.' I wipe my mouth with a napkin, fit to burst.

'It was. In fact, it was better than mine,' says Doll. 'Or at least as good as.' She winks.

When we think the evening is winding down a little, Helena announces she has a surprise for us. Hannah rejoins the table then, as Panos appears to have gone off somewhere.

'All okay?' I mouth to her, and she nods.

'This evening, I would like to present you with a traditional

Greek dancing show,' says Helena, and Judith claps her hands in delight.

A familiar Greek tune can be heard then, and three young men, dressed in traditional Greek costume, assemble in the middle of the flagged floor of the bar. It takes me a moment to realise that one of the young men is Panos. They lace their arms around each other, before slowly moving along to the music, as the rest of us clap along. As the music gets a little faster, Panos pulls Hannah to her feet, and is quickly followed by Yolanda, who gives a delighted '*Opa*'. As the music reaches its crescendo, we are all on our feet once more, laughing and loving life.

'That was just wonderful,' says Tania and as we all break into applause, the Greek dancers give a little bow.

'That took me back to my first holiday to Greece,' I say to Judith. 'I remember dancing like that, then being invited to smash plates.' I recall the excursion from Kavos to a mountain village restaurant, to watch a traditional Greek floor show.

'I bet you don't see any plate smashing these days,' says Doll. 'Not in a global recession.'

'It is true,' agrees Helena. 'No plate smashing, please.'

'Not that we need it. Tonight has been wonderful, without the need to smash plates.'

As the evening winds down, people are milling around and chatting to each other, sharing their life stories. I watch Helena as she proudly witnesses her mother chatting to Yolanda and Judith, laughing with them. I can't imagine what she must have gone through losing her husband so young, and of course Panos and Helena have lost their father.

We offer to help tidy away, but there's nothing to do. Helena and her mother have been silently clearing up throughout the evening, her grandmother sweeping in and out of the kitchen, the sound of plates being stacked into a dishwasher. As we are about to leave, Helena tells Judith that there is still almost seventy euros left of the money Lars placed behind the bar.

'You must keep it,' Judith insists. 'Call it a little tip, for all your hard work.'

Helena tries to protest, saying enough money has been spent in the bar this evening and perhaps she should donate it to the animal shelter, but Judith won't allow it.

'We made plenty of money at the dance evening. Put it in the till, the season will be winding down soon,' says Judith and Helena thanks her.

'What a night.' Yolanda sighs with satisfaction. 'But, please, do not tell me I have to walk home up that hill.' She groans.

Her neighbour who speaks little English talks to her in Greek and Yolanda claps her hands together. 'Thank goodness, we have the lift.'

A few minutes later, her neighbour's husband, who I remember from Tania's BBQ, arrives to collect them, so we wave them off and make our way downhill to the rescue, all of us linking arms as we walk.

'Did you have a good night?' I ask Hannah, as I fall into step with her.

'I did.' She smiles. 'And I'm happy that Panos seems to be friends with me again.'

'I knew that the minute he presented you with some cheesecake. He never offered us any. We had to help ourselves,' I tease. 'So what did you chat about? I won't mind if you tell me to shut up and stop being a nosey cow.'

'As if I would.' She turns and smiles at me. 'You have only ever given me sound advice. And actually, he told me I looked beautiful tonight,' she says.

'You always do, although I think the touch of make-up makes you look extra special this evening.'

'Thank you. Maybe I will wear it for special occasions, such as this evening. I do look good, don't I?' She stops then and gives a twirl, her blue dress spinning around her like a silk cape. 'And it isn't for Panos. It isn't for anyone other than me,' she says and I give her a little clap.

'You go, girl.' I link arms with her again and we walk on, a full moon guiding our way as it shines on the dark road beneath us. No need for our phone lights this evening.

Tania, Doll and Judith are laughing as they walk along in front of us.

'I still can't believe Yolanda made us do the hokey-cokey. It's years since I've done that.' Doll laughs.

'Count yourself lucky they didn't ask you to do some ballroom dancing,' says Judith.

'Oh, I am so glad no one did. It was so nice to just sit and enjoy myself, and watch other people dancing. Especially the Greek dancing, that was wonderful. I was quite happy to sit that out, just watching those young men.' She laughs again. 'Oh dear, I sound like a right old lush, don't I? I think it's this menopause.'

'Surely you're not old enough for that?' says Tania in surprise.

'You'd be surprised,' says Doll, smiling, but she looks tired.

When we reach the bottom of the hill, we can hear the sound of male voices as the men are just returning from their trip.

'Lars, you are back!' exclaims Judith. 'How was the fishing trip?'

'I don't think much fishing actually took place.' He grins, a little unsteady on his feet.

'I can vouch for that,' says Michael. 'It was more a crate of beer on board, and a bottle of whisky. We never actually left the harbour.' He bursts out into laughter, as do Lars and Nicos. 'So we took a taxi home. Marco walked back to his Airbnb.'

'Did you enjoy your night?' asks Lars, as he places his arm around Judith's waist and walks with her.

'Oh, Lars, it was wonderful.' They drift off together, and Tania walks off with Nicos after wishing us all a goodnight.

Michael kisses Doll on the cheek, and walks inside with me and Hannah, and I suddenly wish Marco was here. I think about having another drink, but decide it's probably best not to. I am just the right side of merry, and a hangover in the morning would be a mistake. The animals don't care how we are feeling in the morning.

Hannah heads upstairs to bed and I grab some water from the kitchen. I'm about to switch the lights off when my phone rings.

'Marco, hi.' I couldn't be more thrilled to hear from him.

'I just wanted to hear your voice,' he says, echoing my very own thoughts. 'Did you have a nice night?'

'I did. And, more importantly, so did Judith. It was just wonderful. How was your evening? Although I believe it wasn't exactly a fishing trip.'

'I know.' He laughs. 'Although, if I'm honest, I was rather pleased. I've never really been a fan of fishing. We ended up playing poker on board and sinking a few beers. It was a good night.'

'I'm glad. And I'm glad you called.'

We talk for another minute, before I make my way to bed.

'Goodnight, Beth. I will call you tomorrow,' says Marco as I end the call with a smile on my face. The evening could not have ended any better.

THIRTY-FOUR

I feel surprisingly fresh the next morning, although maybe that is down to the fact that I stayed off the ouzo, apart from the one cocktail we had before leaving. Hannah is already in the shower, and I can hear her singing. A few minutes later she emerges.

'Someone's in a good mood,' I comment as I grab my towel and head for the bathroom myself.

'I am. And I think I ought to thank you,' she says, placing her towel over an air drier.

'Thank me, what for?'

'For all your sound advice. I've seen how you interact with people. You are a natural social butterfly.'

'Do you think so?'

'I know so,' she says firmly.

I shrug off her comment, yet feel flattered all the same. 'Maybe it comes from me working with the general public.'

'I remember you saying to me once that you thought you never had a talent for anything,' says Hannah. 'Well, you were wrong. You have a talent for listening to people, and being honest with them. Not everyone can do that, no matter how many hobbies they have.'

'Thank you, Hannah.' I'm surprised to find I have to stop a tear from trickling down my cheek.

'You're welcome.'

After I shower and dress, we head down to the kitchen for some breakfast.

'So are you seeing Marco later?' Hannah asks.

'Hopefully, yes. He called to say goodnight when we returned from the bar last night. I'm sure we will talk again later.'

'Will he be staying for the wedding?' asks Hannah, which I realise is three days from now.

'He will still be here in Crete, although I don't expect Judith to invite him to the wedding.'

'Are you talking about Marco?' asks Judith, having just walked into the room.

'Yes. I was just telling Hannah that his flight home is a couple of days after the wedding.'

'Then of course he is invited! It's hardly a formal affair,' says Judith. 'It isn't as if we have to rearrange a seating plan.' She smiles. 'And the wedding cake Tania has baked would feed the whole of this village and the next.'

'That's very kind, Judith, if you're sure,' I tell her, not even sure that Marco will want to attend a wedding. Aren't weddings the very things he doesn't believe in?

Michael is on his own in the donkey area, replacing the hay bales when we stroll over.

'Morning, Michael, where is Doll?'

'She's having a lie-in; she isn't feeling too well. Bit of a hangover, I think,' he says, although I don't think Doll drank excessively last night, and walked home in a perfectly straight line. Maybe it's more a lack of sleep, as she was suffering with hot flashes quite a bit last night.

'I'm sorry to hear that,' I tell him. Now is not the time to discuss her menopausal symptoms. 'So how was the stag party?'

He unloads a load of fresh straw and places it into the feeders for the donkeys.

'It was a lot of fun. I won forty euros from Lars in a poker game, but don't tell Judith.' He taps the side of his nose. 'It's a shame we have such an early start, as I would have been right up for a trip to a nightclub,' he says, and I can't help thinking of Marco's comments about nightclubs and stag nights.

I study Michael, who is around the same age as Doll, who is currently lying in bed, probably with a menopausal migraine.

'Ah but don't forget the animals would still need your attention in the morning. They don't care if we are feeling rough. Or should that be "ruff",' I say, imitating a growling sound, and Michael laughs.

'Hangovers have never been a problem for me, I've always been an early riser. I think I'll give the whisky a miss next time, though,' he concedes.

'I believe you met my fiancé, or should I say ex-fiancé.' Gosh, it seems so strange saying that. Especially as he is actually here in Crete spending time with me.

'Marco? Yes, he seems like a nice bloke,' he says, as he carries on working. 'He was telling us all about the restaurant back home. We might pay a visit if we are ever over that way. You can't beat good Italian food.'

'Don't let the Greeks hear you say that,' I warn him and he laughs.

'I won't, but I had the best Italian meal down a little back-street in Rome. It's best to avoid the tourist areas,' he advises.

'Is that all Marco talked about?' I ask, wondering if he might have mentioned me.

'What do you think?' He places the pitchfork he has been using down, and leans on it, a smile on his face. 'He didn't say much until he had a few beers in him, but then he was telling us all how wonderful you were, and how he was attracted to you the minute he laid eyes on you in the restaurant.'

'He said that?'

Marco has never actually said that to me.

'Oh yes. He said you stood out, head and shoulders over the rest of the group of women you were with.'

I find myself being surprised and thrilled by the news.

'He talked a bit about marriage and kids then,' reveals Michael.

'He did?' I can barely take it in.

'Yes. He said he would love to have children one day. After that we just sort of chatted about life in general, before we decided to stay in dock and have a poker game,' Michael tells me. 'Lars had brought a pack of cards in case anyone was interested, which we all were. That's when the whisky came out.' He rubs the side of his head. 'Anyway, I must get on. I'll take a cup of tea to my lovely wife, and see how she is doing.'

'Ask Judith where the caffeine-free tea bags are, I'm sure she mentioned having some. If Doll has a headache, caffeine won't help.'

'Will do, I never thought about that. I might have one of those myself.'

Heading back from walking the dogs with Hannah later in the morning, we walk past Nicos and Tania's place. Tania is in the garden, deadheading some plants and tidying. She walks over to the fence when she sees us.

'Morning, ladies. How are the heads?' She looks as fresh as a daisy.

'Surprisingly okay, well, at least I am.' I glance at Hannah, who has been a little quiet this morning.

'I'm okay.' She smiles. 'But maybe I did have a little too

much wine with the food, I'm not normally a drinker,' she admits. 'It's definitely an early night for me tonight, I think.'

'Judith has told us all about the wedding cake you have baked.'

'Ooh yes, I just have to put the finishing touches to it. When it's finished, you can come and take a sneak peek if you like.'

'Sounds good. Make sure the dogs are locked up, though! We don't want a repeat of Doll's cheesecake.' I can't help smiling.

'Oh, my goodness! Can you even imagine. Don't worry, the cake will be hidden out of sight until the wedding.'

We say our goodbyes and head inside the rescue, where Doll is sitting at the kitchen table with Judith, sipping a drink.

'How are you feeling?' I ask Doll as Hannah nips upstairs to sort out some of her washing.

'Not too bad now, thanks to Judith's TLC.' She points to a box of painkillers on the table and lifts her mug of tea. 'I wouldn't mind, but I don't even think I went over the top with the wine last night.'

'Maybe it's hormonal,' I suggest, thinking about our chat last night.

'Possibly. Or maybe I am just well and truly burnt out.' She sighs.

'Do you think so?' Judith gestures for me to sit down and pours me some tea from the pot.

'I do. The touring can be a little punishing, and Michael will dance at every given opportunity, so we never truly switch off. Oh, I don't mean the show at the restaurant the other night.' She turns to Judith. 'That was a lot of fun, and I'm thrilled at the amount it made for the rescue. But Michael thinks he's half his age sometimes.'

'I thought you couldn't bear the thought of retirement?' I say, thinking about one of her earlier conversations.

'Maybe I'm in denial.' She shrugs. 'No one wants to think they are past it.'

'Past it at fifty! God help me then.' Judith laughs.

'Sorry, I meant in their working life. Dancing is all I've ever known.'

'You're lucky to possess such a talent, but maybe just scale back a bit? I'm not surprised you're exhausted from touring Europe. Perhaps it's time to book a long break in the sun, and just chill. Even though it's gorgeous here, we still have to work,' I remind her.

'Of course, you're right. I wanted to be in the forest, and as I adore dogs, it seemed perfect coming over here. And I am loving it.' She reaches over and squeezes Judith's hand. 'I'm just tired, I'll be fine,' she says, her smile firmly back in place.

'Today, I insist you have the day off,' says Judith kindly. 'We all get sick from time to time, and a ton of volunteers are arriving later this afternoon to walk the rest of the dogs. The other chores are manageable between the rest of us. Go back to bed, read a book if you like. I have some, as does Hannah.'

'Gosh, I can't remember the last time I read a book,' Doll admits. 'I might just go and have another hour upstairs until this headache really shifts. Thanks, Judith. And you, Beth.'

'Take your time,' says Judith kindly.

She heads upstairs then I take our cups to the sink to wash.

'Three days until the wedding, Judith, are you all set?' I ask as she dries the cups with a tea towel, before placing them in a cupboard.

'Oh, I am. I feel so lucky to have found Lars, he is such a wonderful man. And Doll is such a lovely woman. I do wonder why they seem to be spending so much time together. Fancy being jealous at my age.' She shakes her head.

'You can be jealous at any age, I suppose, although I am absolutely sure you have nothing to worry about.'

'I know that, it's just me being silly. Pre-wedding nerves, maybe.'

'But not doubts?'

'No, definitely not doubts.' She smiles. 'I am happier than I have been in a long time. I feel so blessed to have found love twice.'

Judith's comment makes me think about my own feelings. The thrill of seeing Marco and spending the night with him made me feel happier than I have in a long time too. Surely there will never be anyone else who can make me feel like that. I still don't know where he is at with marriage and future plans, but with what Michael said about last night, it sounds like Marco has given it some thought. And I'm not sure I want marriage to come between us now anyway. We are lucky to have found each other, I realise that now. But I do need to know where we stand.

I'm having a chat with Eric the moody donkey, who seems happy to be fussed over today, and spends a while nudging my hand with his head, and braying contentedly when I stroke him. Just as I start scratching behind his ears, a text arrives on my phone. As I read it, Eric saunters off back towards his stall; clearly, he prefers undivided attention.

Morning, beautiful, are you free later? Marco xx

I tap out a reply, and he tells me he will collect me at six thirty. Already I can't wait.

THIRTY-FIVE

'Have you ever been to that mountain village not far from the monastery?'

Marco has collected me just after six, before the sun begins to set.

'I haven't. At least I don't think so. What's it called?'

'I can't remember the exact name now, but I have been reading up on it. Apparently, the view of the sunset is second to none up there, from a rooftop in a particular restaurant. I've booked us a table.'

'That sounds lovely.' I also think it sounds very romantic.

'It's around a half an hour's drive from here, so buckle up.'

We are sitting in a four-by-four and I think of the contrasting style of Artemis's sleek BMW. Marco has a Jeep back home that he loves to nip around town in, and to the food suppliers for the restaurant.

'Tell me all about Judith's hen do,' he asks as we drive. 'Did you have a good time?'

When I tell him about us all dancing the hokey-cokey at Yolanda's request, he laughs loudly. Gosh, I've missed that easy, infectious laugh. We always laughed at things, sometimes things that other people never found amusing. It's good to know that we can still laugh together now.

'And then Helena at the bar surprised us all by introducing a trio of Greek dancers in full costume, they were brilliant. There was no plate smashing, though, a sign of the economic crisis apparently. We had a brilliant evening.'

'Sounds a lot livelier than our evening. I would have been up for a bit of that Greek dancing.' He grins. 'Don't get me wrong, I was chuffed to be invited along by Nicos. I'd have been sitting alone in my room, pining for you otherwise.' He turns and smiles at me and a warm feeling floods through me.

'Really?'

'Of course really. I haven't been able to stop thinking about the other night.' He reaches over and squeezes my leg, and there go those butterflies again.

'I still can't believe you came all the way here,' I say as we descend the mountain road as a soft shaft of yellow sunlight filters through the leaves and bathes the road in a golden glow. 'I'll be home next week.'

'Ah, but I didn't know that. I bumped into Jess in town and asked after you, as I hadn't seen you around. She told me you had gone to Greece, but was very vague about when you were coming back.'

'Did you think I had decided not to come home?'

I realise Jess would have been loyally trying to protect my feelings, as she knew I was coming out here to try and get over him.

'I wasn't sure.' He shrugs. 'But when my mother said that the deputy manager at the supermarket said she would be in the role "indefinitely", I did wonder if you were coming back.'

'She said that?'

I'm not sure why she would say that, when she knows for certain I will be back at work later next week.

'Why would that prompt you to visit, though?' I need to know what's changed, but I can't bring myself to ask so directly.

'I'm hoping I can explain. Maybe I can do that over dinner.'

At the foot of the hills, we head onto the highway, before turning off and following a sign for a village. For a moment, I almost think we are heading to the restaurant I went to with Artemis near the monastery, but we drive on past that sign before following another one, that shows the name of the village.

'You look really lovely, by the way,' says Marco as we climb higher. 'I used to like it when we got dressed up and ready for an evening out back home, a cheeky glass of wine before we hit the pub,' Marco reminds me.

'With you singing at the top of your voice to noughties floor fillers. It's a wonder we never got kicked out of our apartment.'

'Hey, my voice isn't that bad.' He laughs.

I remember those evenings. Sometimes, we would go out alone; other times we would meet some friends and go for dinner. Occasionally, it would be at his family restaurant when he was working, and we would hang around drinking until after midnight when the other diners had long gone, before walking home to our apartment. Good times.

'You scrub up well too.' I return his compliment. Marco looks as though he has really made an effort this evening, with a navy suit and a crisp white shirt underneath. I'm glad I decided to wear one of the pretty floral dresses I brought with me, and some nice earrings.

When we pull into the centre of the village, I'm stunned by how pretty it is. A single cobbled street is flanked by several bars and restaurants, a few gift shops nestled between them. A wooden handcart is displaying locally produced goods such as honey, wine and olive oil, with sprigs of lavender tucked in between the produce.

'This place is gorgeous,' I comment as we walk past a stone

fountain at the centre of the village. People are sitting on benches surrounding it, beneath fig trees, eating ice creams and chatting.

'It is, isn't it?' agrees Marco. 'Even nicer than it looked on Google Images,' he says, smiling to himself, and I can imagine him searching through the comments on Tripadvisor too, leaving nothing to chance.

We walk up an incline in the road, and at the end find a pretty restaurant with flowers threaded through its open roof beams, which are painted white. The wood beams are painted in a traditional blue shade. A friendly waiter informs us that it is two for one cocktail hour, as he escorts us to our table, overlooking the valley below.

'That's good to hear. And the view is pretty amazing too.'

I take in the panoramic view of the valley spread out below, with white houses clinging to the hillside, the sound of a church bell gently ringing on the hour. I can just about make out a strip of sea in the distance.

I turn my gaze to the orange sun that is very slowly beginning its descent behind a mountain as a waiter returns with our cocktails.

'Just look at that.' I sigh. 'You were right about having a beautiful view from here.' I take a sip of my cocktail, and drink it all in. Marco has probably chosen the most romantic location there is, but why? I can't believe I haven't come right out and asked Marco what he thinks has changed between us. Am I afraid to ask him? Is there any way I could go back to being part of a couple, knowing that marriage is never going to happen?

The restaurant is filling up now, and the sound of chatter is ringing around the restaurant. A waitress is lighting candles in the middle of tables, as a string of fairy lights spring into life across the blue painted restaurant walls that are adorned with black and white pictures of the village.

'I'm glad you like it.' He takes a sip of his cocktail, and looks at me with his piercing blue eyes. 'I'm so glad you agreed to come out with me again, Beth. I've really missed you,' he says quietly. 'I've been filling my time with extra hours at the restaurant, so that I could sleep better in the evening,' he reveals. I don't tell him that I frequently indulged in a large glass of wine to send me off to sleep.

'Well, I couldn't have let you come all this way, and not go out with you, could I?'

'You could have, but that might have been a bit mean.' He pulls a sad face.

We place our food order before sipping our cocktails and, as we chat, it feels as though we have never been apart. I think about Marco's comment earlier, when he said maybe his intentions would become clearer tonight, and I'm about to remind him of this, when our food arrives.

We opted for sharing a meze board, and the food, when it is placed down in front of us, looks incredible. Chicken skewers, roasted potatoes and red peppers sit alongside chunks of salty halloumi cheese and a selection of creamy dips. It is accompanied by warm pitta breads, and a fresh Greek salad dotted with olives.

'This looks divine,' I say, grabbing a chicken skewer that has been marinated in herbs, and take a bite of the soft, warm chicken. I barely know what to eat next, but manage to have a sample of just about everything.

'That was amazing,' says Marco sitting back. 'Do you fancy a dessert?'

'You have to be kidding. Although, I did spot an ice-cream vendor on the village street, maybe we could have one of those later? It won't be Italian gelato, though, I'm afraid.'

'That's okay, although I think I will have a try of the dessert here. I spied a waiter taking one to the next table, it looked amazing.'

'You are going to have two desserts?'

'Why not? I am Italian, I like to eat.' He winks. 'In the meantime, just look at that.'

Marco points to the sunset; the orange sun looks almost double in size and seems close enough to touch.

'Oh wow, that is just beautiful.' Marco was right about it being a well-known place to see the sunset and people are snapping away with their phones and cameras. We position our chairs in front of the view, and take a selfie, to capture this moment forever.

'Not quite as beautiful as you.' Marco reaches across the table and takes my hand in his, and kisses it. Everything has been just about perfect this evening, the setting, the food, and most certainly the company.

In the end, neither of us have a dessert and instead enjoy a creamy cappuccino, sipping it as we watch the sun slowly disappear behind a mountain.

'Would you like to go for a walk now?' asks Marco, as he settles the bill.

'I think I need to, or I might be in danger of falling into a food coma.'

The village street is brightly lit now, a hive of activity as tourists browse the gift shops and make purchases from the handcart, the owner handing out goods in brown paper bags. Tables outside restaurants are busy with diners and gentle music can be heard coming from a passing bar.

'Let's go somewhere a little quieter,' says Marco, as we take a left turn away from the main street and follow a path slightly uphill. Presently, we come across a stone ruin that looks as though it may once have been a chapel, with the telltale crumbling remnants of a bell arch. It overlooks a lake, which is silent and dark apart from the lights coming from a few distant houses on the hills, reflected in its surface.

'This is far nicer than I imagined. In fact, it's perfect,' he says, taking in his surroundings.

'Perfect for what?' I ask, feeling a sudden rush of anticipation.

'To explain why I came out here, of course. I'm surprised you haven't asked, to be honest.'

I smile and shrug. 'I didn't want to push, but of course I have thought about nothing else.'

'I came to see you because I missed you. I didn't know when you would be home, and maybe I foolishly thought seeing each other regularly around town might spark something between us once more. Not that the spark between us ever disappeared. Well, not for me at least.'

'Nor me. Oh, Marco, I've missed you too and maybe I shouldn't have been so keen to marry, I—'

Marco silences me then with a thrilling kiss and when we finally pull apart, he gets down on one knee in front of me.

'Marco, what are you doing?' I can feel my heart thumping through my chest.

'Making myself clear. Beth Wilson, you are the love of my life and someone I simply can't be without.' He hesitates for a second, as he takes a deep breath. 'Will you marry me?'

He's done it. He has proposed properly, after me wanting him to for so long. Yet I am almost too stunned to speak.

'But... you don't believe in marriage.'

'Maybe not as much as you *do* believe in it. But if it means keeping you in my life, then I am happy to be married. I would be happy to do anything you asked of me.'

'Anything?'

'Of course.'

'Even shave your head?'

'Okay, maybe not anything.' He touches his hair, and I burst out laughing. 'But I love you, Beth. I never stopped. So what do you think?'

'Well, I know it's what I want, but is it really what you want? I have to be certain.'

'It is,' he says softly, taking my hands in his.

'Oh, Marco, I'm not sure.' I can hear the words coming out of my mouth, but can hardly believe I am saying them.

'What are you saying?' His face falls in confusion.

'Why the sudden change of heart?' I ask, searching his eyes.

'Because I can't lose you again. My heart would not take it.' He places his hand over his heart. 'Being apart made me realise how much I love you. I can't bear the thought of spending my life without you. *Ti amerò per sempre.*'

He has just told me that he will love me forever. Marco knows I love it when he speaks to me in Italian.

'Can we walk?' I ask.

'Of course,' he says, a perplexed look on his face.

Walking on, a dozen thoughts fill my mind. If Marco wants to get married, surely that is everything I wanted, isn't it? Didn't we miss each other dreadfully when we were apart? And hasn't Marco just told me that he can't live without me?

We come across a bench overlooking the valley, and I invite Marco to sit down.

Sitting side by side, we stare silently ahead of us. A moped drives by then, its harsh drone puncturing the stillness of the evening. What am I afraid of? I wonder. I realise this moment may never happen again. Maybe having a little distance between us has convinced Marco that he really wants us to be together forever. Would he have come all this way to see me if he didn't truly love me? He could have waited until I returned home, surely?

I look at Marco's beautiful profile in the moonlight.

'So what now?' he asks, heavy disappointment in his voice.

'I never actually said no to your proposal.'

He turns to face me. 'What?'

'I'm just saying, it wasn't an outright no. I just said I wasn't sure.' I smile at him and his face breaks into a grin.

'Shall I ask you again?' he asks, a look of hope and excitement in his eyes.

'If you like.'

Down on one knee, he proposes to me for the second time and this time there are no doubts. Marco came here to find me. I love him with all my heart. Tears are streaming down my face, as I give him my answer.

'Yes!' I scream at the top of my voice, just as a couple walk past and glance over, probably wondering what is going on in the darkness. Marco slides a ring on my finger then, and I could literally burst with happiness.

'We're engaged,' I call over, wiggling my left hand, and they warmly congratulate us before walking on.

The ring is stunning. It's a vintage-looking gold band with a large emerald at the centre.

'Marco, it's beautiful, But I already have a ring back home,' I remind him.

'But this one is special,' he insists. 'It belonged to my *nonna*. Remember when we rowed and you asked me why I bought you a ring if I didn't want to get married?'

'Of course I remember. It was the worst day of my life when I realised we were going to part,' I tell him honestly.

'Well, perhaps you were right. Maybe I did buy a ring because I thought it was the expected thing to do after three years together. But this time it's different. I mean this, with all my heart. My mother insisted I give this to you. She has always loved you.'

'And I loved her too, and your father, I still do.' I almost choke back tears. 'I loved being part of a family. But, most of all, I never stopped loving you.'

Marco takes me in his arms and kisses me then, and later when we stand looking at the lake, arms wrapped around each other with the reflection of the emerging moon casting white ripples across it, I literally feel as though I am standing on top of the world.

A shaft of sunlight streams into the bedroom, as Marco pushes open the curtains.

'Coffee in bed once more, you are spoiling me.' Marco places coffee and a Danish pastry onto the bedside table.

'You are worth it.' He walks and over and kisses me lightly on the lips.

'Well, if this is a sign of how it's going to be when we are married, I like it.' I stretch my arms over my head and yawn.

'Don't get too used to it.' He winks and I tell him there is still time to change my mind and he attempts to steal my pastry.

'Hey, don't you dare, I'm ravenous.' I slap his hand away.

'I'm not surprised after last night,' he says, and despite our history, I find myself almost blushing.

Marco had informed Judith that I would be staying out overnight and she'd wished him the best of luck, when he told her about his proposal plans. I seem to have made nights away a bit of a habit, but I don't regret this stay at all.

I take a sip of the rich, dark coffee before stretching out my hand and admiring my new engagement ring from Marco. I feel so honoured to be wearing his grandmother's ring, especially with the blessing of his parents, and feel like the luckiest girl in the world.

THIRTY-SIX

The day of the wedding has finally arrived and we were all up early getting the chores done around the rescue, before the ceremony this afternoon at three o'clock.

'Hi, guys, the big day is here! How are you feeling, Judith?' asks Monica from the holiday home, who has swept in with her hairdressing and make-up bag.

'Stupidly nervous,' admits Judith, as she fiddles with a bracelet on her wrist. 'And where on earth has Lars disappeared to now?' She shakes her head in frustration. 'And Doll seems to have wandered off somewhere too, as if there isn't enough to be done around here,' she says, mildly frustrated.

'Don't worry, everything is under control here,' I say brightly. 'And perhaps she is over the road giving Tania a hand. I did see them chatting earlier,' I tell her, which is partly true, as we chatted for a moment over the fence earlier when walking the dogs.

'Oh right, maybe,' she says, sounding a tiny bit unconvinced.

I assume Lars is having a last-minute practice of the waltz somewhere, although he is cutting things a bit fine and could probably have done with having his final dance rehearsal yesterday.

'What you need is a glass of this,' says Monica, waving a bottle of champagne. 'Girls, where are the glasses?' she asks me and Hannah.

'Oh, go on then, but just a small one.' Judith smiles.

She pops the cork of the bottle, just as Doll and Tania enter the kitchen, and shares it out, handing us each a glass that we clink together.

'Here's to you and Lars, Judith. I'm sure I speak on behalf of us all when I say I wish you all the best for a happy and healthy future,' says Tania.

'Thank you, darling, and congratulations on your news, Beth.' She smiles and nods to me.

Monica rushes to congratulate me and admire the stunning engagement ring I am wearing.

'What a romantic story!' she says when I fill her in. 'He came all this way to propose?' She takes a sip of champagne. 'That's amazing! When is the wedding?'

'No idea, to be fair. We haven't really discussed it yet. Anyway, today isn't about me,' I say firmly, getting back to the matter in hand of preparing for Judith's wedding.

'Of course.' She smiles, topping up her drink before diving into her bag and pulling out a make-up pouch.

We leave her to it and head off to shower and get ourselves ready. Marco will be meeting us here and I can hardly wait to see him. Lars has been despatched to Tania's house, and, in line with tradition, will meet Judith at the church later. Judith was thrilled to discover that Lars had arranged to have the ceremony at the flagged terrace at the foot of the church. There's a little-known road which he found out about, next to the remembrance tree. She shed a tear when she told me about it one evening, explaining that there was a remembrance ribbon for Ray on the tree. She said it felt like he would be watching over

her, and somehow giving his blessing and I told her I was
certain that he would be.

An hour later, we all reappear in the kitchen, and give a
collective gasp when we see Judith, who looks absolutely stunning. Her hair is pinned up and dotted with tiny pearls, soft
tendrils curling around her face. Monica has made up her face
up beautifully, using a soft grey on her eyelids that brings out
the colour of her eyes, and a soft peach lipstick.

'Oh, Judith, you look beautiful.' She looks radiant, and ten
years younger.

Her outfit looks amazing too, the fitted dress showing off her
slender figure, set off with some low-heeled ivory satin
slingbacks.

'Monica, you have done a fantastic job,' says Tania. 'I might
book you for my own big day. Not that we are planning a
wedding any time soon,' Tania adds quickly, when she sees the
surprised look on Judith's face.

'Lars is a lucky man. Although I have to say he scrubs up
rather well too, as does Michael.' I saw them both earlier,
making their way across to Tania's, where they will no doubt be
having a little drink of something with Nicos.

'Thank you. You all look beautiful too,' says Judith,
admiring our outfits; her earlier nerves thankfully seem to have
disappeared. Hannah is wearing a little make-up again today,
her sparkling green eyes matching the blouse she has paired
with a pair of wide-legged white trousers. Doll and I are both
wearing summer dresses accessorised with jewellery. Doll's is a
shortish, pink linen shift, mine a knee-length, vintage-style floral
dress.

Monica heads off then to get herself ready, saying she will
meet us at the church, and Tania also disappears to put the
finishing touches to the party at her home later.

'Gosh, I don't want to move in case I spoil anything,' says
Judith as we sit chatting. The rest of us have another small glass

of champagne, as another bottle was sitting in the fridge, but Judith declines, saying a drink might spoil her lipstick.

'I can fetch you a straw if you like,' I offer.

'No, really.' She laughs. 'I'm quite happy sitting here chatting to you all for a while, you are doing a good job of keeping the nerves at bay.'

Ten minutes later, the doorbell rings, and I head outside and take delivery of a beautiful bouquet of cream and peach flowers.

'The flowers, of course! My goodness, I almost forgot about them. Is the delivery driver still there?' she asks, looking a little worried. 'The men are across the road. I hope they have their buttonholes.'

I dash outside after the driver, who tells me the men do indeed have their buttonhole flowers, as he had been over there before coming to us.

'Are you okay?' I ask Judith, who is constantly glancing at her watch.

'What? Oh yes, it's just that I am expecting a couple of visitors,' she tells me. 'I have been trying to keep it a surprise from Tania.'

'That sounds intriguing.'

'She was so disappointed that her mum and dad, my sister and her husband, couldn't come because her dad has broken his leg in a cycling accident. So to cheer her up I invited a couple of the previous volunteers from the summer. Tania was particularly close to them, especially Wes and Liz, and I was thrilled when they told me they would come over for the wedding. Chloe, another of the volunteers, couldn't make it sadly, but says she will call later.'

The doorbell rings again then, and Judith dashes to open it. It's another delivery.

'Who can this be from?' She tears open the cardboard box, which reveals a bottle of champagne sitting on some straw in a wooden crate, with a small box of fancy-looking Belgian chocolates.

'Oh, it's from Chloe, how thoughtful,' she says, turning over a card and reading it. 'Gosh, we were just talking about her. I must send her a thank you message,' she says, reaching for her phone.

Just then, the doorbell rings, and as Judith has just sat down, I answer it. When I open the front door, Marco is standing there.

'Marco, come in. Judith thought you might have been some surprise wedding guests.'

'Sorry to disappoint.' He kisses me on the cheek. 'And you look stunning,' he says, looking me up and down.

'You could never disappoint.' He looks and smells delightful, wearing the blue suit he wore the other night with a pale lemon shirt. I still can't believe we are engaged. And properly this time.

He walks into the kitchen, and I feel proud to introduce him as my fiancé. A few seconds later, the doorbell rings once more, and this time Judith accompanies me to answer it. When she opens it, she almost squeals with excitement at the sight of the two people standing outside.

'You made it!'

'Just about,' says the good-looking guy, before saying hi to me, then crushing Judith in an embrace. 'And you look fantastic.'

'Watch the hair,' she says, stepping back slightly and smiling.

'We would have been here earlier, had someone not booked the wrong name for the taxi at the airport.' He rolls his eyes at Liz.

'It wasn't exactly my fault,' she protests, before looking up at the ceiling innocently. 'Okay, yes, maybe it was.' She breaks out into laughter. 'But we are here now! So let's not worry about that. Judith is getting married!' She hugs her then, before we head inside and everyone is introduced and offered a drink. I can already tell that the pretty dark-haired Liz is a bundle of energy and fun.

Wes, handsome and well-dressed, has a southern American drawl. He and Liz have the sort of banter that might take place between a brother or sister, or a couple of lifelong friends, so I was surprised to discover that they only met in the summer when they volunteered here together.

'I can't wait to see Tania's face when she sees you!' says Judith, before she pours her guests a glass of champagne. Liz glugs hers down and accepts a second glass, as Wes sips his slowly.

'I can't believe you never told Tania we were coming,' says Liz. 'How did you manage to keep it a secret?'

'At times I almost slipped up,' admits Judith. 'But I know you all intended to meet up, and what better occasion than a wedding?'

'Oh completely. I love a wedding,' says Liz, before adding, 'For other people.'

'Are you still with Frank?' Judith enquires.

'I am and we're very happy together.' She smiles. 'I just don't necessarily believe in marriage. Sorry, that was a daft thing to say as I'm here for your wedding.' She pulls a face.

It seems Marco wasn't the only person to have thought that way and I wonder whether Liz will think differently one day.

We chat together easily, the atmosphere happy and relaxed. Michael has nipped back for a minute for his cigars, and is introduced to Wes and Liz. He's about to tell them all about his dance achievements, when I see Doll nudge him gently, and tell him to save it until later as it's Judith's wedding day.

'And remember, not a word to Tania,' Judith warns Michael, as he heads back across to her house.

Soon enough, it's time to leave for the church, just a short drive uphill. Judith's car has been decorated with peach and cream ribbons and she gives a little gasp when she sees it.

'Who's driving?' she asks and Wes steps forward.

'It makes sense if I do, I've barely had a drink,' he offers. 'I'll wear my sunglasses so Tania won't recognise me when we first pull up.'

'I never thought about that,' says Liz, and Wes says she can hide in the back with a blanket over her head if she likes, and she thumps him on the arm. The rest of us follow behind in the hire car, and literally a minute or two later, we arrive at the church.

A table has been set at the front of the church with a floral display and a register to be signed, next to the remembrance tree. The priest is standing waiting, dressed in a purple gown.

Several rows of chairs from the bar have been transformed with ribbons and small sprigs of wild flowers tied to them, the handiwork of Helena. Marco and I find seats next to each other, but after being seated for only a few moments, the priest invites us all to stand.

I glance around at the assembled group, before my eyes turn to Lars, who is standing next to the priest in a cream suit, and when Tania walks Judith down the path to join him, I can feel a lump in my throat.

The stunning church, rising high, looks over the ceremony, and when the branches of the remembrance tree waft gently in the wind, the moment Judith and Lars exchange vows, I think maybe Ray is giving his blessing to their union.

Marco curls his hands around mine and smiles when the wedding vows are over, and when Judith hurls her bouquet over her shoulder and I find myself clutching it, I look at Marco and laugh.

Tania looks around then, taking in the guests and her mouth falls open when she spots Wes and Liz.

'I don't believe it!' She races over and squeezes them both, before she is joined by Nicos, who shakes their hands warmly.

'Just look at that.' I almost have to wipe a teardrop from my eye as I take in the scene. Panos is chatting to Hannah and Lars and Judith look so in love, as their guests warmly congratulate them.

'That will be us one day,' says Marco, joining me for the drive back down the hill. 'Hopefully not too far in the future.' He kisses me on the lips and I feel a surge of happiness.

Back at Tania's house, Tania and Nicos have arrived first to welcome everyone to the party and soon everyone is filtering through the gate. The house looks resplendent, with a gorgeous balloon arch leading onto the large patio, and swathes of white and yellow curtains are stretched across the patio, the handiwork of Yolanda and Helena, as well as her mother, I am told. There are fresh blooms of yellow flowers dotted around the garden and in pots and, beneath a small marquee that has been erected, a banner has the word '*Syncharitiria*' written across it, which means 'Congratulations' in Greek.

'I really can't believe people have gone to so much trouble,' says Judith. 'This all looks wonderful, although I'm not sure I can take any more surprises.'

'There may be one more.' Lars smiles, not giving anything away.

Inside the marquee, a long table is groaning with hot and cold food, and the most beautiful wedding cake stands taking centre stage. As we file inside, Tania makes sure everyone has something to drink before she taps a glass with a spoon and gains everyone's attention.

'Thank you so much, everyone, for coming. Of course, huge congratulations to my aunt Judith and my new uncle Lars,' she says, and everyone cheers. 'Let's raise a glass to them both and wish them a happy life together for many more years.'

'I hope there will be many more, we're getting on a bit,' says Judith and the crowd laugh.

'So without further ado, please find a seat, grab some food and have a good time,' says Tania.

It all feels so wonderfully relaxed, with no table settings or formalities, just people eating and drinking and getting to know each other. It's exactly the kind of wedding I would like for me and Marco.

We get chatting to Liz and Wes, and they tell us all about the summer they spent here.

'Gosh, that all sounds quite eventful,' I say, when they tell us about the fire and one of the volunteers called Chloe, who met a Frenchman and went off sailing with him. And, of course, it's where Tania met Nicos and now lives here with him.

'It was life-changing for me being here,' Wes reveals. 'It made me decide what I wanted to do with my life, and Tania helped me figure it out too, she's really cool.'

'She is,' I agree.

'So, what do you do?' asks Marco, taking a sip of beer from a bottle.

'I'm a musician. I went back to music college last month, and have regular gigs in a nearby town, I sing and play the guitar.'

'Well, good luck to you.' Marco clinks his beer bottle against Wes's. 'I can't think of anything worse than doing a job you have no interest in.'

'So what's your line of work?' Wes asks Marco and he tells him all about the family restaurant.

'Your family own an Italian restaurant?' Liz's eyes widen. 'Italian food is my absolute favourite. Maybe you could give me a couple of recipes?'

'I'm afraid they are family secrets. If I told you, I would have to kill you,' says Marco, narrowing his eyes.

'It's a good job I like my local Italian pizza takeaway then.' She jokingly puts her nose in the air and Marco laughs.

'Maybe this place has an effect on people,' says Marco. 'I know exactly what I want from life now too,' he says, turning to me.

'Congratulations! I love, love, LOVE your engagement ring,' says Liz when we tell her we are engaged to be married.

'Thank you. It was Marco's grandmother's ring.'

People change places and swap stories, villagers mingling with the volunteers and everyone is having a wonderful time.

Music is gently playing and Lars suddenly heads into the middle of the small wooden dance floor.

'And now, ladies and gentlemen, I would just like to sincerely thank every one of you for joining us on our special day. It means so much that you are all here with us. Thank you also for all of your hard work and help to make this such a memorable day. Judith and I will never forget it.

'And now I would like to start the dancing by having the first dance with my beautiful wife.' He nods towards Hannah, who is obviously in charge of music, as just then the sound of a Viennese waltz can be heard.

The sound of applause rings around the room as Judith joins Lars on the dance floor with a look of complete shock on her face.

'May I?'

Lars takes her in his arms, and they glide around the small wooden floor, Lars straight-backed and dancing like a profes-sional. Tania, who is sitting next to me now, clasps her hands together with tears in her eyes, as she records the special moment on her phone.

'You're not a bad teacher,' I hear Michael say to Doll as the newly married couple walk off the dance floor to thunderous applause.

'You taught Lars how to dance?' says Liz. 'So are you a dance teacher then?'

Michael takes no time in telling Liz and Wes all about their dance prowess and Liz's eyes light up.

'Oh, Latin American dance is my absolute favourite. I'll be up for a dance later, if you are,' she tells a delighted-looking Michael. 'I've been going to Zumba classes for ages.'

'It would be my pleasure.' Michael beams.

Yolanda is the first on the dance floor after the couple's first dance and soon everyone else joins her. It's a delight to watch Helena's mother and grandmother going for it on the dance floor, dancing to some traditional Greek music, throwing their head back and laughing.

'The red shoes have had two outings,' Yolanda says to Tania when she finally takes a breath.

'Make sure you look after them. Judith's seventieth birthday is approaching,' she tells Yolanda, who looks visibly delighted.

Just then, the music changes from Greek music to English. A jaunty Beatles number is recognised by almost everybody, and soon the small dance floor is filled, ties are loosened and everyone is having a whale of a time.

'What have you done with the dogs?' I ask Tania as we graze on some delicious food from the buffet table. The glorious cake at the centre is decorated beautifully, with pink and white icing, and adorned with delicate roses. Having sampled Tania's cakes, I can imagine it tastes every bit as good as it looks.

'They are in the stables,' she tells me, as I take a bite of a slice of *spanakopita* I was told Yolanda had made. 'They had a good run around the rear garden early this morning and are now happily devouring a huge lamb bone each, leftover from some of the lamb dishes I have cooked. Could you imagine them being let loose?' She giggles.

'I know. I bet there wouldn't be much left of this buffet

table,' I say. 'Especially with Smudge,' we both say at exactly the same time, and we crease up with laughter.

Judith and Lars join us then, Judith still hardly able to believe how Lars danced.

'I'm completely thrilled.' She turns to Lars with a huge smile on her face. 'I can't believe you learned how to dance, just for me. You could have knocked me down with a feather. I'm looking forward to many more dances together now, I hope you realise that.'

'I can hardly wait,' Lars replies with a smile, kissing her on the cheek.

'Your dancing was absolutely beautiful.' I turn to them both and Lars thanks me, before Michael steals him away for a whisky.

'I still can't believe it. And I must go and thank Doll properly for teaching Lars to dance. I'm afraid I was a little suspicious of the amount of time they spent together,' she confesses to me and Tania.

'I can see how it might have looked,' I admit. 'But it's obvious Lars only has eyes for you.'

I see Judith chatting to Doll, who smiles and nods her head. She approaches Michael and says something to him and his face visibly lights up, as they head off out of the marquee.

Around twenty minutes later, Judith takes centre stage and addresses the guests.

'Some of you may know, others may not, but I would like to tell you that we are in the company of world-class dancing champions today,' she says, and there is a an audible 'ooh' around the room.

'In fact, I had no idea one of the dancers has been kindly training Lars to dance a waltz at our wedding,' she continues. 'It was the best wedding gift I could have received. And now, they have kindly agreed to dance for all of us,' she tells the crowd, and they respond with a loud cheer.

A few bars of a tune can be heard, and Doll and Michael sashay onto the dance floor, in full dance outfits that they had clearly sloped off to change into.

They put on another dazzling dance display, and everyone is on their feet clapping, thrilled with the unexpected floor show. Hannah and Panos are standing side by side, as Hannah snaps away with her camera phone, something she has been doing throughout the day, I've noticed.

They go through several dance routines, and when the thrilling display comes to an end, they join us for a drink.

'THAT was something else,' says Liz. 'And maybe I won't dance with you after all. I would be a huge disappointment,' she says to Michael.

'Nonsense. Let me have a breather, and we will dance that Zumba,' he offers.

'Oh good,' says Doll, flopping down onto a chair with a drink Tania has placed into her hands. 'I don't think I have another dance in me.'

'Thank you so much, Doll. You have turned a simple wedding into a day to remember,' says Judith.

'You didn't need us for that,' she says kindly. 'You are surrounded by those you love. You are lucky to have such wonderful people in your life.'

'We are indeed, aren't we?' says Judith, glancing around, as Lars covers her hand with his.

THIRTY-SEVEN

As the day moves into early evening, a few of the volunteers, including myself, head across the road and give the dogs their second feed, and make sure everything is okay. When we head back, things have quietened down on the dance floor, and Tania requests Judith and Lars make their way to the buffet table to cut the cake.

Once more, Hannah is in the background taking photos as the couple cut into the enormous cake. Tania places generous slices onto paper plates that are immediately passed around for the guests to enjoy.

'This is amazing,' says Marco, forking a huge piece of cake into his mouth. 'Maybe you ought to make our wedding cake.' He turns to me and winks. The cake is loaded with fruit, and so moist it tastes nicer than any wedding cake I have ever tasted.

After a quiet spell, more dancing ensues and the sound of 'Opa' can be heard coming from Yolanda and her village friends, and makes me smile when I think of dancing the hokey-cokey at the hen party. Eventually, as the evening draws on, the lively music gives way to some slow songs, as some of the older village residents filter off, crushing Judith and Lars in warm embraces as they leave.

Hannah and Panos head to the dance floor for a slow number, and when Panos circles his arms around Hannah's waist, I can't stop myself from smiling.

'Fancy a dance then?' Marco asks, already leading me to the floor.

As we dance, he draws me to him and nuzzles my neck before pulling me even closer to him and it feels just wonderful.

Eventually, most of the village have left, and things are cleared away in the marquee, which will be collected by a friend of Nicos's tomorrow.

Outside, there are several of us sitting around a table on the front porch, grazing on the last of the buffet, and chatting. I comment on Liz's gorgeous shoes that she tells me she customised herself.

'Tania persuaded me to go to college and study design and dressmaking, and it is the best thing I have ever done,' she tells me. 'It's actually at the college where my boyfriend teaches art. I met him here, though.'

'That's it, I think we need to rename this place Love Island,' I say and the others laugh.

'I've been dying for a cuppa all day,' says Judith as she sips some tea, before slipping her shoes off and rubbing her feet. Her carefully pinned-up hair is coming loose a little, so she feels for the tiny clips and lets it all loose. 'Ooh, that's better. Gosh, I've had such a wonderful time, although I'm wondering whether we ought to have got a photographer to record the day a little more, although I know you took some photos,' she says, turning to Tania.

'There was no need,' says Hannah, waving her phone. 'I recorded the wedding ceremony on here, and I have been taking photos all day. I have a top of the range phone with a brilliant camera installed. I'll email all the pictures to you. Call it a little wedding present.'

'Oh, Hannah, you absolute darling.' She reaches over and kisses Hannah on the cheek. Hannah gives the widest smile and Panos looks at her in admiration.

Doll and Michael have just returned from the rescue, having changed once more, this time into tops and sweatpants, and report to Judith that everything is okay.

We chat, drink and eat when suddenly Wes asks Judith if she still has a guitar at the rescue.

'I do. Why do you ask?'

'I thought you might like me to round off the evening with a song,' he offers, and Judith looks thrilled.

'Wes, really? How wonderful.'

'I'll go and get my earplugs then,' teases Liz.

Lars offers to go over and retrieve the guitar, and when he returns, Nicos has lit a fire pit, and pulled some chairs around it in a circle.

'Do you have any special requests?' Wes asks Judith, as he tunes up the guitar.

'I'll let you choose,' says Judith, warming her hands in front of the fire as the temperature has cooled a little.

Just then, Liz's phone begins to ring, and she answers a videocall. A pretty blonde woman appears on the screen and waves.

'Hi, guys! And Judith and Lars, congratulations!'

'Chloe! How wonderful to see you.' Judith and Lars wave at the camera and chat.

'I must look a right sight now,' says Judith, laughing. 'I've just taken my hair down; it was beautifully sculpted earlier.'

'You look just beautiful. And I would have called before, but didn't know the right time to call with the time difference. We're in Los Angeles.'

'Living your best life, I'm happy to see. Thank you so much for the champagne and chocolates once again, it was very thoughtful of you.'

'Not at all. Thanks for the invite, I'm just sorry we couldn't make it.'

Her boyfriend Phillipe appears then and wishes Judith and Lars congratulations, before they have a quick catch-up with Tania, Wes and Liz.

'That was nice,' says Judith when the call ends, and I can see why everyone who comes across Judith gives her a special place in their heart.

'Have you decided on a song then?' Liz asks Wes.

'I hope it isn't cheesy, but I thought this might be nice.'

Wes has the most beautiful, mellow voice and when he begins to sing, everyone falls silent.

By the time he gets to the final bars of a well-known, romantic ballad, we have all joined in.

'I can see why you have chosen music as a career, you have a big talent,' says Marco kindly.

'Thanks, buddy.' Wes smiles.

Reluctantly, we call it a night as Wes sings a final song, drawing the night to a natural conclusion.

'That was what I call a beautiful wedding.' I sigh as I link arms with Marco, who is walking me home.

Wes and Liz, who are staying with Tania and Nicos, headed off to bed and the rest of the volunteers are walking along ahead of us. Panos is walking with Hannah before going home. Marco was going to take a taxi to his accommodation, but Tania insisted he stay with her too, as they have enough room.

'I agree,' he says as we stop for a moment to admire the black sky dotted with bright, white stars.

'It was a beautiful wedding, but there is another wedding I am looking forward to even more.'

'Oh yes, anyone I know?'

'Yes, and hopefully someone I will know for the rest of my life.' He turns to face me then, and I look into his hypnotic blue eyes. 'And I happen to know that this wedding will be just perfect,' he says, before moving in for a lingering kiss.

EPILOGUE

'I'm going to miss you.'

Two days later, I am packing a case and preparing to take a flight home with Marco.

'I'll miss you too.' I turn to Hannah. 'But you have Panos to keep you company now, as well as everyone here.'

'I know, but I'm so happy I met you at the airport that day,' she says, sitting on her bed opposite me. 'I might have turned around and gone home if not. I wasn't certain I would get on the plane.'

'Well, you did. And I actually think you would have been fine, whether I was there or not,' I tell her sincerely.

'That's the thing,' she says, looking at me directly, and not from under her glasses. 'You made me believe in myself.'

'I did? Well, I'm pleased to hear that, but I think all you needed was a little nudge to go after what you want. I think we all need that from time to time,' I reassure her.

'Maybe. You also helped me loosen up a bit. I was worried about falling for Panos, but so what if I do? When I return home, we will continue to email each other, just as we did when we first met.'

'There we are then. And if things are meant to be, then love will find a way.'

'"Love will find a way through paths where wolves fear to prey." Lord Byron,' Hannah quotes.

'There you go then. Who is going to argue with him?' I say as I lock my case and Hannah smiles.

'I will text you when I get home, Hannah. Enjoy the rest of your time here.'

'I will.' She steps forward and we share a long, affectionate hug.

She walks me downstairs, where I say my goodbyes to everyone, just before Marco arrives to collect me.

'I won't walk you to the car, I hate waving people off,' says Judith. 'Thank you for everything, and good luck to you both.'

'Thank you, Judith.' I swallow down a lump in my throat when I say a final goodbye.

'And don't forget to book that beach holiday,' I whisper in Doll's ear. 'Take a break.'

'Already on it.' She winks.

As we drive towards the airport, I turn and glance at my handsome fiancé and thank my lucky stars.

'So what are your plans when we get home?' I ask Marco.

'I have a couple of important things to tackle,' he says, turning to me and smiling. 'The first one is to move into a new place. An apartment in town that I know, if there is still a bed available, that is.'

'Sounds interesting. And the second thing?'

'To take a look at some wedding venues. If my fiancée is agreeable to that.'

'She most certainly is,' I say, my heart soaring.

'Then we will do it as soon as possible. Someone once told me that wedding venues book up quickly. And I think my fiancée deserves the wedding of her dreams.'

A LETTER FROM SUE

Dear reader,

I want to say a huge thank you for choosing to read *All You Need is Greece*. If you did enjoy it, and want to keep up to date with all my latest releases, just sign up at the following link. Your email address will never be shared and you can unsubscribe at any time.

www.bookouture.com/sue-roberts

I hope you loved *All You Need is Greece*; I certainly enjoyed returning to Pine Forest Rescue and spending time with some characters old and new, and of course the wonderful animals! If you did enjoy the story, I would be very grateful if you could write a review. I'd love to hear what you think, and it makes such a difference helping new readers to discover one of my books for the first time.

Once more, I found this book such a joy to write. I particularly loved writing about the forest setting, and the volunteers that come and go. I hope the trips to the beach gave it the summer holiday feels too!

I love hearing from my readers – you can get in touch on my Facebook page or through Twitter.

Thanks,

Sue Roberts

facebook.com/Suerobertsauthor
twitter.com/SueRobertsautho

ACKNOWLEDGMENTS

I would like to thank my lovely editor Natalie Edwards and everyone at Bookouture, for once again helping to get this book out in the world to all you lovely readers!

I do hope you enjoyed returning to Pine Forest Rescue. The idea to include an animal rescue in the two stories came from coming across such a place in Crete. Navigating the mountain roads, we had stopped at a viewing point that gave wonderful sea views, when we heard the sound of dogs barking in the distance. A couple passed by, walking some of the dogs from the nearby rescue centre, and had we been staying longer, we may have done the same. There are many animal rescue centres, at home and abroad, and thank goodness there are. The plight of abandoned animals doesn't bear thinking about otherwise.

Thank you for some of the lovely messages I have received from you readers, telling me how much you love my books. It is always such a joy to receive such messages. And of course, a huge thank you to all of you book bloggers, and all your sharing and recommendations to read my books.

Finally, thanks to all my family and friends (including real life Annie and Smudge!). You all inspire me daily and make me laugh. I can't imagine life without any of you.